GHOST

Cerberus Personal Security Specialists

Book 1

ELLIE MASTERS

MASTER OF ROMANTIC SUSPENSE

JEM Publishing

Dedication

This book is dedicated to my one and only—my amazing and wonderful husband.

Without your care and support, my writing would not have made it this far.

You pushed me when I needed to be pushed.

You supported me when I felt discouraged.

You believed in me when I didn't believe in myself.

If it weren't for you, this book never would have come to life.

Also by Ellie Masters

The LIGHTER SIDE

Ellie Masters is the lighter side of the Jet & Ellie Masters writing duo! You will find Contemporary Romance, Military Romance, Romantic Suspense, Billionaire Romance, and Rock Star Romance in Ellie's Works.

YOU CAN FIND ELLIE'S BOOKS HERE:

ELLIEMASTERS.COM/BOOKS

Shop Ellie Masters Romantic Suspense and Steamy Contemporary Romance by series.

Angel Fire Rock Romance

Guardian HRS: Alpha Team

Guardian HRS: Bravo Team

Guardian HRS: Charlie Team

Guardian HRS: Delta Team

Cerberus Personal Security

The LaRouge Triplets

The One I Want Series

Angel's Peak Series

Billionaire Boy's Club

The Lovers

Changing Roles

Rescuing Eve

Rescuing Lily

Rescuing Jinx

Rescuing Maria

Bravo Team

Rescuing Angie

Rescuing Isabelle

Rescuing Carmen

Rescuing Rosalie

Rescuing Kaye

Cara's Protector

Rescuing Barbi

Charlie Team

Rescuing Rebel

Rescuing Stitch

Rescuing Mia

Jenna's Protector

Rescuing Sophia

Rescuing Malia

Rescuing Ally (Part 1)

Rescuing Ally (Part 2)

Delta Team

Rescuing Ember

Rescuing Aria

STANDALONES IN THE GUARDIAN HOSTAGE RESCUE

SERIES YOU CAN READ ANYTIME

Military Romance

Guardian Personal Protection Specialists

Sybil's Protector

Lyra's Protector

Angel's Peak Series

Steamy Instalove Small Town

EACH BOOK IN THIS SERIES CAN BE READ AS A STANDALONE AND IS ABOUT A DIFFERENT COUPLE WITH AN HEA.

SNOWED IN WITH THE MOUNTAIN DOCTOR

Rescued by the Mountain Guide

Stranded with the Resort Owner

Matched with the Small-Town Chef

Trapped with the Forest Ranger

Snowbound with the Vineyard Owner

Reunited with the Hometown Hero

Colliding with the Coffee Shop Owner

Falling for the Firefighter

Wrecked with the Reclusive Author

Tangled with the Single Dad

Whirlwinded by the Helicopter Pilot

Sheltered by the Veterinarian

Bound by the Sheriff

The One I Want Series

(Small Town, Military Heroes)

By Jet & Ellie Masters

EACH BOOK IN THIS SERIES CAN BE READ AS A STANDALONE AND IS ABOUT A DIFFERENT COUPLE WITH AN HEA.

Saving Abby

Saving Ariel

Saving Brie

Saving Cate

Saving Dani

Saving Jen

The LaRouge Triplets

Asher

Brody

Cage

Billionaire Romance

Billionaire Boys Club

Hawke

Richard

Contemporary Romance

Cocky Captain

Romantic Suspense

EACH BOOK IS A STANDALONE NOVEL.

The Starling

The Swan

~AND~

The Ties that Bind

Alexa

Penny

Michelle

Ivy

HOT READS

Becoming His Series

The Ballet

Learning to Breathe

Becoming His

Dark Captive Romance

She's MINE

To My Readers

This book is a work of fiction. It does not exist in the real world and should not be construed as reality. As in most romantic fiction, I've taken liberties. I've compressed the romance into a sliver of time. I've allowed these characters to develop strong bonds of trust over a matter of days.

This does not happen in real life where you, my amazing readers, live. Take more time in your romance and learn who you're giving a piece of your heart to. I urge you to move with caution. Always protect yourself.

Grab the First Book in The Guardian Hostage Rescue Specialists Series for Free

https://elliemasters.com/RescuingMelissa

ONE

Willow

THE TRUCK FISHTAILS ACROSS THE ICY ROAD, TIRES SHRIEKING AS they lose traction. A white-out swallows the headlights, transforming the world into a spinning tunnel of snow and black asphalt.

I clutch the wheel with bloodless fingers, heart slamming against my ribs, eyes straining to find something—anything—to orient myself. The guardrail looms too fast. I yank the wheel, but it's too late. Metal screams against metal, a shrill, gut-twisting wail that cuts through the storm.

Not like this. Not when I'm so close.

Impact. Everything tilts. My body slams sideways. Silence falls in the aftermath, broken only by the hiss of steam from the radiator and the tick-tick-tick of a dying engine. The world settles at a sick angle, and the truck crumples against the guardrail like a broken toy.

Pain arrives in waves—sharp, splintering agony radiating from my ribs, a wet warmth seeping down my chin.

Blood drips from my split lip onto the steering wheel. The

metallic taste floods my mouth, a familiar tang I've grown used to. Not from this crash. No, this is older. Deeper.

The blood mixes with the copper pennies I've been swallowing since Steffan's boot caught me under the ribs. Every breath feels like a razor, sending lightning-hot shards stabbing through my chest.

I reach under the passenger seat with hands that won't stop trembling, my fingertips scrabbling for the hidden drive I planted months ago. There—cold and solid. I find the small backup drive I taped there three months ago.

It's identical to the one Steffan ripped from my hands in his study, the one he crushed under his heel while Drake held me down.

He thinks he destroyed everything. He's wrong.

Three years of marriage. Three years of brutality hidden behind charm and tailored suits.

Steffan Reynolds.

Federal judge, rising political star, master manipulator, he treated me to three years of his fists, his belt, and his careful cruelty disguised as discipline and command. Behind closed doors, he's a monster. His cruelty is surgical, meticulous, the kind that leaves no trace unless he wants it to.

And Drake—his shadow, his enforcer—was always watching, always smiling.

The engine ticks as it cools. The cab fills with steam. I cough, wince, force myself to move.

Move or die.

The truck sits at a sickening angle, front end crumpled against the twisted guardrail, steam hissing from the punctured radiator. The driver's side is wedged into the guardrail, but the passenger door opens toward the forest.

Hope flickers. I crawl across the bench seat, every shift igniting white-hot pain in my chest.

The door handle fights me, warped from the impact. When it finally gives way, the door screams against its hinges, metal grinding against bent metal, the sound lost in the howling wind.

I tumble out into knee-deep snow. The cold hits like a slap, shocking my system awake. Wind slaps against my face, driving snow into the cuts on my cheek where Steffan's ring caught and ripped skin.

My breath catches, ragged in the frozen air. I stagger, turn back toward the road, and see headlights.

No! No. No!

Headlights, low and fast, slice through the storm. Still distant, but unmistakable. I know that truck. I know who's driving it.

Drake.

Steffan's enforcer. His shadow. The man who held me down while my husband's belt found its mark, who smiled when I screamed, who took his turn when Steffan was finished breaking me.

Panic ignites like a fuse in my bloodstream. He'll see the wreck. He'll know where I went off the road. There's no time. No time for plans, no time to think.

Terror floods my system, hot and electric despite the killing cold. Snow sucks at my feet with every step, dragging me down. My canvas sneakers are soaked instantly, offering neither warmth nor protection.

I didn't plan this escape well, not really. I had a window and I took it. I ran for the truck and didn't look back.

I should have grabbed a coat. Should have planned better. Should have—

I should have never married Steffan Reynolds.

The blizzard howls around me as I push into the forest. Pine branches tear at my hair and whip across my face. My lungs burn, ribs screaming with each ragged breath. The cold sears my throat, each inhalation like swallowing broken glass.

Run. Willow. For God's sake, run!

Behind me, somewhere beyond the white curtain, an engine dies. Doors slam. Voices carry on the wind. Harsh, clipped commands. Fragments of words, tactical coordination. They're following on foot now.

I push harder, stumbling over roots and rocks hidden beneath the snow. My foot catches a root. The world tilts, gravity claims me. I hit the ground hard, pain detonating through my shoulder where Drake dislocated it last spring—a memory that lives in bone and sinew, awakening with fresh agony.

The flash drive flies from my grip, a small dark speck disappearing into the endless white.

No, no, no—

Panic claws at my throat. I scramble through the snow, blind and frantic, my fingers already numb, searching. My chest heaves. The wind picks up, driving powder into my eyes, my nose, my mouth. I taste blood and snow and desperation.

The cold finds every weakness, burrowing under my sweater, freezing the sweat on my back. The blood from my lip has frozen to my chin. My hands ache with numbness, my fingers turning stiff.

I can't breathe. I can't see.

There. The small metal rectangle, cold as death against my palm. It documents three years of Steffan's crimes. Three years of evidence, every wire transfer and illicit deal. Every bribe. Every threat. Every backroom meeting with arms dealers and human traffickers. Every time he bent justice to his will while bending me over his desk.

I risked my life to record threats and copy financial records. Three years of surviving hell to reach this moment.

I clutch it tight, pushing upright on trembling legs. The forest spins around me, white and dark bleeding together. The blizzard turns relentless—snow driving horizontally, stinging like hornets.

Numbness creeps up my arms and legs, death claiming me inch by inch.

Just like Steffan promised. "One day you'll push me too far, sweetheart. And when that day comes..."

Voices rise behind me. Close. Too close.

I keep moving. Because if I stop, I die. If I stop, they win.

Time stretches and compresses in the white-out. The forest becomes a fever dream of white and shadow, pain and cold. My legs move without feeling, stumbling over obstacles I can't see. The taste of copper mingles with the metallic bite of snow.

Behind me, shouts carry on the wind. Coordinates being called out. The systematic closing of a net.

I angle toward a denser section of trees, but a light sweeps across my path. They're everywhere—shadows moving through the white hell of the blizzard.

A root catches my foot. I go down hard, face-first into the snow. The impact drives the air from my lungs and sends fresh agony through my broken ribs. For a moment, I can't move, can't breathe, can only lie there as the storm tries to bury me alive.

Get up. Get up or they win.

I push myself to hands and knees, spitting snow and blood. The flash drive has somehow stayed clutched in my death grip; a small mercy in a night of disasters. Around me, the lights converge, voices growing louder.

The cold is winning. I feel it in my bones, in the growing numbness that starts at my extremities and creeps inward like death itself. My coordination fails—I trip over logs I can't see, walk into branches that appear from nowhere in the white void.

The blizzard has become my enemy and my salvation. It hides me from Drake's men, but it's also killing me degree by degree, heartbeat by heartbeat.

Each inch forward feels like a mile, a war waged with my own broken body. My breath comes in shallow, panicked gasps, misting in the cold air, but I keep going. Because I have to. Because the only thing behind me is pain and the promise of death.

I don't know how long I wander through the white maze. The forest closes around me like a frozen cathedral, pine boughs heavy with snow creating a canopy that muffles sound and dims what little light filters through the storm.

The cold has moved beyond pain into something deeper—a bone-deep ache that speaks of systems shutting down, of a body preparing to surrender.

Keep moving. Movement means warmth. Stillness means death.

And just when the last shred of hope starts to unravel, when the darkness feels endless and the cold has worked its way through my bones, a branch cracks somewhere in the white void ahead.

I freeze, heart hammering weakly against my ribs. Through the driving snow, a shape emerges—tall, broad-shouldered.

He stands still—too still for a man who doesn't know what's coming. He has no flashlight, no radio. He doesn't speak right away. Doesn't rush to help me. He just watches, calm, grounded, real.

Dogs flank him.

Drake doesn't use dogs.

This man isn't part of the hunt.

He moves like he belongs here, like the storm is simply weather instead of a weapon.

A massive dog bounds toward me through the snow, tail moving—not aggressive, but curious. Protective. The other dog holds its position, alert but not threatening.

"Who's there?" His voice cuts through the wind like a blade, deep and authoritative, low and steady, as if we're the only two people left in the world.

"Please," I whisper, the word torn from my frozen throat. "They're hunting me."

Steam rises from his breath in the frigid air. Snow clings to broad shoulders covered in winter camouflage. A scar bisects one eyebrow, and his eyes are pale gray—winter sky after the storm passes.

"Who's hunting you?"

The honest concern in his voice breaks something inside me. I sway on my feet, the last of my adrenaline finally failing. Blood loss, hypothermia, exhaustion—all of it crashes over me at once.

He moves toward me, like he's seen this before. Like nothing about me—bloody, half-broken, filthy—makes him hesitate. When his arms wrap around me, it's not the rough grab I brace for. It's strength wrapped in control. Hands that lift without hurting, that ground without caging.

"I've got you," he says, and something in his voice—calm certainty, unshakeable protection—breaks the last of my resistance.

I collapse into him, this stranger who smells like pine and gunpowder and safety. The flash drive cuts into my palm where I still clutch it desperately.

Three years of evidence. Three years of documenting a federal judge's corruption while he destroyed me piece by piece. It has to matter.

"They'll kill me," I manage against his chest, my voice barely a whisper in the storm. "If they find me."

His arms tighten around me, and when he speaks again, his voice has gone deadly quiet—not a threat, but a promise carved from winter steel.

"Then we better make sure they don't find you."

Something shifts inside me. The fear doesn't vanish, but it's no longer everything. I still feel the cold, still hear the men behind me. But now, I'm not alone.

TWO

Mason

The woman in my arms weighs nothing and everything. One hundred and twenty pounds of frozen responsibility I swore I'd never carry again.

Not after Rachel.

Not after the night that rewrote every line I thought I could safely walk.

Fifteen minutes ago, I was tracking a six-point buck through fresh powder. Now I'm cradling a half-frozen stranger while my planned route back to the cabin dissolves in the thickening white-out.

Funny how fast priorities shift.

How quickly training overrides common sense.

Her skin is ice, brittle, and pale. Bruising darkens her throat in finger-shaped smears, fresh and ugly. Her hair is matted with blood where someone struck her temple hard enough to swell a knot beneath the skin.

Scrapes and abrasions mar her arms—defensive wounds. The kind that speaks of struggle. Of someone who fought back until she couldn't.

Chaos's low growl cuts through the wind as he scents the trail behind us. The Malinois's ears prick forward, his posture screaming danger. Bear circles us, his massive Newfoundland bulk already positioning to shield us from the wind, dark fur collecting snow like a living shroud.

"Bear, guard."

The Newfoundland immediately shifts his weight, placing himself beside the woman as I lower her gently to the ground. His massive body radiates warmth, buying me necessary minutes.

"Chaos, perimeter sweep. Double-back." The Malinois disappears into the white like smoke, silent and efficient.

They're the only company I keep now. Dogs don't flinch at scars or ask questions I can't answer. They know what I am and accept it.

The storm's building fast.

The temperature's dropping faster than my comfort zone allows. What started as a manageable snowfall has evolved into nature's version of psychological warfare.

The forecast said light snow, but it's turned into a white-out. The wind howls through the pine tops like artillery fire, and visibility's down to about ten feet.

Her tracks behind us are already half-obscured, disappearing like ghosts in the fresh powder. Another hour, maybe less, and they'll be completely buried. Along with us, if I don't make the right call.

The cabin's three miles north. In this storm, it might as well be on another planet.

"Goddammit." The curse freezes in the air between us.

This would be manageable solo. I've survived worse conditions with less gear, but the woman changes everything. Her breathing is shallow, lips tinged with a blue that has nothing to do with cosmetics. The gash on her temple has mostly stopped bleeding, but the dried blood has frozen into macabre crystals along her hairline.

Decision time: risk movement to the cabin or build a temporary shelter? One look at her blue-tinged lips makes the choice for me.

Shelter first. Then triage.

The woman's carotid pulse flutters beneath my fingertips—thready, irregular. Her core temperature is dangerously low. She's not dressed for this kind of weather.

I spot a shallow depression ahead. It offers some protection. The towering pines will break the wind, and their lower branches give me material to work with. I unsheathe my K-bar, and pine boughs fall under its blade. A decade of special operations etched this process into my bones.

I build the lean-to in fifteen minutes. String out an emergency blanket for insulation. Pack snow walls tightly to trap heat. It gives maybe twenty degrees of temperature advantage.

Every degree counts when you're fighting hypothermia.

I layer the ground thick with pine branches, creating insulation from the frozen earth. It's not pretty, but it'll keep her alive through the night if necessary.

I return to her. Bear hasn't moved. His massive form shelters the woman from the worst of the wind. She stirs slightly when I lift her, her body instinctively curling toward warmth.

Toward me.

It shouldn't matter.

But it does.

Something breaks within me, wishing I was worth that kind of trust.

Inside the shelter, I lay her on the pine bough bed.

"Bear, cover." The Newfoundland settles against her side while I begin my assessment. Head to toe, methodical. Her pulse is weak and erratic. Skin like ice. She won't make it without intervention.

Her clothes are soaked. They have to go.

Field protocol. Dry her. Warm her.

Probable concussion from the gash on her temple. But then I uncover other marks that have my jaw clenching until I taste copper. The bruising visible beneath her torn clothing speaks of systematic abuse.

My hands catalog each injury with growing fury. Precise bruising along the ribs. Fingerprints around the throat. The kind of calculated violence that leaves plenty of nightmares for the victim.

I bite back the growl rising in my throat. The world narrows to three priorities: stabilize her, keep her warm, and protect her.

That last hits like an IED, setting off warning bells in my head. She's not mine. Can't be mine. The last time I claimed responsibility for someone's life…

No. Focus on the mission.

Chaos returns, materializing from the white void like a specter. His posture tells me we're temporarily clear, but his agitation confirms my suspicions—someone's out there, hunting through this storm.

Hunting her.

The wind picks up, driving the temperature lower. The storm's no longer just a threat—it's a full-scale assault. We're officially in white-out conditions. The kind that swallows men whole and spits out frozen corpses in the spring thaw.

The storm provides cover, but traps us. It traps those hunting her too.

I'll take the win.

Because there's no way out until the weather breaks and she's stable. I grab my spare thermals out of my pack. They'll swamp her small form, but they are dry. I wrap her in an emergency blanket, tucking her against Bear's flank. Then I take the other side, sharing my body heat with her. My sidearm rests within easy reach.

Her head rests in the crook of my arm.

I should feel nothing.

Instead, I feel everything.

She fits too perfectly.

Feels like heaven.

Smells like redemption.

I should be back at my cabin, processing that buck I was tracking, stoking the woodstove against the storm. Instead, I'm hip-deep in someone else's nightmare, with an unconscious woman who carries more secrets than answers, two dogs, and a blizzard bearing down that could last days.

Whatever she's running from, whoever marked her with such cruelty, they'll have to go through me to get to her.

Hours pass in a blur of howling wind and soft breaths. The storm rages beyond our snow walls, but inside we've created our own warmth. Bear's massive bulk heats her left side while I'm pressed against her right, my body curled protectively around her petite body.

Her color improves. Pulse steadies. Her body seeks heat, burrowing instinctively closer, into me.

Her soft curves pressed against me are a special kind of torture—one I've earned, maybe, for thinking I could play protector again.

My body thrums with awareness, combat instincts tangled with baser needs I can't afford to acknowledge. I spent a year drowning that part of me in whiskey, isolation, and silence. She brings it all raging back to the surface.

Chaos maintains his vigil by the entrance, occasionally shaking snow from his coat. Bear's bulk and thick coat shield against the wind.

The night stretches, marked only by the howling wind and the steadily warming body in my arms. The professional part of my brain monitors her vital signs: stronger pulse, better color, regular breathing. The rest of me catalogs things I shouldn't: the delicate curve of her neck, the way she unconsciously burrows closer, seeking heat.

Dawn creeps in, barely visible through the thick clouds still spitting snow. The storm's fury has ebbed, but the snowfall continues—lighter now, almost peaceful. Nature's perfect camouflage for whoever might be tracking her.

Her cheek brushes my chest. My fingers twitch.

Don't move. Don't react.

She stirs.

Whimpers.

Then her eyes open.

Green. Gold-flecked. Sharp and too clear.

She sees me.

Panic detonates.

She jerks upright. Cries out. Collapses.

I catch her before she hits the ground.

"Easy." The command voice comes naturally, pitched low but authoritative. "You're safe."

The words feel like a lie.

No one's safe with me.

Her eyes snap open—sharp intelligence cuts through the confusion and fear. For a moment, she's perfectly still. Then recognition hits—not of me, but of the situation. Of being restrained, confined. She jackknifes upward, then crumples with a cry of pain. My arm shoots out, combat reflexes catching her before she can aggravate those ribs.

The contact sends electricity through my system, awakening hunger I've denied for too long. But there's no time to dwell on it. She's panicking, her breath coming in sharp gasps as she registers the strange clothes, the emergency blanket, the confined space.

"No, no, no—" She thrashes. Voice rising in terror. "You can't… He sent you… I won't go back…"

Bear whines but maintains position, rock-steady under his training. Chaos moves to the threshold.

I recognize the panic response—mine mirrors hers on the bad nights. But I also see something else; how she instinctively stills at my touch, even in her panic. The way her body unconsciously responds to authority.

"Stop." The word cracks with parade-ground authority. My hand cups the back of her neck, exerting precisely calculated pressure. The dominance flows without conscious thought, a part of me I've tried to bury.

She freezes at my command, the reaction instantaneous. Her pupils dilate, breath catching for a different reason now. The submission in her response is like a key clicking into a lock I thought I'd thrown away.

Something primal stirs in my chest at how perfectly she yields to that tone. It hits like a tactical breaching charge.

Every muscle goes instantly pliant under my hand. Her breath catches, pulse leaping beneath my fingers. Recognition flares in those gold-flecked eyes. Not of me, but of what I am.

What she is.

The knowledge arcs between us like an electric current. That immediate surrender kicks my protective instincts into overdrive, along with other impulses I've kept locked down tight.

"Focus on my voice. You're safe. I'm Mason. You're in Montana, in a snowstorm. My dogs and I have your six."

"I—" She swallows hard, eyes darting between me and the dogs. "Why am I wearing—where are my clothes?"

"Hypothermia. Your clothes were soaked. You're in my spare thermals." I maintain the steady pressure on her neck, feeling her pulse race beneath my fingers. "I'm former Special Forces. The dogs are trained protection animals. We found you in the storm. Brought you to shelter. Nothing more."

She watches me like a cornered animal. Slowly, logic begins to win. Her eyes sharpen.

"You're not one of them? You don't work for him?"

"I don't work for anyone." *Not anymore.*

The words come out rougher than intended. "Just me and the dogs up here. Speaking of—Bear, ease up."

The Newfoundland gives her a few inches of space, but stays close enough to lend warmth. She watches him, then looks back at me with dawning understanding.

"You saved me."

"That remains to be seen." My hand falls away from her neck, and I immediately miss the contact. "Storm's not over. Your pursuers might still be out there. And you've got some explaining to do."

A shudder runs through her, but there's trust in her eyes now. Trust I haven't earned. Don't deserve. But damned if I don't want to keep it.

"I'm Willow," she whispers, and the simple offering of her name feels more intimate than our shared body heat. "And I think—I think you just saved my life."

Something shifts in the space between us.

Outside, the snow continues to fall, but in here, something far more dangerous is building—something that threatens the carefully constructed walls of my self-imposed isolation.

I'm already addicted to the way she yields to my command, and that's inherently dangerous.

"How about we start with some hydration?" I maintain a steady and professional tone. It's easier to focus on immediate survival needs than the way she unconsciously leans toward me, seeking protection.

I lift the canteen. One hand supports her neck as she drinks. Her throat works under my fingers, fragile and soft. She lets me guide her. The simple trust in that gesture hits harder than any firefight—the way she lets me control the flow, support her weight.

Something dark and possessive uncoils in my chest as her throat works beneath my fingers.

Lock it down, asshole.

The storm softens. Snow still falls, but the wind's dropped. Chaos remains alert, but there's no movement outside the shelter.

"I'm Willow Reynolds," she whispers when I take the canteen away. Her eyes meet mine, fear warring with determination. "My husband—"

"The one who gave you those bruises?" The words emerge as a combat growl.

She flinches but doesn't withdraw. If anything, she leans closer, like she's starved for protection rather than afraid of male aggression. Bear rumbles, responding to my tension, and I force my hands to unclench.

"Federal Judge Steffan Reynolds. He found my flash drive. Evidence. Witness tampering. Money laundering. Worse. I've been gathering proof of his corruption for months. Years. Offshore accounts, doctored verdicts, connections to..." She swallows hard. "The men tracking me are his head of security. Drake and his men. They're all Ex-Delta Force." Her fingers twist in the thermal shirt I gave her. "They're not here to bring me back alive."

I process this while checking the storm through the lean-to's entrance. The snow's lighter now, but visibility's still shit. Wind chill's hovering around dangerous.

We're on borrowed time.

"When's the last time you ate?" The question surprises her,

but I need to know what I'm working with. Her physical condition will determine our next course of action.

"I… Yesterday morning, I think. Everything after that is…" She shivers, and I automatically pull her close, sharing body heat.

"Here." I dig through my pack, producing a protein bar. "Small bites. Slow. Let it settle." My hand stays at the small of her back as she eats, monitoring her breathing, the way she favors her left side.

Combat medical training catalogs each detail: probable bruised ribs, mild concussion, severe bruising, and possible internal injuries.

She manages half the bar before her hands start shaking. Delayed shock, maybe, or just the weight of everything catching up. I take the wrapper, tuck it away—no trace left behind, automatic after years of spec ops.

"Can you walk?"

She nods, determination replacing panic. I help her dress in the spare clothes from my pack, cataloging each wince and swallowed gasp. The bruises on her skin burn in my tactical memory, building a target package I file away for future use. Each mark feeds the predator I've kept caged, the one that wants to hunt down every man who hurt her.

"The evidence," she says suddenly. "It's on a thumb drive. I managed to—" She pats her pockets, panic flaring. "No, no, no—"

"Inside pocket of your coat," I tell her, remembering the small lump I felt while changing her. "It's safe. We'll get it once you're stable."

Relief hits her like a body blow.

She's not just running from an abusive husband—she's carrying proof that could bring down a federal judge. No wonder this Drake asshole was sent to eliminate the threat.

"Listen carefully." I cup her face, making sure I have her full attention. "My cabin's three miles from here. Uphill most of the way. It's defensible, stocked with supplies. But getting there won't be easy. Tell me now if you can't make it, and we'll figure out another option."

She stares at me like I've just rewritten her world. "You'd do that? Change your plans based on what I can handle?"

The question carries weight beyond its obvious implications. I hear the years of being ignored, her limits dismissed, and her needs trampled. My jaw clenches.

"I protect what's mine." The words slip out before I can catch them.

Shit! Rein it in, Mason. Not now.

Her eyes widen, pupils dilating.

"We work within your limits, but you have to be honest about them. Can you do that?"

"Yes." The word comes out soft but certain. There's trust in her eyes, mixed with something else—something that calls to the dominant I've kept locked away.

"Good g—" I barely hold in the *Good girl* that comes as naturally as breathing. But she's not mine. Not like that. *Never* like that. "Um, that's good."

God help me, I want to keep her. Keep her safe. Keep her protected. Make her mine.

A stranger.

I'm so fucked.

We break shelter. Chaos clears ahead. Bear makes the trail.

"Stay behind me. Step where I step. If I say drop, you drop. Clear?"

"Yes, sir."

Two simple words. They slam into me like a physical blow. Rachel used to say them the same way—soft, trusting, completely surrendered. Until the night I woke from a nightmare about

Syria, watching my team die while I survived, and found my hands around her throat.

The absolute horror in her eyes as I came back to myself… I swore then I'd never put another submissive at risk. Never trust myself with that kind of power again.

But Willow's "yes, sir" does things to me I can't control. The delicate curve of her neck as she bows her head slightly. The way her breath catches when I move close. The subtle softening of her entire body at my command. Even injured, even terrified, she responds to dominance like she was made for it.

Made for me.

STOP IT!

Fuck.

The snow's thigh-deep in places, each step a battle against nature itself. Bear forges ahead, his massive bulk creating a path, but it's a double-edged sword. The trail he leaves might as well be a neon sign pointing straight to my cabin. Behind us, Chaos ghosts through the white, covering our tracks as best he can, but it won't buy us much time against experienced operators like Drake and his team.

Willow stumbles for the third time in ten minutes, a soft cry of pain escaping before she can bite it back. Those ribs are slowing her down more than she wants to admit. She keeps pushing, trying to match my pace, but her body's reached its limit.

"Stop." I turn back, catching her before she can fall. Her small frame fits perfectly against me, triggering every protective instinct I've spent years suppressing. "New plan."

"I can keep going." She looks up at me, snowflakes caught in her lashes, cheeks flushed with cold and exertion. "I'm not weak—"

"No, you're injured." My voice comes out rougher than intended. "Pushing through pain is different from pushing through damage."

The ridge ahead looms like a white wall. The easier path will take us around, adding an hour to our trek. The direct route requires climbing—nothing technical, but with her injuries…

A sound escapes her—frustration mixed with fear.

"They'll find us."

"Let them try." The words emerge as a growl. I shouldn't enjoy how she shivers at that tone, or how her body unconsciously yields to my authority. "Bear, break trail. Chaos, sweep, and clear."

The dogs respond with years of training evident in every movement. I turn back to Willow, forcing myself to focus on the tactical rather than how perfectly she fits against me.

"New plan. Arms around my neck." When she hesitates, I add the command tone that makes her pupils dilate. "*Now*."

She obeys instantly, the response so natural it hurts.

I lift her easily—she weighs nothing compared to my combat load—but the intimacy of the position is dangerous. Her breath against my neck. The way she instinctively burrows closer. Every subtle submission chips away at defenses I thought were ironclad.

We climb.

The snow hides treacherous footing, and the wind picks up, driving ice crystals like needles against any exposed skin.

It takes three times as long as it should, but we finally reach my cabin.

One room, one bed, minimal comfort.

I've kept it that way deliberately, part of my self-imposed exile.

Now it will become torture with no escape from this hunger she's awakening in me. The part of me that wants to heal every mark on her skin and replace them with my own.

The cabin's dark shape emerges through a curtain of snow— my fortress against the world. High-tech sophistication hidden beneath the wilderness façade. Motion sensors gleam dully beneath snow-laden eaves. Reinforced shutters wait to transform windows into armor. Solar panels peek through frost, powering a military-grade security system.

"Almost there." I adjust my grip, hating how naturally she yields to the movement.

She doesn't know that the same instincts driving me to protect her could easily turn destructive. One flashback, one nightmare, and all that control shatters.

Bear leads and Chaos flanks us. Everything in me screams to get her inside, to shelter her, and make her mine.

That's what makes me dangerous. The same drive that makes me want to protect can instantly turn deadly.

Whatever, there's nothing to do about that now. My fortress waits.

One room. One bed.

No escape.

From her.

From myself.

Until those men come hunting.

And they will come hunting.

But when they come, they'll find something they didn't expect.

Not a helpless victim.

They'll find me, and all the parts I've tried to bury.

The monster I've been keeping leashed, the one that already sees her as mine to protect.

God help us both.

THREE

Willow

EACH STEP THROUGH THE DEEP SNOW SLICES FIRE THROUGH MY ribs. I match Mason's pace, forcing each foot to follow his tracks. Only his stride is much longer than mine.

He set me down as we neared this cabin of his. A cabin, deep in the wilderness. Sounds *safe*. I'd laugh if I had any energy left.

The wind cuts through the borrowed thermals, but it's his presence that steals my breath. The way he moves, deliberate, powerful, silent. The way his hand reaches back to steady me when I stumble.

I shouldn't be noticing him. Not like this. Not when Drake and his men could be closing in.

But something in me—something bruised but not broken—recognizes safety in him. Strength in his hands. Calm in his voice. Authority wrapped in restraint.

When he carried me through the storm, I felt weightless and anchored all at once.

Mason's authority feels different. Natural. Safe. Trusting.

It hits me—how easily I yield to his voice. How instinctive it feels to obey.

He scans the woods with lethal focus. His dogs melt into position—one flanking, one guarding. The storm thins just enough for me to see him. Scars cut across one side of his face, but they don't mar his looks—they tell a story. Strength. Survival. His eyes, pale steel, land on me with heat I feel in my knees.

"Almost there."

His hand touches the small of my back, and a current sparks across my skin. I lean into the contact, craving it like warmth and life.

I must be delirious.

A cabin emerges from the swirling snow like a fever dream of safety and strength—all raw power masked by rustic charm, just like its owner.

Mason's hand settles at the small of my back, guiding me up the covered porch. That simple touch sends electricity arcing through my nervous system. My body recognizes safety in his strength even as my mind catalogs potential threats—a survival reflex beaten into me by Steffan.

But where Steffan's touches carried underlying cruelty, Mason's speak of protection and salvation.

When I dare to look up, I find his eyes on me—something dangerous flares in that steel-gray gaze—not threat but banked heat. Recognition floods me. He feels this too, this crackle of electricity between us. A magnetic pull that has nothing to do with survival and everything to do with primal attraction.

Mason disarms three different systems before unlocking the door. Each beep and click echoes in the storm-muffled air like a combination lock tumbling open.

The dogs take up defensive positions without command—Bear pressing against my legs while Chaos prowls the perimeter.

"Clear." His voice is a growl of certainty. Commanding. Grounding. Pure alpha male, natural dominance, and protective instinct.

Inside, heat wraps around me, stealing the air from my lungs.

Mason secures multiple locks and security systems. I watch, transfixed, as he strips off layers of gear. Each movement is efficient and practiced, yet unconsciously sensual.

The thermal shirt beneath clings to his torso, revealing a chest broad enough to make my mouth go dry. His arms flex as he hangs his gear—arms that could easily pin me against the wall, that could…

I can't stop the flush that creeps up my neck.

Whoa, where the hell is my head at?

The cabin's interior takes my breath away. Sophistication and survival blend seamlessly, with clean lines and modern technology hidden within mountain aesthetics. A massive stone fireplace dominates one wall, radiating bone-deep warmth that makes me realize how cold I am. Floor-to-ceiling bookshelves line another wall, crammed with everything from military tactics to medical texts.

A single king-sized bed commands the far corner, partially screened by a rustic partition. Heat floods my cheeks as my body remembers the feel of him carrying me from the snow.

Those powerful arms could so easily…

I shut down that train of thought, but not before Mason notices my reaction. His jaw tightens, muscles ticking beneath his scars.

"Don't worry. I'll take the floor." His voice drops an octave, rough with unspoken things.

But Mason doesn't give me time to gawk. He's already moving, securing locks, and checking systems. The fluid grace of his movements—economical, purposeful, like a predator comfortable in his territory—mesmerizes me. He commands this space with absolute authority, and my gaze lingers longer than it should.

Bear shakes snow from his coat and immediately claims a spot by the fire. Chaos prowls the perimeter, alert but relaxed.

"Sit," Mason says, and it's not a request.

His hand settles on my lower back—firm, decisive, guiding me exactly where he wants me. The warmth of his palm burns through the borrowed jacket, and something deep in my belly clenches in response.

I shouldn't feel this. Not after everything Steffan and Drake did to me. Not after the way they—

But this is different. This touch doesn't take. It gives.

I sink into the chair he's chosen for me, and part of me—a part I thought was dead—responds to his quiet authority with something that feels dangerously close to submission. The realization should terrify me. Instead, it awakens something I didn't know I was capable of feeling anymore.

Mason retrieves a first aid kit—military grade, not the basic drugstore variety. He kneels beside my chair. Pine soap, leather, and something uniquely masculine fill my nostrils, making my pulse quicken and my thighs clench involuntarily. His movements are careful and clinical as he examines the cut on my temple, but his breathing changes, and his hands aren't as steady as they were moments ago.

"Look at me," he says softly, and I obey without thinking. The command in his voice is gentle but absolute, and my body responds before my mind can protest.

"Concussion?" I ask, trying to keep my voice light, trying to ignore how his proximity affects me, how something low and needy is stirring to life.

"Mild, maybe. Your pupils are responding normally."

His fingers probe gently around the wound, and I have to bite my lip to keep from making a sound. When our eyes meet, there's something there—a flicker of dark awareness that has nothing to do with medical assessment and everything to do with the way I'm looking at him like I want to be devoured.

"This needs cleaning, but it's not deep enough for stitches."

The antiseptic stings, but his touch is so gentle I barely notice. My gaze travels over his face—the strong jaw, the way his dark lashes cast shadows on his cheekbones, the tiny scar near his left temple. My body betrays me, responding to his nearness with a heat I thought was dead forever.

When his fingers trace the bruises on my throat, his jaw tightens, and something dangerous flickers in his eyes. His touch becomes impossibly tender, but there's a possessive quality to it too, as if he's claiming what someone else has damaged.

"Your husband did this?" The question comes out deadly quiet, but there's something in his voice that makes arousal pool between my thighs despite everything.

"Steffan. Yes." I meet his eyes, see the flash of something protective and possessive that should frighten me, but doesn't. Instead, it makes me wet. "Among other things."

Something dark and predatory flickers in his gaze—not just anger, but decision. Like he's already decided I'm his to protect, his to heal, his to…

The thought sends heat racing through me.

"Show me," he says quietly.

The command is soft but implacable, and I find myself obeying before I can think about it. My hands move to the buttons of the jacket before the decision fully forms. His eyes track every movement, dark and hungry.

When I reveal the bruises on my ribs, the marks on my arms, he makes a sound low in his throat that sends liquid heat straight to my core.

"These ribs—lift your arms above your head." It's phrased as an instruction, not a request, and my body responds to his authority even as my mind reels.

I try, wince, and shake my head. His hands hover near my ribcage, not quite touching, but the heat radiating from his palms makes me shiver with want.

"Bruised, not broken. You were lucky." He sits back on his heels but doesn't move away. His gaze travels over my exposed skin with clinical assessment that somehow feels more intimate than any touch. "When's the last time you had a proper meal? A shower? Real sleep?"

The questions are so practical, so concerned with basic human needs, but it's the way he's looking at me—like I'm something precious that needs tending—that undoes me completely.

Like, I'm his responsibility now.

His to care for.

"I… It's been a while."

Mason studies my face, seeing too much. His thumb brushes away a tear I didn't realize had fallen, the touch so gentle yet possessive it makes my breath catch and my nipples tighten against the fabric.

"Shower first. Then food. Then we'll talk about what comes next."

The way he decides for me, takes control so effortlessly, should make me panic. Steffan's control was suffocating—every decision stripped away to isolate me, to diminish me, to make me smaller until I disappeared entirely. His dominance was about ownership of my fear, feeding on my helplessness like a parasite.

But this… Mason is different.

Mason's control doesn't take from me.

It gives.

Where Steffan demanded submission through terror, Mason earns it through protection.

Where Steffan made decisions to trap me, Mason decides to free me from the burden of choice when I'm too broken to bear it.

His authority doesn't diminish me—it cradles me, holds me steady while I remember how to breathe.

Instead of panic, it makes me ache. For the first time in years, someone else is making the decisions, and my body is responding with a hunger that terrifies and thrills me.

Not because I'm afraid of him, but because I'm afraid of how much I want to yield to him.

The realization hits me like a physical blow. Submission is woven into my DNA like breathing. I yield to authority—always have, even before Steffan weaponized it against me.

It's why I followed his commands for so long, why I stayed when every instinct screamed to run.

Here I am, doing it again with Mason when it's the last thing I should do, when I should be running, fighting, and protecting what's left of my fractured independence.

But there's something about Mason that makes it feel—safe.

Natural.

Inevitable.

Like I can finally exhale and let someone else carry the crushing weight I've been dragging. He won't hurt me. I know this with a certainty that defies logic, that bypasses every rational defense I should have.

Where Steffan took my submission and twisted it into something ugly, Mason handles it like something precious.

I know it's probably a trauma response. I should fight this instinct that's gotten me into so much trouble, but with Mason, yielding doesn't feel like losing myself.

It feels like coming home.

He leads me to a bathroom that's surprisingly luxurious for a wilderness cabin. Heated floors, a rainfall shower, and thick towels stacked neatly on shelves.

As he sets clean clothes on the counter, I'm acutely aware of the small space we're sharing, the intimacy of him preparing these things for me. The way he's taking care of me.

"Take as long as you need," he says, but when he turns to leave, our bodies brush in the narrow doorway. The contact is electric, and for a moment, we're frozen, looking at each other with something raw and hungry.

I see the moment he notices my hardened nipples through the thin fabric, the way his pupils dilate.

"These will be too big, but they're warm. I'll be right outside if you need anything."

The promise in those words—that he'll be listening, that he'll come if I call—sends a rush of warmth and comfort through me that leaves me breathless.

"Mason." I can't look him in the eye. He's too much, too caring, too devastatingly perfect.

He pauses at the threshold, his knuckles white where he grips the doorframe like he's fighting not to turn back.

"Thank you. For—all of this."

Something softens in his expression, but there's heat there too, possession.

"Get clean. I'll take care of the rest."

The way he says it—like it's already decided, like I'm already his to tend—sends shivers through me that have nothing to do with the cold and everything to do with the ache building between my legs.

FOUR

Willow

THE HOT WATER IS A REVELATION, BUT I CAN'T STOP THINKING about Mason's hands on my skin, the way he looked at me like he wanted to map every bruise with his tongue.

I shouldn't be feeling this. After what Steffan did, after Drake's brutality, I should be terrified of male attention. Instead, I touch myself under the spray, imagining Mason's hands replacing mine, his mouth on my throat where Steffan left his marks.

The borrowed soap smells like pine and something uniquely masculine, and using it feels like being claimed in the most intimate way. When I finally emerge, wrapped in a towel that could double as a blanket, the clothes he left are indeed enormous.

Thermal underwear, wool socks, and a flannel shirt that hangs to my knees. But they smell like him, and wearing them without anything underneath feels unexpectedly erotic.

He's in the kitchen, stirring something that smells like heaven. He's removed his jacket, and the play of muscles under his shirt shouldn't be legal. The way the fabric stretches across his broad shoulders entices.

When he turns to look at me, his eyes darken as they take in the sight of me in his clothes, and I can see him imagining what's underneath—or what isn't.

"Better?" Mason asks, his voice rougher than before, his gaze lingering on the way his shirt hangs loose on my frame.

"Much." I settle into the chair he indicates, hyperaware of how his gaze follows my movements, how the flannel rides up slightly when I sit. "Your cabin is—not what I expected."

A ghost of a smile touches his lips, while I stare at his mouth, wondering what his lips would feel like against mine.

"What did you expect?"

"Honestly? A one-room shack with a wood stove and maybe a sleeping bag." I gesture at the high-tech security panel, the sophisticated electronics, trying to distract myself from the way he's looking at me like he wants to strip his shirt right back off me.

"This is like something out of a spy movie."

"Former military contractors tend to be particular about their security." He ladles soup into a bowl and sets it in front of me. When he hands me the spoon, his fingers deliberately brush mine, lingering longer than necessary.

The contact sends heat shooting up my arm and straight between my thighs.

"Venison stew. Easy on the stomach."

I take the first spoonful, and he watches me eat with an intensity that makes me squirm. There's something almost predatory in the way he observes every swallow, like he's cataloging my responses, learning what I need. The soup is rich and warming, but I'm more focused on the way Mason's attention makes my skin feel too tight, makes me want to arch into his gaze.

"Good girl," he murmurs when I finish half the bowl.

The praise lands on me like a physical caress. My thighs

clench involuntarily, and from the slight smile that curves his lips, he notices.

"The dogs," I say desperately, trying to focus on something other than the way two simple words have made me wet. "They're not just pets, are they?"

"Working dogs. Bear's a Newfoundland—trained for search and rescue, though he thinks his main job is comic relief." Mason's smile is genuine when he looks at Bear, but when his attention returns to me, there's something darker there. "Chaos is a Belgian Malinois. Military working dog, like me."

"Like you are, or were?" I ask gently, studying the way the firelight plays across his features.

His expression shuts down slightly, but there's something vulnerable there. "Some things you never stop being." His eyes meet mine. "Some instincts never fade."

The way he says it, the weight behind the words, makes me wonder what instincts he's talking about. The way he's looking at me suggests they have nothing to do with military training and everything to do with the tension building between us.

"You built this yourself?" I ask, impressed despite myself, trying to ignore the way my body is responding to his proximity.

"Most of it. Took about a year." He refills my bowl without asking, his movements bringing him closer. When his knuckles brush mine, neither of us pull away immediately. "Good project for a man with too much time and too many things to forget."

The honesty in that statement hits me like a punch to the chest. This isn't a cabin—it's a fortress. A sanctuary. A place to heal from whatever haunts him. And he's brought me into it.

"I'm sorry," I say quietly. "For bringing trouble to your sanctuary."

Mason's eyes meet mine, steady and sure, and the intensity there steals my breath.

"You're not trouble, Willow." He reaches out, cups my chin

with fingers that are gentle but firm, tilting my face up to meet his gaze. "You're someone who needed help, and I was in a position to give it. That's all that matters."

But it's not all that matters, and we both know it. My mouth opens to argue, but his thumb traces along my lower lip, stealing the words. The urge to suck it into my mouth, to taste his skin, overwhelms me. The air between us is charged with possibility, with want, with something that feels inevitable.

"Finish your soup," he says softly, but there's command in it, and my body responds before my mind can protest. I obey, taking another spoonful, and the approval in his eyes makes warmth spread through my chest.

We fall into comfortable silence, but the tension between us is palpable. Every glance feels loaded, every accidental touch electric. I finish the second bowl of stew, feeling more human than I have in months, more alive than I've felt in years. But underneath the contentment is something else—a building need that has nothing to do with food or shelter.

Mason moves around the kitchen, cleaning up. I should offer to help, but I'm mesmerized by the economical grace of his movements, the way he commands even this domestic space. When he catches me staring, his eyes darken.

"The bookshelves," I say, fighting the urge to ask him to touch me again. "Law books. Are you studying something specific?"

Mason pauses in his dishwashing, his shoulders tensing. "International maritime law. Jurisdictional issues. Extradition treaties." He doesn't elaborate, but I catch the implication—and the danger that still surrounds him.

"Preparing for something?"

"Always." He meets my eyes, and there's something in his expression that makes my pulse quicken and my thighs clench. "A man in my line of work needs to understand the legal landscape."

The reminder that he's dangerous, that he lives in a world of violence and shadows, should frighten me. Instead, it intensifies the ache between my legs. After Steffan's weak cruelty, after Drake's mindless brutality, there's something intoxicating about Mason's controlled strength.

Exhaustion is creeping back in, but underneath it is something else, something that makes me want to stay awake, to explore this connection building between us. My eyelids are growing heavy, but I'm fighting it, not wanting to break this spell.

"Rest," Mason says, noticing my drooping eyelids. His voice is gentler now, but there's an undercurrent of command. "I'll keep watch."

"I should help with—"

"You should rest. That's an order." But he moves closer, and when he adjusts the chair so I can recline slightly, his hands linger on the armrests, caging me in.

The position should trigger every alarm in my system. Steffan used to trap me like this—hands braced on either side of me, using his size to intimidate, to remind me how small and helpless I was beneath him. Drake's version was worse—pinning me down while I fought, holding me captive while he took what he wanted, my struggles only feeding his excitement.

But Mason's cage feels nothing like theirs. Where Steffan's proximity felt like a storm cloud ready to break, Mason's presence is steady warmth. Where Drake's weight was crushing, suffocating, Mason's body creates a shelter rather than a prison.

His arms aren't bars—they're walls protecting me from everything beyond this moment. I should be panicking, should be flashing back to all the times being trapped meant pain was coming.

Instead, I feel safe. Cherished. Like something precious being carefully contained, not to control, but to protect.

For a moment, we're frozen like that, his face inches from mine, both of us breathing a little too hard.

The scent of his skin, the heat radiating from his body, surrounds me. My lips part slightly, and his gaze drops to my mouth. The moment stretches, taut with possibility. My body leans forward before my mind catches up, wanting…

He pulls back abruptly, but not before I catch the hunger in his eyes. "Sleep, Willow."

The command in his voice makes my body go pliant, makes me want to obey in ways that have nothing to do with exhaustion. I settle back in the chair, and someone—Bear, probably—has arranged himself so I can rest my feet against his warm bulk. But it's Mason's presence I'm most aware of as my eyes drift closed, the way he watches over me like a sentinel.

Just for a moment, I tell myself. Just until the storm passes.

But sleep claims me anyway, deep and dreamless and safe. And in my dreams, it's Mason's hands on my skin, Mason's voice commanding my pleasure, Mason claiming what Steffan broke.

I wake to the sound of Mason moving quietly around the cabin, checking locks, monitoring his security systems. The fire has been stoked, casting dancing shadows on the walls. There's a blanket draped over me that wasn't there before—soft wool that smells like him. Outside, the storm still rages, but here in this fortress of warmth and safety, it feels like nothing can touch us.

For the first time in three years, I'm not afraid. But I am aware…

Of Mason's presence.

Of the way my body responds to his nearness.

Of the attraction that's been building since the moment he touched me.

I shift slightly, and the movement makes me acutely aware of how ready I am.

Mason catches me watching him and offers a small smile that

does dangerous things to my pulse. In the firelight, he looks like something out of a dark fairy tale—beautiful and dangerous and mine.

"Feel better?" he asks, moving closer.

"Much." I stretch deliberately, knowing his shirt rides up, knowing he's watching. "Thank you. For everything."

"Don't thank me yet. We still have to figure out how to get you somewhere permanently safe."

The reminder of the outside world, of the danger still lurking, should terrify me. Instead, all I can think is that leaving here means leaving him, and that thought is almost unbearable.

I don't want safe. I want him.

Before I can respond, a new sound cuts through the storm's howl. Faint but distinct.

Thump-thump-thump.

Helicopter blades.

Mason's entire body goes rigid, every muscle coiled for action. His eyes meet mine across the room, and in them I see not just protectiveness, but something fierce and possessive that makes my heart race for entirely different reasons.

"Stay exactly where you are," he commands, and my body responds to the authority in his voice even as—

The sound grows louder. Closer.

And everything changes.

Mason stills. Completely.

The breath he takes is sharp, shallow. His entire body coils like a wire about to snap, and then—he moves.

Not the smooth, calculated movement I've come to expect. Not the steady-footed warrior I trust with my life.

This is different.

He stumbles toward the bathroom, like the floor's shifting under him. Like, he doesn't know where he is. I ignore his order and leap to my feet, knowing instinctively that he *needs* me.

By the time I reach him, he's at the sink, sleeves shoved to his elbows, scrubbing his hands under scalding water. Over and over. Nails digging into his palms. Skin turning red.

Steam curls around his head like smoke. His eyes don't see me. They don't see anything.

He's somewhere else. Somewhere bloody and loud and godawful.

I don't think.

I just move.

My arms slide around his waist, careful but firm. I press my cheek to the thick heat of his back. He's rigid, heart hammering through his spine, but he doesn't push me away.

"You're safe," I whisper, anchoring my voice low and steady. "You're home. Montana. Your cabin. The storm's still outside. Nothing's coming."

He shakes once. Just once. A full-body tremor like a dam cracking behind his ribs.

I hold on tighter.

Because right now, he's the one drowning.

And I need him to know he's not alone.

I barely know this man. I shouldn't be reaching out to someone lost in his nightmares, but somehow, it feels right.

As if comforting him is the most instinctive thing in the world.

Maybe it's crazy.

Maybe it's reckless.

But with Mason, it feels—right.

The moment my fingers touch his skin, electricity crackles between us. His heart thunders against my touch, its frantic rhythm gradually steadying as I hold him.

He stiffens at the contact, a tremor running through his powerful frame, but he doesn't pull away. He allows the contact, though his muscles remain coiled tight.

"Feel my arms around you. Feel the solid floor beneath your feet. You're here, not there."

Wherever that is.

I reach forward, shutting off the tap, then gently dry his hands. He lets me.

"Talk to me," I whisper.

A shudder runs through him. One hand comes up to cover mine, resting against his chest, his grip almost desperate. "Just—stay," he manages, his voice rough. "I need to feel something real."

"I'm here. I'm real." I go still, letting him ground himself through the contact.

Gradually, his heartbeat slows. Then, carefully, he turns within the circle of my arms. His hands slide to my waist, drawing me close as my cheek finds his chest. The solid thud of his heart beneath my ear anchors us both to the present.

One hand cradles the back of my head, pressing me more firmly against him. His fingers tangle in my hair, grip tightening as the memories release their hold. The helicopter's sound has faded, leaving only the storm's howl and our shared breathing.

"Good girl," he murmurs, the words rumbling through his chest against my cheek.

The praise slides through me like warm honey, melting my spine. Mason's dominance feels natural, perfect, and protective rather than possessive and cruel. When he claims, he offers shelter in return. My body softens against him, offering submission as sanctuary.

When he finally looks down at me, his eyes are clear again, though shadows lurk in their depths. His hand cups my cheek, thumb tracing my bottom lip. The touch is feather-light, giving me every chance to pull away. Instead, I lean into his palm, offering myself as comfort.

Something shifts in his gaze as I yield to his touch. Those

steel-gray eyes darken, and his pupils dilate until only a thin ring of color remains. The transformation steals my breath—the way his expression changes from vulnerable to predatory in the space of a heartbeat.

His thumb presses more firmly against my lip, and I can't help but part them on a shaky exhale. The small surrender makes his nostrils flare, and his other hand tightens in my hair.

I should be terrified of this—of the raw hunger I see in his eyes, of the way his powerful body cages mine against the wall. Instead, I arch closer, seeking more of his heat, strength, and control.

The air between us crackles with tension, a silent understanding passing between us without a word spoken. I'm open to whatever comes next, ready to let this stranger lead me into uncharted territory.

For once, I want to let go—completely.

I lick the pad of his thumb. A whisper of contact.

A *yes*.

He growls low, a sound from deep in his chest. One arm wraps around me. Pulls me flush. His thumb lingers before sliding along my jawline. The tension between us winds tight like a coiled spring. His other hand moves to the small of my back, drawing me closer until there's hardly any space left between us.

My heart pounds. My breath catches.

And still, I don't look away.

I want this.

God help me—I want everything.

I don't think about it. Can't think about it. Just rise on my toes and press my lips to his. Offering comfort. Seeking solace from him.

FIVE

Willow

One moment, we're breathing the same air, suspended in fragile stillness. Next, his mouth crashes into mine, all fire and desperation. I gasp as he walks me backward, gripping my thighs and lifting me like I weigh nothing.

My back hits the wall. My legs wrap around his hips, my body reacting on instinct. Heat floods my core as his hardness presses against me, and I whimper into the kiss.

"Tell me to stop." The command growls from his throat, hands already under my borrowed shirt, branding my skin. The dominance in his tone makes me shiver, but it's the restraint behind it that undoes me. He's giving me control even as he claims it.

"Please don't."

A sound like pain rips from his throat. His mouth claims mine again, harder this time, all restraint shattering.

I roll my hips against him. Need sparks like lightning through my body, electrifying everything Steffan tried to beat into silence. Mason devours my mouth, one hand gripping my hip, the other sliding up my ribs, leaving fire in his wake. When he pulls back to kiss down my throat, I arch into the contact, offering more.

Every touch erases another memory of Steffan, replacing fear with fire. When Mason breaks the kiss to trace his lips down my throat, I tilt my head back in willing surrender.

His teeth graze the tender skin below my jaw. A question. A dare.

Instead of retreating, I pull him closer, fingers curling into his hair.

He pauses, his breath warm against my skin.

His teeth press a little more firmly, testing my boundaries, waiting to see how far I'm willing to go. My heart pounds in my chest, excitement and anticipation swirling within me. I slide my fingers into his hair, pulling him close, signaling that this is what I want.

He groans, low and primal, and his hand moves to the small of my back, yanking me tighter to him. The world beyond this cabin—the storm, the danger, my past—vanishes beneath the weight of this moment.

I never imagined I could feel this way with someone I barely know. But maybe that's the key. With Mason, there's no pretense, no expectations. Just raw, unfiltered desire. And perhaps, for the first time, I can truly be free to explore the depths of my longing.

"This is madness." He lifts his head slightly, his eyes searching mine for any sign of reluctance. Finding none, a subtle smile curves his lips before he captures my mouth once more, deeper this time. I meet his fervor with my own, ready to see where this uncharted path leads us.

He breaks the kiss just enough to look at me.

"Look at me," he demands, and I force my heavy lids open to meet his gaze. The possession I see there makes me tremble. "If this isn't what you want… If it's too much—tell me to stop."

"Don't stop." My breath catches, words tangled on my tongue. "Please, don't stop."

He studies me, searching for doubt, and I meet him with fire.

"Are you sure?"

"Yes."

He studies me for a moment longer, ensuring he's reading me correctly. Seeing the resolve in my eyes, the tension in his shoulders eases. His hand moves to cup my face gently, his thumb brushing against my cheek as he leans in. The space between us disappears, and I surrender completely to the moment, trusting him to lead the way.

"I'm not gentle." The words come out as a warning, even as his thumb traces my bottom lip with aching tenderness. "Not like this. Not when you make me feel this way, but I can try… You're injuries…"

"Please don't be gentle with me. I don't need gentle," I whisper, nipping at his thumb, a silent invitation for him to let go, to take what he needs from me. "I need real."

Something snaps behind his eyes—a primal, feral hunger that sends a shiver down my spine. His voice drops lower, rougher, more intense. His forehead presses against mine, his breath ragged and hot on my skin.

"I don't want to hurt you. I can't promise I'll be gentle. I need you to know that."

"Take what you need. I can handle it." I look into his eyes, seeing the raw hunger and the underlying concern. I reach up, cupping his cheek, my thumb brushing against his stubble. "I'm strong enough for you."

His response is instantaneous and overwhelming. His control shatters.

He sets me down, strips me with shaking hands, and rips his shirt over his head. His scars glint in the low light, powerful and brutal. He shoves his pants down, eyes locked on mine, watching for any sign of fear.

There is none.

Then he's on me again, lifting me like I weigh nothing. My back hits the wall as my legs wrap instinctively around his hips. The feeling of skin against skin is electric—all heat and need and desperate hunger. His hardness presses against me, drawing a whimper from my throat.

"Last chance," he growls, his voice a low rumble that resonates in his chest. "Last chance to tell me to stop."

"Not going to do that." I meet his gaze steadily, my voice filled with determination and need. I roll my hips against him, feeling the hard length of him pressed against my core, drawing a sound like pain from deep within his chest.

A primal, feral hunger flashes in his eyes, and his control snaps. His teeth find my throat, biting down, marking me as his. His hands grip my thighs hard enough to bruise, a claim of possession that sends a wave of heat through me. With one powerful thrust, he enters me, swallowing my cry of pleasure with a fierce, demanding kiss.

There's no gentleness, no hesitation. Only raw, primal connection. Each stroke claims me more thoroughly than the last, erasing every bad memory with pure, overwhelming sensation. His hands roam my body, claiming every inch of me as his own. His mouth devours mine, his teeth nipping at my lips, his tongue invading, possessing.

The wall is cold and unyielding against my back, a stark contrast to the heat of his body pressed against me. His grip on my thighs is bruising, his fingers digging into my flesh, holding me in place as he drives into me with relentless force. The sound of our bodies coming together fills the room, a raw, primal symphony that drowns out everything else.

His mouth moves to my throat, his teeth grazing my skin,

marking me, claiming me. Each bite, each suck, each lick erases another memory of Steffan, replacing pain with pleasure.

My body burns for him, desperate, greedy. The cold wall digs into my back. His body pins me in place like a living weapon.

He growls something against my skin, and I don't catch the words, only the fury and hunger beneath them. I answer with my own cry, lost in sensation, in the way he claims me like I'm his to take.

And I am.

I want to be.

His.

A fantasy come to life.

Every thrust steals another piece of my past and gives it back, laced in pleasure.

I surrender to his possession, letting him drive every thought from my head except the feel of him, the scent of him, the sound of his rough groans against my skin. His body claims mine, his cock filling me, his hands gripping me with bruising force, his mouth marking me as his.

He growls against my throat, his voice thick with desire and dominance.

Animalistic.

I cling to him, taking what he gives.

His thrusts become harder, faster, and more desperate. Each stroke drives me higher, closer to the edge. Pleasure coils low in my belly, building, intensifying, until it explodes through me, a wave of pure, unadulterated ecstasy. His name tears from my lips, a cry of surrender and release, as my body clenches around him, pulling him deeper, claiming him as much as he claims me.

His release follows closely behind, his body tensing, his thrusts becoming erratic. He buries his face in my neck, his teeth sinking into my flesh as he chases his pleasure and finds his release. His body shudders against mine, his breath hot and ragged in my ear.

As we cling to each other, our bodies still joined, our hearts pounding in sync, I know this is more than just sex. It's my fantasy come to life.

And I want it all. I want him, all of him, every dark, wild, possessive inch of him.

He holds me against the wall until my trembling legs can support my weight again. Then he lowers me, legs barely holding. Scoops me into his arms like I'm weightless and carries me to bed. He pulls the covers back and lays me down gently, his touch reverent.

"Get in," he says, pulling back the covers. His voice is still rough with need but gentler now, the primal edge softened by satisfaction and concern.

I slide between the sheets, watching as he follows, immediately drawing me against his chest. His arms cage me protectively, his body a warm, solid shield against the world. He presses a kiss to the top of my head, his lips lingering, his breath ruffling my hair.

"Well," he chuckles, a sound that vibrates through me, filled with disbelief and amusement, "that was *definitely* unexpected." He shakes his head, as if still trying to process what just happened between us. "When I first saw you, I didn't think we'd end up like this—especially not with me fucking you against the bathroom wall."

His fingers trace the marks he's left on my throat, my shoulders, my hips, each touch a silent apology, a tender caress that soothes the lingering sting.

"I hope I didn't hurt you," he says, his voice soft with concern. "I didn't mean to be so rough, but you… That was the best damn thing that's happened to me in a long time," he admits quietly.

"Only in the best possible way," I murmur, pressing closer to his warmth. His chest rumbles with satisfaction at my words. I can't help but smile, my fingers tracing lazy patterns on his chest. "It was incredible. The best wall sex I've ever had."

"Was it?"

"Yes."

"Have you ever been fucked against a wall before?"

"No." I laugh. "That was a first for me."

"I shouldn't have done that."

"I shouldn't have let you, but I really needed something like that."

"Sex with a stranger?"

"Sex with a savior," I correct. "You have no idea what that meant to me."

"It wasn't too—rough?" He looks down at me, his eyes searching mine, a soft smile playing at the corners of his mouth.

"No."

"Seems like you enjoyed it."

"It was perfect and amazing. I'm still tingling, and no, it wasn't too rough."

"Duly noted." His arms tighten around me, holding me closer, his body a haven of safety and comfort. As we lie there, wrapped in each other's arms, the world outside fades away, leaving only the two of us, lost in our private sanctuary.

He presses another kiss to the top of my head, his voice a soft rumble in his chest. "We should get some sleep," he says, his fingers still tracing lazy patterns on my skin. "Tomorrow's going to be a busy day."

"If you say so." I roll over and stare deeply into his eyes. "You're the one in charge."

"Is that so?"

"I hope so." How do I explain to this man, this stranger, how his natural dominance feeds a need deep within me? How do I explain it to myself, when it's brought so much pain?

Sleep proves elusive, however.

Each time one of us shifts, sparks reignite. His hands find me in the darkness, claiming me again with the same desperate need. He covers me with his body, pinning my wrists above my head. The position makes me feel deliciously vulnerable and completely at his mercy. His other hand traces down my side, grip possessive.

"You like that, don't you?" he asks, voice rough with desire. His eyes search mine, gauging my reaction. "Being restrained? At my mercy?" His eyes, fierce and hungry, lock onto mine, gauging my reaction.

"Not going to lie." What other answer can I give him when he's tapping into my deepest fantasies?

I'm trapped, helpless, at his mercy. A thrill of pleasure and fear courses through me, but there's no trace of the old terror I used to feel with Steffan.

I let out a shuddering breath, unable to speak, but my body arches into his touch, betraying my need. He leans down, his mouth next to my ear, his voice a low rumble.

"I'm going to fuck you now. Take my time. Make you scream. Make you beg." His grip tightens on my wrists as he claims my mouth in a bruising kiss.

His hand leaves my wrists, trailing down my side, gripping my hip with bruising force. I keep my hands over my head, locked where he left them. He shifts, settling between my thighs, his hardness pressing insistently against me. His gaze locks onto mine, dominant and possessive.

His hand slides up to my throat, wrapping around it gently, a promise of control.

"Is that too much?"

I arch into his touch, begging for him to tighten his grip.

"Fuck, look at what you do to me. You bring out the beast within me."

I whimper, a sound caught between pleasure and protest, but

my body betrays me, my hips lifting to grind against his. He smirks, a satisfied and dangerous expression.

"You *really* like that, don't you?" he murmurs, his hand tightening slightly around my throat. "Yeah, you love that."

I can't speak, can't even nod, but my eyes flutter closed, my body quivering with need. He leans down, capturing my mouth in a brutal kiss, his teeth nipping at my lips.

"That's what I thought," he growls against my mouth.

Suddenly, he flips me onto my stomach, his strong hands gripping my hips, pulling me up onto my knees. He presses one hand firmly between my shoulder blades, pushing me into the mattress, forcing me to arch my back, presenting myself to him completely.

My breath hitches, and I push back against him, silently begging for more.

With Steffan, sex was always about fear and pain, about submission through terror. With Mason, it's about surrender and exquisite pleasure, about submission through trust and desire.

He positions himself at my entrance, and with one powerful thrust, he enters me, stealing my breath away. Each stroke is hard and deep, claiming me, owning me, driving away every memory of Steffan, every moment of fear and pain.

"*Fuuuuuuck*, you feel so fucking good." His voice rasps rough with desire.

He leans over me, his hand still pressed firmly between my shoulder blades, keeping me pinned to the mattress. His other hand grips my hair, yanking my head back and to the side so he can claim my mouth in a fierce, dominating kiss.

He drives into me, his body tensing, his thrusts becoming erratic. "You like that, don't you?" he growls against my mouth. "You like being fucked like this."

"Yes," I gasp, my body quivering with pleasure, my heart pounding in my chest.

With a final, brutal thrust, he finds his release, his body shaking with the force of it. I cry out, my orgasm crashing over me, waves of pleasure drowning out the past, leaving only the present, only Mason.

As he collapses on top of me, his body still claiming mine, his breath hot and ragged in my ear, I'm struck by the sudden realization of what I'm doing. I'm having aggressive, brutal sex with a man whose last name I don't even know.

After everything Steffan put me through, I should be terrified, should be guarding myself against more pain and abuse. But there's something about Mason, something in his touch, his voice, his eyes, that makes everything okay.

I feel safe with him.

Ironically, I feel safer with a stranger than my husband.

We lie there, our bodies entwined, our hearts pounding in sync. Then he rolls off me, pulling me into his arms, holding me close. His hand gently strokes my back, his touch now tender and caring.

"You're incredible," he murmurs, his voice soft with awe. "The way you respond, the way you give yourself to me... It's more than I ever hoped for."

"It's you." I smile, pressing a soft kiss to his chest, feeling his heartbeat steady and strong beneath my lips. "You give me space to yield."

He kisses the top of my head, his arms tightening around me. His touch is gentle and tender. "You're safe with me, I promise. I will never take your submission for granted."

I smile, pressing a soft kiss to his lips.

As I drift off to sleep, wrapped in his embrace, a sense of peace and contentment washes over me. I don't know his last name, and I know nothing about him except how he makes me feel.

The reality of what I've just done hits me in waves.

I had the most erotic sex of my life with a man I barely know —a man who, only hours ago, was a stranger. A man who saved me from a blizzard, brought me to safety, and who might be able to protect me from the very real danger that Steffan poses.

I should be terrified. I should be guarding myself against more pain, more abuse. I should be thinking about the consequences of my actions, about the potential danger I'm putting myself in. But as I lie here, wrapped in Mason's arms, I'm not afraid.

I don't regret what I've done.

Instead, I'm filled with a sense of wonder and disbelief. A sense of *rightness*. As if *this* is what I've always desired.

I wish I could keep real life from intruding on this moment. I wish I could stay here, in this cocoon of pleasure and surrender, forever. Because this moment is pure bliss. It's everything I never knew I needed, everything I've been craving.

Everything I never had.

As I drift off to sleep, reality waits outside this secluded cabin. Drake and his team are out there, posing a very real and dangerous threat. I can't hide forever, which means I can't lose myself in Mason's touch.

But this moment is mine.

Mason is mine.

And I want more.

SIX

Willow

MASON LIES BESIDE ME, ONE ARM FLUNG OVERHEAD, HIS SCARRED chest rising and falling with the rhythm of sleep. There's a softness to him now, a quiet vulnerability that tugs at something deep inside me.

The scent of wet fur and cedar greets me before I even open my eyes. Morning light seeps through the cracks in the cabin walls, cold and pale, but there's warmth pressed to my feet—dense, immovable warmth that snores in low, thunderous gusts.

Bear.

I crack one eye. He's sprawled across the foot of the bed like a fallen boulder, tongue lolling, one massive paw twitching in some dream of snow or squirrels. His fur smells like pine smoke and mountain water, like he belongs out there instead of in here. He lets out a grunt as I shift, tail thumping once, half-heartedly, before going limp again. Lazy power in a two-hundred-pound shag carpet.

But it's not Bear who tenses when the floorboard creaks beneath my heel.

It's Chaos.

I don't have to look to know he's behind the front door. I can feel him—coiled stillness in the shape of a predator, breath slow, ears sharp. He doesn't sleep so much as wait. Not Bear's brand of guardianship. No. Chaos is a blade tucked in shadow. Precision wrapped in fur.

I sit up slowly. Chaos doesn't move. Doesn't blink. But he tracks every breath I take.

I swing my legs over the edge of the bed. Bear groans and rolls onto his back, all belly and drool and zero dignity. His tail flops. I rub it absently. He saves lives, Mason said, but right now, he's just a glorified rug with bad breath.

Chaos, though—he waits until I take a step toward the kitchen before he rises. Silent. Controlled. His gaze locks onto mine, neither aggressive nor soft. Just—assessing.

Guard mode. Always.

Bear protects with brute instinct and slobber.

Chaos?

Chaos calculates.

Together, they're safety in stereo.

One soft. One sharp.

One warm. One warning.

Both of them have accepted me into their pack.

And our leader is Mason—still no last name.

Scars map his chest, telling stories of battles survived. Need coils low in my belly as I watch him, my body aching in the most delicious ways, remembering his possession.

I reach out, brushing my fingertips across his ribs where faint bruises from our earlier frenzy bloom. He stirs, lashes fluttering, eyes opening slowly. When they land on me, they're shadowed—not from sleep, but something deeper.

Regret, maybe.

"I was too rough," he murmurs, voice low and ragged. "Should've stopped, should've pulled back. I lost control." He reaches out, his fingers gently tracing the bruises he left on my skin, each touch a silent apology for his earlier roughness.

"You didn't take anything I didn't give freely." I cup his cheek, feel the rasp of stubble against my palm. "You didn't hurt me, Mason. You gave me something I didn't think I could have again." I press my fingers to his lips, feeling them tremble against my skin.

He kisses my fingertips, but the shadows don't fully retreat. Tension tightens in his body, and self-recrimination simmers in his gaze. He's a man used to being in control, and last night, he walked a fine line, testing my boundaries and pushing my limits.

I loved every minute of it, but the concern in his eyes worries me.

Before I can overthink it, I shift, moving down his body, my intent clear. His eyes widen in surprise, but he doesn't stop me. When I take him into my mouth, his eyes snap shut instantly, hands automatically gripping my hair.

For a heartbeat, he holds me there, a low groan rumbling in his chest. Then he moves, lifting and lowering my head, fucking my mouth as desire overcomes him.

"*Fuuuck*," he growls, his voice ragged with pleasure. "You don't have to, but there's no way I'm stopping you. Your mouth feels so good."

I hum in response, the vibration drawing a hiss from him. His fingers tighten in my hair, holding me where he wants me, using my mouth for his pleasure. I can feel him holding back, can sense the restraint in his touch.

I don't want his restraint.

I want his passion, his wildness, his fire.

I look up at him, meeting his gaze as I swallow him deeper. His eyes darken, the guilt and regret replaced by hunger and need. He keeps me there, my mouth filled with him, until he's on the edge, then he flips our positions. His weight pins me to the mattress as his mouth claims mine, erasing any doubt about reciprocal desire.

"Brave girl, sucking my cock like that," he growls against my throat. "Playing with fire."

"Then teach me a lesson." I arch into him, my breath hitching with anticipation.

His eyes darken, and a primal, feral hunger takes over. He searches for any sign of doubt or fear, but there is none.

I want this.

He sits back, his gaze roaming over my body, a primal hunger in his eyes. This is my fantasy coming to life, and now that he knows what I need and crave, he gives it to me.

"Turn over," he commands, his voice rough with desire. "On your hands and knees."

I comply without hesitation, presenting myself to him, offering him everything. He grips my hips, his fingers digging into my flesh, his touch possessive, dominant. He presses one hand firmly between my shoulder blades, pushing me into the mattress, forcing me to arch my back.

"Stay," he commands, his voice leaving no room for argument.

I comply, my body tense with anticipation, my breath coming in quick, shallow gasps, my body quivering with need, my back arching further, offering myself to him completely. He grips my hips with bruising force, his fingers digging into my flesh, marking me as his. He positions himself at my entrance, and with one forceful thrust, he enters me, filling me completely.

He sets a brutal pace, each stroke hard and deep. His hands grip my hips, his fingers digging into my flesh. He leans over me, one hand gripping my shoulder, the other tangling in my hair, pulling my head back and to the side, exposing my throat to his mouth, his teeth.

"Fuck, you feel incredible," he growls, his body tense behind me.

I moan, my body stretching to accommodate him, my nerves alight with sensation. Each thrust sends a jolt of pleasure coursing through me, pushing me higher, driving me further into that realm of sensation where only he and I exist.

He releases my hair, his hand trailing down my spine, pressing between my shoulder blades, holding me against the mattress. It's a power move, and I love it.

My body pulses with pleasure.

My heart pounds in my chest.

My mind retreats to the bliss of submission.

His words send a rush of heat through me, pushing me closer to the edge. His thrusts become harder, faster, more desperate. He leans over me, his body covering mine, his breath hot and ragged in my ear.

Pleasure explodes through me, a wave of pure, unadulterated ecstasy. I cry out, my body convulsing beneath him, my heart pounding in my chest. He continues to thrust, riding me through my orgasm, his release following closely behind. He comes with a roar, his body shaking with the force of it, his cock pulsing deep inside me.

We collapse onto the mattress, our bodies entwined, our hearts pounding in sync. He pulls me into his arms, holding me close, his touch gentle and tender. He presses a soft kiss to my lips, a smile playing at the corners of his mouth.

"You're incredible," he murmurs, his gaze full of wonder. "I've never met anyone like you."

"I wish we could stay like this."

"What do you mean?"

I meet his gaze steadily, letting him see the truth in my eyes.

I exhale slowly. "I've lived in fear for years. Submission became a prison instead of a choice. Steffan… He raped me.

Over and over. And he let his chief of security do it too. Drake. Steffan watched. He approved and encouraged."

Mason goes still. The air thickens around us.

"You're saying—" His voice breaks with fury. "The motherfucker let his security chief touch you?"

"Touch me. Punish me… Rape me." I don't know why Mason gets to hear about all the ugly parts of my life. There's just something about him that makes me feel safe. Like I can trust him with the worst of my life.

"I've been living in hell." My throat tightens as I share the worst moments of my life. "Always afraid, always waiting for the next punishment. Last night… With you?" How do I explain to this man the gift he's given me? "It was different. You didn't take anything from me. You let me give. I felt wanted. Safe. Protected."

He exhales hard, scrubbing a hand through his hair as he leans back against the headboard. "You said that was the best sex you've ever had."

"It was." My voice is quiet but certain. "I've never come apart like that in someone's arms. Never felt that safe. That free."

A slow, wicked grin spreads across his face. "Careful. You say things like that, and you're gonna give a guy a god complex."

I arch a brow. "A god complex?"

"Yeah. Giant ego. Swagger for days. Probably start carving notches in the headboard."

"Huge ego." I laugh, the sound easing some of the heaviness still pressing on my chest. "And for the record, you already have a swagger."

He leans in, voice dropping to a husky murmur. "That's not the only thing I've got that's huge." He glances down at the sheets, and the indisputable evidence rises between us. Eager and ready for more.

"You did not just say that." My cheeks flame, and I swat him with the nearest pillow.

His grin widens as he catches the pillow mid-swing. "Babe, you're the one who said *best sex of your life*. I'm just living up to expectations."

I roll my eyes, but the smile won't leave my lips. "Unreal. One night and you're already impossible."

"You started it." He shrugs, completely unapologetic.

"I'm trying to be serious here."

"I'm very serious when it comes to sex." He waggles his brows and lifts the sheets, checking. "Yup. Very serious."

"Truly impossible, and while I'd love more, we need to talk."

"About your asshole husband and the fucktard he sent to bring you back?"

"Fucktard? Haven't heard that one before."

"Didn't feel like asshole was strong enough for this Drake dude."

"Anyway…" I slap him playfully. "I want more sex. A lot more sex. But we need to talk about what's out that door."

"If you insist."

"Steffan won't let me go. Drake and his team are still out there, hunting me. This is a dream, a wonderful dream, but a dream nonetheless. I can't stay here."

"We deal with Steffan. Together. No arguing about that part."

"I can't ask you to—"

"You're not asking." His dominance flows naturally into his words, sending a familiar shiver down my spine. "I'm telling. Or did you forget you're mine to protect?"

"You've known me for less than a day. I would never ask that of you… I would never expect it. All I've done is bring trouble into your world and a day of… Well, a day and night of the best sex of my life."

But even as I embrace the moment, even as I lose myself in

his touch, his kiss, his love, a part of me can't help but mourn the inevitable end. Because I know, deep down, that this can't last. That eventually, I'll have to go back to my real life, back to a world where this kind of passion, this kind of trust, this kind of love, is just a distant memory, a beautiful dream, a fleeting fantasy.

As the day turns to night, we stay in bed, our bodies entwined, our hearts pounding in sync. Mason pulls me into his arms, holding me close, his touch gentle and tender. He presses a soft kiss to my lips, a smile playing at the corners of his mouth.

"You're incredible," he murmurs, his voice filled with awe and satisfaction. "The way you give yourself to me…"

A bittersweet smile touches my lips as I look into his eyes. "Mason," I say softly, my voice barely a whisper, "this is a fantasy. The best fantasy I've ever had. This kind of sex… It's not real. It can't be real. It's a beautiful and intense, but I don't know how to have this in a normal life. I don't know how to maintain this or let go like this outside of this cabin."

He looks at me, his eyes filled with understanding and sadness, but there's also a fierce determination in their depths, a resolve that burns like a flame. He cups my face in his hands, his thumbs gently stroking my cheeks, his gaze steady and sure.

"You're wrong about that," he says, his voice firm yet gentle. "This is something that can be real. We can have both—the intensity, the passion, the trust, and the escape—in our real lives. It doesn't have to be just a fantasy."

I look at him, my eyes searching his, a glimmer of hope flickering to life within me, warring with the doubts that plague my mind. "Do you really believe that?" I whisper, my voice filled with both longing and doubt. "Because I have a life outside of this cabin. A husband who wants me dead. A job. Responsibilities. How does this fit into that?"

His expression turns serious, his eyes intense. "I believe that what we have here, what we've found together, is something rare and special. Something worth fighting for. Something worth taking risks for."

"But, Mason…" I start, my voice trembling with fear and uncertainty. "He's not going to let me go. He'll come after me. He'll hurt you. I can't let that happen."

Mason's gaze hardens, a protective fierceness shining through. "I'm not afraid of Steffan," he growls. "I'm not afraid of anyone who tries to hurt you. I will protect you, no matter what it takes. I will keep you safe."

"But how?" I ask, my doubts growing stronger. "How can we make this work? How can we have this kind of passion, this kind of trust, in the real world? It's not that simple. It's not that easy."

He presses a soft kiss to my forehead, his arms tightening around me, his voice filled with conviction.

"I never said it would be easy, but I promise you, it will be worth it. We will find a way. Together. Because this is the reality I want to live in. A reality where you are mine, and I am yours. A reality where we fight for what we have, protect what we have, and cherish what we are."

I look into his eyes, seeing the reflection of my feelings mirrored in their depths, but also seeing the shadows of my doubts, the fears that hold me back.

"I want to believe you," I whisper. "I want to trust in this, but I'm scared. I'm scared of what happens when I leave this cabin. I'm scared of what happens when reality catches up with me."

He holds me closer, his voice a low, steady rumble in his chest. "I know you're scared. I know you have doubts. I'm not letting you go without a fight. I'm not letting this be just a fantasy because you are worth fighting for. Because *this* doesn't happen often. *We* are worth fighting for."

His words ignite a spark of determination within me, a flame that burns brighter than my doubts, stronger than my fears. I take a deep breath, steeling myself for the challenges ahead.

"Okay," I say, my voice filled with resolve. "Okay, let's fight for this. Let's make this our reality. But promise me, promise me that no matter what happens, no matter what we face, we face it together."

He smiles, a fierce, determined smile that sends a shiver of anticipation down my spine. "Together," he says. "No matter what. That's a promise."

As we lie there, wrapped in each other's arms, the world outside fades away, leaving only the two of us, lost in our private sanctuary.

"Speaking of..." he says. "Tell me about this drive that's so precious. What does it have on your husband?"

SEVEN

Willow

THE SOFT BLUE GLOW OF THE LAPTOP ILLUMINATES MASON'S FACE
as his fingers move across the keyboard, his expression severe. I
watch from the kitchen, two mugs of coffee steaming in my
hands. The last day has shown me another side of him—
methodical, tactical, a mind as lethal as his body.

The USB drive containing my evidence against Steffan sits
connected to Mason's high-security laptop, its contents now laid
bare.

"It's worse than I thought." His voice holds the flat tone I'm
learning means controlled rage. "Your husband has connections
to arms dealers in six countries. At least three judges in his
pocket. And the offshore accounts..." He shakes his head. "How
did you get all this?"

I place his coffee beside him, savoring the brush of his
shoulder against mine. "Three years of playing the perfect wife.
People talk freely around women they underestimate." I pause,
remembering the careful cataloging of each scrap of information. "I was a public defender before I married him. I knew what
to look for."

He looks up at me then, something like admiration in his steel-gray eyes.

"You're remarkable."

The compliment warms me in places his hands haven't touched. But there's still caution in my soul, a voice that whispers: *You barely know this man. Don't make the same mistake twice.*

The silence stretches between us, comfortable yet charged with unspoken questions. Outside, the storm has settled into a steady snowfall, quieter than yesterday's rage but just as effective at keeping us isolated. A perfect cocoon for secrets and revelations.

"Mason," I begin carefully, "who are you? Really?"

His fingers pause over the keyboard. For a moment, I think he'll deflect again with a non-answer about being a wilderness guide. Instead, he closes the laptop and turns to face me fully.

"Former special operations. Delta Force, then something without a name." His eyes hold mine, gauging my reaction. "I specialized in high-value target extraction and intelligence operations."

"And now you live alone in the woods," I say softly. "That's quite a career change."

A shadow crosses his face. "I had my reasons."

"Rachel?" I whisper the name I heard him call out during last night's nightmare, when he thrashed beside me, lost in memories I couldn't see.

His whole body goes rigid. The mug in his hand freezes halfway to his lips. When he sets it down, the careful control of the movement speaks volumes about his internal struggle.

"How much do you want to know?" he asks finally.

"Everything," I answer without hesitation. "I want to know everything I can."

He nods once, sharply, then rises from the chair. I follow him to the fireplace, where he stokes the flames higher before settling onto the sofa. When I move to sit beside him, he pulls me into his lap instead, arranging me so my back rests against his chest, his arms locked around me like a fortress.

"It's easier to say this when I'm not looking at you," he admits, his breath warm against my hair.

I cover his hands with mine, offering silent support. Whatever demons haunt him, I'll face them alongside him.

"Rachel was my submissive," he begins, voice low and steady. "And my fiancée. We met after I returned from my third tour and lived the lifestyle. I was—*struggling*. PTSD, though I wouldn't admit it then."

His breathing shifts, becomes more controlled. "About six months into our relationship, I had an episode. Woke up in the middle of the night with my hands around her throat, choking her." The words emerge like broken glass. "She was fighting me, clawing at my hands, trying to wake me up. By the time I came to, she had bruises. I nearly killed her."

The self-loathing in his voice is devastating. "I tried to leave her that night. Packed my shit, told her I was too dangerous, that she deserved better than a broken soldier who could kill her in his sleep. But Rachel..." His voice softens with memory and pain. "She wouldn't let me go. Said she knew the man I was beneath the damage, that we'd figure it out together."

His arms tighten fractionally around me. "She was my center. My rock. Helped me develop strategies to manage the episodes— sleeping arrangements, ways to ground myself when I felt one coming on. She gave me a reason to keep my shit together, to fight for something better than just surviving."

The fire pops and crackles, filling the silence as he gathers his thoughts.

"After we got my episodes under control, I was recruited for specialized operations—the kind with no official record. The work was brutal but effective. I was good at it. Too good. Rachel knew not to ask questions, but she supported me. Gave me a safe place to come home to, a way to reconnect with humanity after the things I had to do."

His voice remains steady, but I feel the tension in his body, the slight tremor in his hands beneath mine.

"Three years in, I was assigned to gather intelligence on a Russian arms dealer named Viktor Orlov. The mission went sideways. My cover was blown. I barely made it out alive. The rest of my team didn't."

He stops, his breathing carefully controlled.

"I should have known they'd track me back to Rachel. Should have had better security protocols in place." The self-loathing returns, sharp and cutting. "I came home one night and found our apartment door ajar. Inside…"

He stops, his breathing carefully controlled.

"They tortured her. For information she didn't have." The words emerge with precision, each one carved from stone. "She died because of me. Because I brought my work home. Because I thought I could have both—the mission and a life with her."

I turn in his arms, needing to see his face. The raw pain in his eyes steals my breath.

"Mason…" I whisper, but he continues, needing to finish.

"When that helicopter came over, I was back there. Back in Afghanistan, watching my team die. The sound triggered a flashback, and I was trying to fight my way out of it when you put your arms around me." His hands frame my face, thumb tracing my cheekbone. "That's never happened before. No one's ever been able to pull me back like that. Rachel couldn't do it. My therapists couldn't do it. But you—a woman I barely knew—you touched me and just—pulled me out."

His voice drops to a whisper, filled with wonder and confusion. "Do you understand how impossible that is? How incredible? It's why when you kissed me, I kissed you back. Why I couldn't resist you. The sex we've had, the intimacy we've shared—it's not just physical. There's something about you, something I can't explain."

The weight of his confession settles between us. "You brought me back from that flashback, but that doesn't make me safe. It makes me more dangerous, because now I care about you too much to think clearly about the risk I pose."

"What happened to Rachel wasn't your fault," I whisper, cupping his face in my hands.

"I was trained to anticipate threats. To protect assets." His voice hardens. "I failed her."

"You weren't her protector—you were her partner," I say firmly. "The blame lies with the people who killed her."

His jaw clenches beneath my palm. "After her funeral, I hunted them down. All of them. It wasn't sanctioned. Wasn't clean. When it was done, I… I disappeared into these mountains where I couldn't hurt anyone else."

The confession hangs between us, heavy with implications. I search his face, seeing the warrior beneath the guilt, the protector beneath the pain.

"I've been up here almost two years," he continues. "Just me, Bear, and Chaos. No visitors. No contact. I came here to disappear. To make sure I didn't hurt anyone else."

Something fractures in my chest. This man, this protector, this storm-forged warrior has been punishing himself for something he couldn't control.

"You've been alone that long?"

His smile is crooked. "Not anymore."

Silence stretches between us. Warm. Complicated. Full of truths too big to say aloud.

"I know what happened between us came from a heightened place," I whisper. "You saved me. I was scared and hurting and needed something to hold onto. I don't want you to feel like you owe me anything."

His hand tightens on mine. "You think that's what this is?"

"I hope not, but I need you to know I don't expect anything from you."

He nods slowly, then shifts, pulling me gently onto his lap. His voice, when it comes, is quiet but unyielding.

"I hear you, but I need you to understand something. Even if you hadn't come apart in my arms, even if we'd spent the night on opposite sides of this cabin, I would still protect you. I would still stand between you and whatever's hunting you. That's not because of the sex. That's because it's who I am."

Tears sting my eyes. "That's not something I'm used to hearing. Especially from a man. Especially not one I barely know."

"You're not used to a man being a man," he says. "To someone standing up for you just because it's right."

"Steffan has ties in every department," I whisper. "Cops, FBI, even judges. I didn't mean to drag you into this."

"You didn't." Mason's expression hardens with quiet conviction. "I have friends too. Not official channels. Not the kind who wear uniforms. But they're loyal. Smart. Trained. They're already en route."

"What?"

"I made a call while you were sleeping."

I blink at him. "You—did?"

"You deserve peace. You deserve to live. I can give you that." He cups my jaw, his thumb brushing my bottom lip. "And once this is over, if you're still willing, I'd like to explore this. *Us*. Not as a one-night thing. But as something more."

"I'd like that," I whisper.

"Good, because this is happening." His eyes darken, pupils dilating. One hand slides up to cup the back of my neck, thumb tracing my pulse point. "I swore I'd never take responsibility for another submissive. Never trust myself with that power again. Then you said '*yes, sir*' in that soft voice, and everything in me wanted to claim you."

Heat pools low in my belly at his words. "I never responded to Steffan that way, even before the abuse started." I meet his gaze steadily. "With you …" Now it's my turn to pause. "I don't know how to explain it, but it comes naturally."

A growl rumbles through his chest. "Dangerous words, little one."

"The truth often is." I press closer, my lips a whisper from his. "I trust you. All of you—even the parts you're afraid of."

His control snaps. He claims my mouth in a bruising kiss that steals my breath. His hands brand my skin through the borrowed clothes, marking me as his. When he finally pulls back, we're both breathing hard.

"I've been hiding from my life long enough. Punishing myself for Rachel. But finding you…" He shakes his head, wonder mixing with determination. "I'm done hiding. I'm done letting ghosts dictate my choices."

Pain flickers across his face. "Rachel would hate what I've become. This—half-life." His thumb traces my lower lip. "She would have liked you, though. Your courage. Your resilience."

Tears prick at my eyes. "I wish I could have met her."

"So do I." The simple honesty in his voice breaks my heart and heals it in the same moment.

Twin growls suddenly shatter our peace. Chaos and Bear are alerting to something. Mason tenses, immediately alert as he sets me aside and moves to the window.

In an instant, Mason is off the bed, grabbing the tablet and flipping through perimeter camera feeds. Bear lumbers to the window, fur bristling, a low growl rumbling from his chest.

"Movement," he says, voice shifting to tactical precision. "Someone is watching the cabin."

"Drake?" Fear slithers down my spine.

"Most likely." He turns to me, soldier replacing lover. "They lost you in the blizzard—white-out conditions should have made tracking impossible. We spent the night in the shelter, then I brought you here. There's no trail for them to follow, no reason they should suspect you're here."

His jaw tightens as he studies the feeds. "Most likely, they're searching grid by grid. It's what I would do. Checking every structure, every possible shelter within a fifty-mile radius. It was only a matter of time before they reached this area."

"What does that mean?"

"It means they're thorough, and they won't stop until they find you." He sets down the tablet, his expression grim. "The storm's easing. They'll make their move soon. We need to prepare."

"For what?"

"For war." The deadly certainty in his voice should terrify me. Instead, it steadies me.

EIGHT

Willow

MASON FOCUSES ON THE MONITORS. EXTERIOR CAMERA FEEDS
blink in and out of view. Shadows shift in the trees.

"What do we do?" My voice is tight. Thin.

Mason turns to face me, and the transformation steals my
breath. Gone is the tender lover who held me through the night.
In his place stands a warrior, eyes sharp as steel, every line of his
body coiled for violence. Calm, focused, and terrifying. This is
the soldier, the man who survived whatever hell carved those
scars into his flesh.

A man who knows exactly how to hunt and how to kill.

"We prepare." He moves to a seemingly ordinary panel in the
wall. It slides open at his touch, revealing an arsenal that would
make a military general weep with envy. Rifles, handguns,
tactical vests, and equipment I can't even name. It's enough to
fight a small war.

"And we fight." He starts suiting up like it's second nature,
pulling on a tactical vest and arming himself. The calm in his
voice should terrify me. Instead, it steadies something inside me. I
trust this man with my body—why not with my life?

"Tell me how to help." I stare for a heartbeat too long before snapping myself into motion.

His eyes meet mine, assessing. Then he nods once, decision made.

"Wear something warm and layers you can move in. We have work to do."

I move quickly, pulling on the clothes he laid out for me yesterday. Thermal leggings. Flannel shirt. Wool socks. My hands tremble as I dress, but I force them to be steady.

Mason buckles on his gear. Every movement precise. Measured. Deadly. He straps a combat knife to his thigh and checks the chamber of a sidearm before holstering it.

Each knife and firearm becomes an extension of him, as natural as breathing.

"Drake had three men with him at the crash." I try to be helpful. "Although he usually works with at least two teams of three each."

"He's had two nights to prep and search." Mason pauses, his eyes sharpening on me. "Tell me everything about them. Training, weapons, tactics. Leave nothing out."

I close my eyes, forcing myself to remember details I've tried so hard to forget. "Drake was Delta Force before Steffan hired him. Harris, his second, is Marine Recon. They have two other regulars—Reeves and Jackson. Both military, though I'm not sure which branch. They're…" I swallow hard. "They're very good at hurting people without leaving evidence. I don't know the names of the others."

Something dangerous flashes in Mason's eyes, but his voice remains controlled. "Combat experience?"

"Drake was in Syria and Afghanistan. Four tours, I think. The others, I'm not sure."

"Weapons preference? If you know it."

"Drake carries a Sig Sauer P320. Custom grip. Harris favors

a Glock 19. Both use suppressors when they're working. They keep rifles in their vehicles—AR-15 platforms, though Drake mentioned something about a-a PSR for longer range work?"

"Impressive." Something hard flickers through Mason's eyes—respect. Maybe something else.

"I spent the last three years of my life planning my escape. That meant learning everything I could about my enemy."

"PSR means Precision Sniper Rifle. Military issue, not something civilians can easily acquire." Mason strides to the window. "Your husband has serious connections."

"His reach goes beyond the legal system. He's tied to arms dealers, politicians…"

Mason scans the tree line through a reinforced window. "Then you already know this isn't just a cleanup crew. They're here to bury every trace of you."

"I don't *think* they know about the backup drive. If I don't make it…"

"You will. They don't know I'm part of the equation now." Mason's jaw tightens. "That gives us an edge. Don't worry, Willow. You *will be* walking away from this."

"You're not scared?" I wish I were as certain as him. I reach into my pocket reflexively, feeling the small, hard shape through the fabric.

I stare at him, heart pounding.

"No. Assume they know everything. It makes any surprises hurt less." He turns, his expression raw and wounded, before the soldier mask slips back into place.

"I'm scared."

"Don't be. I *will* protect you." His hand cups my cheek, thumb brushing my lower lip in a gesture already familiar and necessary. "You're the bravest person I've ever met," he says softly. "And I've served with men who ran into gunfire to save their brothers."

Heat floods my cheeks at the praise, and I lean instinctively into his touch. His thumb presses more firmly against my lip, a gentle reminder that grounds me even as fear threatens to overwhelm me.

"I need you to do exactly as I say, when I say it." His voice takes on that dominant edge that makes my knees weak. "Can you do that for me?"

"Yes, sir." The words come without thought, natural as breathing.

"Good girl." His approval means the world to me. "First things first. I need you to know what we're working with."

He leads me to a sturdy table where he spreads out what looks like architectural blueprints of the cabin and the surrounding area.

"The cabin sits in a natural depression," he explains, one finger tracing the topographical lines. "Anyone approaching has to come downhill through these trees, which gives us lines of sight and natural choke points." He points to several X marks on the map. "Motion sensors here, here, and here. They triggered one of the outer alarms."

He points to a section further out on the map. "They're definitely professionals, because they didn't breach the secondary detection layer. Right now, they're probing my setup to see what they're up against."

"Sounds bad."

"It's good."

"Good? How?"

"It gives us time." Mason pulls at his chin. "I'm guessing they'll come at night. They don't know my outer sensors detected them."

"How do you know that?"

"Because they pushed through, but stopped at the secondary

layer. That means they're thinking things through. Easier to attack at night, and it gives them all day to search."

I blow out a breath, my cheeks puffing out as I do.

"That gives us a few hours to prepare. The storm worked in our favor. The snow is thick, and that will slow them. They'll wait for the snow pack to harden and visibility to improve."

His competence should be reassuring, but fear still claws at my throat. "Mason, these men... They're killers. Professional. Well-equipped."

"So am I." A smile touches his lips, and there's nothing warm about it. It's the smile of a predator anticipating the hunt.

He moves to a locked cabinet, entering a code I can't see. Inside sits a satellite phone and what looks like specialized communications equipment. He punches in a number and speaks in clipped tones. Military jargon I can't follow flows with practiced ease. He ends with, "Confirmed. Ghost protocol. Six-hour window."

When he turns back, determination has hardened his features to granite.

"Who was that?"

"Friends who will fight for you." He doesn't elaborate, and I don't push. "I don't like the timing. Drake will make his move before they arrive."

"So we run?" The thought of leaving this sanctuary makes my stomach clench.

Mason shakes his head. "Running makes us vulnerable. We'd be exposed, trackable." His eyes hold mine, gauging my reaction. "We stay. We defend. We choose the battlefield."

An hour passes in a flurry of preparation. Mason fortifies entry points, rigs simple but effective traps at likely approach vectors, and shows me how to use the security systems. He pauses only when the dogs grow restless. Chaos paces by the rear entrance, hackles raised. Bear stations himself at my side, massive body pressed against my leg.

"They're moving." Mason's voice is calm. Too calm.

The casual way he checks his weapon should terrify me. Instead, I mirror his steadiness, that same stillness I cultivated through three years of surviving Steffan's unpredictable rages.

He hands me a small pistol. "Glock 43. Nine-millimeter. Seven rounds in the magazine, one in the chamber. Safety's here." His fingers guide mine over the weapon, his touch businesslike. "Last resort only. I don't want you fighting unless absolutely necessary."

"I've never fired a weapon before." The gun feels alien in my hand, heavy with responsibility.

"Point and squeeze. Don't pull the trigger—*squeeze* it, like you're trying to press a button without moving anything else." He positions my hands, adjusting my grip. "If you have to use it, aim for center mass. Don't try for headshots like in the movies."

"What's the plan?" I nod, committing his instructions to memory.

"You hide. I hunt." His voice brooks no argument. "There's a concealed basement, a safe room. You'll hide there. It has more than enough room for you and Bear. He'll protect you if anyone gets past me."

"And what about you?" Fear tightens my chest. "You can't face them alone."

"I won't be alone." That predatory smile again. "I have Chaos, and don't forget, I've called in reinforcements."

"And if something happens to you?"

He slides a tracker into my palm. "Hit this. My team will come."

As if on cue, the satellite phone chirps. Mason snatches it up, listens for a moment, then says, "Confirmed."

He turns to me, something almost like excitement glittering

in his steel-gray eyes. "Good news. The cavalry is arriving ahead of schedule. A weather window opened briefly to the east."

Relief floods through me, but Mason's expression remains vigilant. "Don't celebrate yet. We still need to hold out until they arrive. Drake's men will move sooner than I thought. They have the same weather data we have."

The dogs suddenly go rigid, Chaos emitting a low growl that raises the hair on the back of my neck. Mason moves swiftly to the security console, scanning the feeds. His posture changes instantly, shoulders squaring as adrenaline visibly floods his system.

"Movement. Southwest approach." His voice drops to that combat-ready rumble. "Three figures, tactical gear. Two hundred yards and closing."

Terror grips me, but beneath it rises something unexpected—resolve. I've spent three years surviving a monster. I refuse to die now, not when freedom is finally within reach.

"What now?"

"Get to the safe room. Take the USB drive and this." He kisses me hard. Fast. "If I don't come back for you in two hours, activate the tracker. My friends will find you. Now go."

I hesitate, caught in the sudden, visceral fear that this might be the last time I see him. "Mason…"

"This isn't a request, Willow." Command fills his tone. "It's an order. Go. Now."

My body responds before my mind can argue, submission flooding my system at his command. I turn toward the bedroom but pause at the threshold, looking back.

"What's your last name?" The question sounds ridiculous even to my ears, but suddenly it seems vital to know.

A ghost of a smile touches his lips. "Blackwood. Mason Blackwood."

"Stay alive, Mason Blackwood." I try for lightness, but my voice betrays me. "I've only just found you."

Something softens in his expression. "I've got too much to live for to die today." His eyes hold mine, a promise in their depths. "Go, little one. I'll come for you when it's over."

Bear follows me to the bedroom, his massive body a reassuring presence at my side. The hidden compartment in the closet floor opens with a pressure mechanism, revealing a large room underneath. It's lined with what looks like Kevlar and contains emergency supplies—water, energy bars, a first aid kit, even an oxygen mask.

Mason's fortress within a fortress.

I slip inside. Bear follows, his warmth a comfort in the confined space. Chaos remains with Mason, a more effective weapon than I realize. The panel slides silently closed above us, plunging us into darkness until my eyes adjust to the thin strips of light filtering through nearly invisible ventilation slots.

The world goes silent, and we wait.

Then—

BOOM!

An explosion rattles the walls.

NINE

Mason

THE DOGS DETECT THEM BEFORE THE SENSORS DO. CHAOS'S hackles rise as he positions himself by the door, a four-legged weapon primed and ready. Bear's already with Willow in the safe room—right where I need them both.

Protecting Willow is my singular focus, a mission that eclipses everything else. Not because she's an innocent caught in the crossfire. Not because she carries evidence that could bring down a corrupt federal judge. But because in less than twenty-four hours, she's somehow become essential.

Necessary.

Mine.

The thought should terrify me.

After Rachel, I swore I'd never let another person get close enough to become a liability. A target. Yet here I am, prepared to unleash hell on anyone who threatens the woman I protect.

Movement flickers across the security monitor. Three heat signatures approaching from the southwest, using the trees for cover. Their formation suggests military training—staggered approach, with overlapping fields of fire.

Professional.

Methodical.

Good.

Professionals are predictable.

I check my weapons one last time. Glock 19X at my hip, suppressed. KA-BAR tactical knife strapped to my thigh. M4 carbine modified for close-quarters battle slung across my back. Flash-bangs and smoke grenades on my tactical vest. Overkill for most situations, but against trained operatives hunting an injured woman, I'm not taking chances.

The nearest figure disables my outermost motion sensor rather than tripping it.

Definitely professional.

"Time to introduce ourselves."

I move to the gear closet, pulling out the white camouflage snow suit designed specifically for these conditions. Each piece is applied methodically—tactical thermals first, then the reinforced snow pants and jacket, both of which are layered with ballistic material at vital points. The hood features a mesh face covering that allows me to breathe without creating visible vapor clouds. When fully suited, I'll be nearly invisible against the pristine snowscape outside.

"You're leaving?" Willow asks, fear edging into her voice.

"Only technically." I nod toward the small structure visible through the kitchen window—what appears to be a simple outhouse just ten yards from the cabin. "That's not what it looks like. It's an access point to a tunnel system that runs beneath the entire property."

Her eyes widen in understanding. "A tunnel?"

"Runs thirty yards out, emerges beyond the tree line." I secure my weapons, checking each one methodically. "They're watching the cabin, looking for movement, tracks in the snow. It looks like an outhouse, so tracks in the snow won't seem out of place. They don't know about the tunnel system."

She glances at the pristine white blanket outside. The heavy snowfall has covered everything, creating an untouched canvas around the cabin's natural hollow.

"No footprints," she whispers. "They'll never know you're out there."

"Exactly." I finish the final straps on the snow camouflage. "Bear stays with you in the safe room. Chaos comes with me."

At his name, the Malinois's ears prick forward, his body vibrating with anticipation. Where Bear is the shield, Chaos is the sword—designed and trained for precisely this kind of operation.

I reach down, fingers brushing the thick fur of Chaos's ruff. His body quivers with anticipation, every muscle taut, waiting.

Chaos and I head outside. I stamp the snow between the cabin and outhouse, making it look like a well-travelled path. Inside, I secure the lock and open the hatch to the narrow concrete tunnel below.

Chaos follows silently, his nails clicking softly on the concrete. The passage is tight but navigable—six feet high, three feet wide, reinforced to withstand both weather and potential discovery.

Fifty yards of careful movement brings me to the exit point— a concealed hatch inside a small grouping of boulders. I pause, listening for movement above, then carefully push open the hatch designed to allow snow to fall away without creating an obvious opening.

The cold hits like a physical wall as I emerge. Chaos slips out beside me. The pristine snow stretches unbroken in all directions. My white camouflage renders me nearly invisible against the landscape as I pull the hood up and secure the mesh face shield.

Using the snow-laden pines for cover, I circle behind their

position. My breath clouds briefly before the specialized mesh disperses it, preventing the telltale vapor that could give away my position. The storm has eased slightly, but visibility remains poor —an advantage for the defender who knows the terrain.

"Intercept and herd," I murmur low, my voice just for Chaos.

The Malinois's ears flick. One soft huff is the only acknowledgment before he slips into the shadows, silent as smoke, vanishing like a ghost into the snow.

I trigger the first trap—a simple but effective distraction on the northwest side of the cabin. The small explosion sends birds scattering from the trees.

The advancing team halts.

Reassesses.

Standard procedure when encountering unexpected resistance.

More importantly, now they know.

They're not dealing with some backwoods hick holed up in a cabin with a shotgun and a grudge. I hope they jump to the conclusion I'm some paranoid prepper living out in the woods.

They have no idea they're dealing with someone who's trained.

Prepared.

Someone who's likely more dangerous than they are.

What they do next will tell me everything I need to know.

If they pull back, regroup, and wait for a better opportunity —that's a tactical mind at work. Measured. Disciplined. It will give me the time I need until my team arrives.

But if they continue? They're desperate.

Getting Willow matters more to them than caution, more than logic.

And desperate men make mistakes.

Let's see which kind I'm dealing with.

The familiar calm of impending violence settles over me—the stillness that earned me my call sign: Ghost.

While I circle left, Chaos moves right. His military-grade training activates. He knows to remain silent, observe, and wait for the command.

I spot the first man through my scope, checking his gear, adjusting his comm unit after the distraction. His attention is focused forward, toward the cabin. He never hears me approach from behind.

The takedown is silent, efficient. One arm across his carotid, pressure in precisely the right places, and he slumps unconscious. I ease his limp body into the snow, zip-tie his wrists and ankles, and relieve him of his radio and weapons.

Through the trees, Chaos scents one of the assailants. His posture goes rigid. When our eyes meet, I give the signal—a single finger point, the command we've practiced a hundred times.

Attack. Disable. Don't kill.

Chaos moves like liquid shadow, launching from his hidden position. The operative has no warning—one moment he's advancing cautiously, the next seventy pounds of military-trained canine hits him from the side. The man goes down hard, a startled cry cut short as Chaos clamps onto his weapon arm with precision, the pressure calculated to immobilize without severing arteries.

By the time I reach them, the man has stopped struggling, his eyes wide with fear as Chaos maintains his grip, a low growl vibrating through his powerful jaws.

"Good boy," I murmur, administering a sedative to the operative before securing him. Chaos releases on command, circling once to check for additional threats before returning to my side, mission focus unbroken.

That leaves Drake.

The most dangerous.

The one Willow fears the most.

I signal Chaos.

Track.

He lifts his nose, head tilting slightly, as he catches the scent molecules drifting through the cold air. His entire demeanor transforms from silent shadow to precision instrument. The Malinois moves in a zigzag pattern, nose working the air currents, processing information no human could detect: microscopic skin cells, the chemical signature of weapon oil, and the distinct human pheromones of heightened alertness and aggression.

His ear flicks back toward me once—confirmation. He's on target.

Chaos drops low, belly nearly touching the snow as he advances through the underbrush. His movements are fluid and economical—the result of countless hours of specialized training.

Twenty yards ahead, he freezes, one paw lifted, tail perfectly still—the classic pointer stance that tells me exactly where our quarry is positioned.

Drake has taken cover behind a large pine, approximately forty yards ahead. Perfect tactical choice—good sightlines, protected position, multiple escape routes. But he doesn't know about Chaos.

I signal again, two quick hand gestures.

Circle. Contain.

The dog acknowledges with an almost imperceptible ear movement before melting into the forest. His tan-and-white winter coat disappears against the dappled light filtering through the pines. He'll circle behind Drake, cutting off his retreat options, becoming a silent sentinel ready to launch on command.

I track Drake through the trees, moving like a shadow. He's good—better than his companions. His head swivels constantly, checking his six, maintaining awareness of his surroundings even as he approaches the cabin. When the second missed check-in comes through, he immediately goes defensive, taking cover behind the massive pine exactly where Chaos indicated.

"I know you're out there," he calls, voice carrying in the still air. "Let's talk like professionals."

I remain silent, circling to his flank. He's expecting an attack from the direction of the cabin, not from deeper in the forest. Chaos is positioned perfectly through a gap in the trees—completely still, almost invisible, waiting for the command that would send him launching at Drake's blind side.

"Reynolds just wants what's his," Drake continues. "The woman and the drive. No need for bloodshed."

The casual ownership in his tone when referring to Willow ignites something primal in my chest—a killing rage I haven't felt since Syria. Since I watched my team die while I survived.

I tamp it down, force it into the cold calculation that keeps operators alive in hostile territory.

Drake shifts position, still scanning. "She's not worth dying for, whoever you are. She's damaged goods. Judge Reynolds has used her up, wrung her out. Nothing left but a shell."

Each word feeds the fury building in my chest, but I channel it into focus, into precision. I want nothing more than to put a bullet between his eyes, to end the threat he poses to Willow.

But I need him alive.

I need to know if more teams are coming. Need to guarantee her safety beyond the immediate threat.

I slip closer, using his voice to mask the sound of my approach. Twenty feet. Fifteen. Ten.

"Last chance," Drake calls. "Give us the woman, and you walk away. This isn't your fight."

Five feet.

"You're wrong about that." My voice startles him, but he's good—already turning, weapon rising.

Not good enough.

I close the distance before he can acquire his target, driving my shoulder into his sternum while deflecting his weapon arm upward. His shot goes wild, echoing through the trees. We crash into the snow, a tangle of limbs and murderous intent.

TEN

Mason

DRAKE FIGHTS LIKE THE PROFESSIONAL HE IS—NO WASTED movement, each strike aimed at vulnerable points. In another life, in another context, I might have respected his skill, but all I see is the man who watched while Steffan Reynolds tortured the woman currently hiding in my cabin, and then took his turn.

The man who participated in her abuse.

Who *touched* her against her will.

His fist connects with my jaw, snapping my head back. Stars explode in my vision, but the pain only focuses me. I counter with an elbow strike to his throat, following with a knee to his solar plexus. He grunts but doesn't fold, retaliating with a headbutt that splits my eyebrow.

Blood trickles into my eye as we grapple in the snow. Drake manages to jerk free long enough to reach for a backup weapon, but I'm already moving, driving the heel of my boot into his wrist.

Bones crack with an audible snap. He howls, more in rage than pain, as the pistol disappears into the snow.

"Who the fuck are you?" he snarls, blood staining his teeth. "A mountain man with a hero complex?"

I don't answer, don't waste breath on words. My fist connects with his temple, dazing him long enough for me to pin him, one knee crushing his sternum while my forearm presses against his throat.

"The woman," I say, voice deadly quiet. "Tell me who else is coming for her."

Drake's laugh is wet with blood. "You have no idea what you've stepped in, do you? You think you can protect her? You're a dead man walking."

I increase the pressure on his throat, watching his eyes bulge. "Names. Numbers. Timetable. Now."

"Fuck you." He tries to buck me off, but my weight and leverage are too much. "She's Reynolds's property. His to deal with. You're just delaying the inevitable."

The rage I've been containing breaks free at his words. My vision tunnels, clouded with red. All I see is Willow's bruised body, her flinches at sudden movements, the terror in her eyes when she woke in a stranger's care.

This man participated in that.

Enabled it.

Maybe even enjoyed it.

My control slips, just for a moment, but it's enough. My hands close around his throat, thumbs compressing his trachea. His eyes widen in genuine fear as he realizes what's happening— that he's pushed too far, triggered something beyond his calculation.

A distant part of me recognizes I'm crossing a line. I need him alive for information. Killing him solves the immediate problem, but creates others. Unfortunately, that rational voice is drowned out by the roar of protective fury pounding in my veins.

Drake's struggles weaken, his face purpling as oxygen deprivation sets in. Just a few more seconds, and the threat he poses to Willow will be permanently eliminated.

Gunfire erupts from the direction of the cabin. Three shots in rapid succession, unmistakably from a rifle. Not my weapons.

Not Willow's pistol.

I release Drake's throat, slamming his head into the frozen ground hard enough to ensure unconsciousness without killing him. Zip-ties secure his wrists and ankles while I retrieve his weapons, adding them to my arsenal.

More gunfire from the cabin. My blood runs cold. There were only three heat signatures on the perimeter.

Unless—

Unless they split their forces. Unless the three I engaged were a distraction while others approached from a different vector, counting on me to focus my attention southwest.

Willow.

I sprint through the forest, no longer concerned with stealth. Snow whips against my face, branches claw at my tactical gear, but I barely notice. Every cell, every fiber of my being, is focused on reaching the cabin, on protecting what's mine.

The world narrows to running footsteps and rasping breath, to the primal need to reach her before it's too late.

I break through the tree line as more gunfire erupts—but this time, it's coming from inside the cabin, directed outward.

Through the swirling snow, I make out two figures taking cover behind an overturned snowmobile. Their attention is fixed on the cabin windows, where someone returns fire with precise, disciplined shots.

Not Willow.

She's safe in the hidden compartment.

Which means—

The pieces click into place as a figure materializes from the trees to my right—tall, bearded, moving with the unmistakable economy of special forces. Ryan. My second-in-command.

The cavalry arrived ahead of schedule.

Relief floods through me, followed immediately by renewed focus. I signal Ryan with a quick hand gesture—two tangos, northwest position—and receive a curt nod in response. Two more shapes emerge from the forest to the east. Martinez and Jackson complete an improvised pincer movement.

The men by the snowmobile never stand a chance. Caught in the crossfire from four directions, they're neutralized in seconds— one dead from Ryan's shot to the head, the other wounded and subdued by Martinez and Jackson.

I approach the cabin cautiously, weapon at the ready, but a familiar whistle from within confirms it's secured. When I push through the door, I find our team's sniper, Cooper, positioned at the window, rifle trained on the tree line.

"Ghost." He nods without taking his eyes from his scope. "Welcome to the party."

"Status?" I scan the cabin for signs of disturbance, relieved to find everything relatively intact. The hidden door to the safe room remains closed, undisturbed.

"Five tangos total. Two on the snowmobile, three in the woods." Cooper's voice is as calm as if he's discussing the weather. "You got the ones in the woods?"

"Two down, one secured for questioning." I move toward the bedroom. "Perimeter?"

"Secured. Martinez has drone surveillance up. No more incoming detected." He raises and eyebrow at the blood on my face. "You look like shit."

"You're late," I counter, already moving toward the bedroom.

Cooper's laugh follows me. "No, man. You're just always early to the fight."

In the bedroom, I trigger the hidden mechanism. The floor

panel slides back with a soft click, revealing Willow's pale face blinking up at me.

Bear's positioned as a living shield—his two-hundred-pound frame curled around her, one massive paw resting on her arm. The dog's protective instincts transform him from a gentle giant to a deadly guardian. His head lifts the moment the panel moves, a low rumble vibrating deep in his chest.

The Newfoundland's dark eyes assess me first, checking for threats before giving a soft woof of recognition. He nudges Willow protectively, as if asking if she's okay, then turns that massive head toward me and snorts, a quiet reprimand for staying gone too long.

Willow's relief hits like a punch to the sternum—raw and immediate—but it's quickly chased by concern as her gaze locks on the blood tracking down the side of my face.

"You're hurt." She surges upright, her fingers flying to her mouth. "What happened?" She reaches for me, fear and worry warring in her eyes.

Bear shifts as she moves, making space but staying close, his body still angled between her and the door. He's absorbed her fear, made her safety his singular mission. The bond between them, formed in such a short time, speaks to both Willow's gentle nature and Bear's extraordinary instincts.

"Not mine," I lie, extending a hand to help her out. "It's over. We're secure."

She takes my hand, letting me pull her to her feet. Bear follows, shaking himself and immediately moving to investigate the new scents in the cabin. Willow steps into my arms without hesitation, her body trembling against mine as delayed shock sets in.

"I heard an explosion and then gunfire," she whispers against my chest. "I thought—"

"I'm here." I tighten my grip, one hand cradling the back of her head. "I've got you."

She pulls back just enough to look at my face, fingers gently touching the cut on my eyebrow. "This is yours," she accuses softly.

"Barely a scratch." I capture her hand, pressing a kiss to her palm. "Are you hurt?"

She shakes her head, then stiffens as voices in the main room register. "Who's here?"

"Reinforcements." I keep my tone reassuring, though I can feel the questions building in her. "They're here to help."

Fear flickers across her face. "Can we trust them?"

The question cuts deeper than it should, reminding me that her experience with men in positions of power—men who should protect rather than harm—has been nothing but betrayal and pain.

"With my life," I say simply. "And more importantly, with yours."

She studies my face, searching for deception, for the cracks that would reveal a lie. Finding none, she nods once, decision made.

"Is Drake…" She can't seem to finish the question.

"Alive." For now, I don't add. "We'll question him, find out if more teams are coming."

Relief and dread battle in her expression. "And then?"

"And then we take the fight to your husband." The promise in my voice is iron-clad. "This ends on our terms, not his."

Fear ghosts across her features, but beneath it rises something stronger—determination. The same steel that helped her survive three years of abuse, that drove her to gather evidence against a powerful, connected man who thought himself untouchable.

"Together?" The single word carrying the weight of so many questions. So much trust.

"Together," I confirm, sealing the promise with a gentle kiss to her forehead. "Now come meet the team that's going to help us burn your husband's world to the ground."

I lead her into the main room, where four men in tactical gear have established a temporary command center on my dining table. Maps spread across the surface, communication equipment set up, weapons checked and rechecked with practiced efficiency.

All conversation stops as we enter, four pairs of eyes instantly assessing Willow, noting her injuries, cataloging the protective way I position myself slightly in front of her. Ryan—ever the XO—speaks first.

"Ma'am." He inclines his head respectfully. "I'm Ryan Ellis. That's Cooper, Martinez, and Jackson. Formerly of the 5th Special Forces Group, now private contractors with Cerberus Security."

"Willow," she replies, her voice steadier than I expected. "Thank you for coming."

"Ghost calls. We come." Ryan shrugs as if it's the simplest equation in the world. For men who've bled together, I suppose it is.

"Ghost?"

"That's me." I turn to Willow with a smile.

Cooper eyes our joined hands, a smirk tugging at his lips. "So Ghost finally found someone worth haunting for, huh?"

I feel Willow's questioning glance, but ignore it for now.

"Status report."

Ryan takes over, all business. "Five hostiles neutralized. One dead, one critically wounded, three secured for questioning. Immediate perimeter secure, drone surveillance active." He gestures to the maps. "We've established a secure corridor to the extraction point. Chopper on standby, wheels up as soon as weather permits."

Martinez chimes in, tablet in hand. "Preliminary intelligence suggests Judge Reynolds has at least two more teams on standby. One local, one coming in from out of state."

Willow pales but stands her ground. "He won't stop. Even if we get away, he'll keep hunting. He has connections everywhere. Police, FBI, local courts…"

Jackson looks up from checking his weapon. "With respect, ma'am, so do we."

"The USB drive," Ryan says, eyes sharp. "Cooper says you have evidence that could take the judge down."

Willow hesitates, then reaches into her pocket, producing the small device that's cost her so much. "Three years of documentation. Financial records, witness tampering, weapons deals with terrorist organizations. Everything."

Martinez whistles low. "No wonder he wants you dead."

"He doesn't just want me dead," Willow says quietly. "He wants me to suffer first."

The room goes silent, tension thickening the air. These men understand violence and comprehend the darkness humans are capable of inflicting on one another. But the clinical brutality of domestic abuse—the prolonged, calculated torture disguised as marriage—hits differently.

Jackson breaks the silence, voice tight with controlled rage. "Let's make sure that doesn't happen."

Cooper nods toward the back room. "Drake's secured. Chaos is guarding him. Want first crack at him?"

Willow flinches at the name, her grip on my hand tightening. I squeeze back reassuringly.

"Wash up first," Ryan suggests, eyeing the blood on my face. "You look like hell."

I lead Willow back to the bedroom. She's silent, then turns to me with questions in her eyes.

"Ghost?" she asks softly.

"Call sign. Not important." I move to the bathroom, wetting a cloth to clean the blood from my face. The cut on my eyebrow has already stopped bleeding, but I'll need stitches eventually.

She follows, taking the cloth from my hand with fingers that tremble just slightly.

"Let me."

I let her. Let her blot the blood from my temple, let her clean the graze on my cheekbone like I'm something fragile instead of someone forged in violence. Each touch carries a reverence I haven't known in years—maybe ever. Not even Rachel, for all her sweetness and submission, ever looked at me like this. Like I'm something worth saving.

Willow swallows hard, eyes flickering between the blood and my eyes. "I thought what we had… What happened between us —was just adrenaline and circumstance. Escapism."

"Was it?" I keep my voice even. I won't push her. She needs to arrive at her truth without being cornered into it. "Just comfort in crisis? A distraction?"

Her gaze drops to our hands—her small, strong fingers wrapped around mine.

"No," she whispers. "It's more, and that terrifies me almost as much as Steffan does."

I tilt her chin gently. "I terrify you?"

"Not you." Her head shakes instantly, a crease forming between her brows. "The way you make me feel." Her voice cracks. "Like I could trust again. Like I could want something more than just surviving. That kind of hope feels dangerous."

Understanding hits low and sharp. "After what he did… After everything he stole from you… Of course it feels dangerous."

Tears glitter in her eyes, and one escapes, sliding down her cheek. She doesn't wipe it away.

"What if I'm broken? What if I don't know what I want

anymore? I want to trust what I feel, but I don't know if I should."

Her honesty guts me.

"We probably shouldn't have crossed that line." I admit. "It was too fast. Too raw. Hell, we barely knew each other's names. I don't regret it." I step closer, lowering my voice. "I meant what I said. Even if we had slept on opposite ends of this cabin, I'd still be standing between you and them. That doesn't change because we happened. That's just who I am."

Her lower lip trembles. "I can't believe any of this. You risked your life. You called in a team. You didn't even know me."

"We already talked about this." I cup the side of her face, thumb catching a fresh tear. "But I get it. This is intense. You're scared. Your emotions are all over the place. And you don't know what's real."

She nods. "Exactly. I don't know if I can trust myself. What if I'm doing it again? Jumping headfirst into something dangerous because it feels better than being alone?"

"Then we slow down," I say. "We breathe. We survive this. After that, we figure it out together."

Her voice is barely a whisper. "I don't know how to trust someone like you. I've only ever trusted men who hurt me."

I lower my forehead to hers. "Then don't trust me yet." My voice is soft. Steady. "Just watch me. Watch what I do when things get hard. Watch how I show up for you. Let me earn your trust."

Her fingers curl into my shirt. She doesn't pull away. Doesn't run.

And that's enough.

For now.

The vulnerability in her question breaks something open inside me—a tenderness I thought had died with Rachel. I brush the tear away with my thumb, marveling at the trust she's placing in me by showing her fear.

"You're not broken, Willow. Wounded, yes. Healing, yes. But you're not broken." I press my forehead against hers, our breath mingling in the small space between us.

ELEVEN

Mason

THE WIND STOPS HOWLING, LEAVING AN UNNATURAL STILLNESS IN its wake. Out here, silence is rarely a comfort—it's the quiet before the storm, the breath held before the strike, the pause between heartbeats when instinct knows danger is near.

I glance at my team as we trudge through knee-deep snow toward the storage shed where we secured Drake and his men. Ryan walks two paces behind me, ever the faithful XO. Jackson and Martinez flank our sides, weapons at the ready. We left Cooper in the cabin with Willow—his sniper skills are best utilized as overwatch.

"Four tangos secured," Ryan says, his breath clouding in the frigid air. "One KIA by the snowmobile. The critically wounded one might not make it."

I process the information. "Status on the wounded?"

"GSW to the chest, through and through," Martinez supplies. "Jackson patched him, but without proper medical, he's got maybe hours."

"And Drake?"

Ryan's mouth tightens. "Conscious. Angry. Zip-tied hand and

foot. Bastard's already threatened to skin us alive when he gets loose."

"Charming." The word emerges as a growl.

The storage shed appears through the trees—a solid structure I built to house equipment too large for the cabin, reinforced against both weather and unwanted visitors. We've repurposed it as a temporary detention facility, one that won't allow sound to carry back to the cabin.

To Willow.

The woman's been through enough without hearing what's about to happen.

Jackson clears the perimeter before I unlock the reinforced door. The interior is dimly lit, illuminated only by a single battery-powered lantern that casts long shadows across the walls. The smell hits immediately—blood, sweat, fear. Four men secured to support posts, spread far enough apart that they can't assist each other.

Drake's eyes lock onto mine the moment I step inside, a calculating hatred burning in their depths. To his credit, he doesn't flinch. Doesn't cower. Just watches me with the cold assessment of a predator.

"You're officially dead men." His voice is surprisingly steady for someone with zip-ties cutting into his wrists. "All of you."

I ignore him, turning to the wounded man slumped against the far post. Blood has soaked through the field dressing on his chest, his breathing shallow and labored. His eyes are glassy, unfocused.

"He needs a hospital," Martinez mutters.

"We all do," one of the other men snaps—younger than Drake, with a military buzz cut and a busted lip. "This is fucking kidnapping. We're licensed security contractors."

Ryan snorts. "That's what they're calling hitmen these days?"

I crouch beside the wounded man, checking his pulse.

Thready. Weak. "Who's your medic?" I ask Drake without looking at him.

"Go to hell."

"Your man is dying." I meet his gaze evenly. "I've got supplies that might stabilize him, but I need to know what field training he's had, what medications he's on, and his blood type. Right now."

A flicker of uncertainty crosses Drake's face—the first crack in his armor.

"Harris is our medic," the young one supplies, earning a venomous glare from Drake. "But he's the one you killed by the snowmobile."

Jackson moves to the wounded man, medical kit already open. "I can help him, but he needs evac ASAP."

I nod, a decision crystallizing. "Martinez, contact the chopper. We're moving up extraction. Weather's clearing enough for a medical evac."

Drake laughs, an ugly sound that scrapes against the walls. "Softening already? Judge Reynolds will be disappointed."

I turn to him, letting my expression go flat.

Empty.

It's a look that made hardened terrorists in Afghanistan piss themselves.

"Don't mistake mercy for weakness. Your man gets medical attention because I'm not like you. The rest of you..." I let the sentence hang.

"Your boyfriend's a pussy," Drake spits at Ryan. "Reynolds would've let him bleed out and used the corpse to send a message."

Ryan doesn't take the bait. Just checks his watch with exaggerated casualness. "I'm thinking we've got about four hours before that chopper arrives. Lots of time for a chat."

I move to the center of the shed, positioning myself where

all four men can see me. "Here's how this works. I ask questions. You give answers. The quality of those answers determines how comfortable, or uncomfortable, the next few hours become."

"Fuck you." Drake strains against his restraints. "You got no idea what's coming. Reynolds owns half the state. He's got teams mobilizing from three directions."

Jackson steps back from the wounded man, having administered morphine and replaced the field dressing. "Patient stabilized, but he needs blood and surgery within the next six hours."

I acknowledge this with a nod, then turn back to Drake. "Let's start simple. How many teams, where are they staging, and what's their timetable?"

"I'm not telling you shit." Drake's sneer is pure bravado. "Reynolds will find her. And when he does, what he'll do to her will make the last three years seem like a honeymoon."

Something snaps inside me—a thin tether of control I've maintained since Syria. I'm across the room before I realize I've moved, my hand wrapped around Drake's throat, thumb pressing precisely into the pressure point beneath his jaw.

"Wrong answer." My voice emerges strange even to my ears —flat, emotionless, yet somehow charged with lethal intent. "Let's try again."

Ryan steps forward. "Mason." A single word of caution. He knows what happened in Syria. Knows what I'm capable of when that control slips.

I release Drake, stepping back while he gasps for air.

"You think this is about Reynolds?" Drake manages when he can speak again. "You've stumbled into something so much bigger. The judge has connections you can't imagine—cartels, foreign governments, people who make rendition flights when problems need to disappear."

"Names," I demand. "Locations. Timeframes."

Drake spits blood onto the snow near my boots. "Like I said, fuck you."

I exchange glances with Ryan. We both know Drake's training. Delta operators are taught to resist interrogation techniques that would break most people. Physical intimidation won't work —not quickly enough, anyway.

"We've got time," Ryan says casually. "Lots of time to work with."

I crouch down to Drake's eye level. "Here's what's going to happen. I'm going to step outside with my team to discuss our options. While we're gone, you're going to think about something." I lean closer. "I'm not military anymore. I'm not bound by rules of engagement, Geneva Convention, or operational protocols. You hurt someone that matters to me. So, I'm pissed and not in a forgiving mood."

Something flickers in Drake's eyes—not fear exactly, but calculation.

"Five minutes," I tell him, then signal my team to follow me outside.

Once we're in the clear, Ryan speaks low. "He won't break with standard approaches. Not in our timeframe."

"I know. We need leverage."

Martinez jerks his head toward the wounded man. "What about him? Drake seems to at least marginally care about his team."

"Or," Jackson interjects, "what about the younger one? Carver. He's already shown a willingness to talk."

I consider this, weighing options and ethics against the clock ticking down to Reynolds's reinforcements arriving.

"Divide and conquer," I decide. "Martinez, move Carver to the other side of the shed, out of earshot. Tell him we know he's not fully committed to this, offer him immunity in exchange for cooperation."

"And if he doesn't cooperate?"

"Make him think Drake already sold him out."

Jackson nods toward the wounded man. "I'll play up the severity, tell Drake his man will die without immediate evac."

"Good. Let's go."

We re-enter the shed. Drake watches us warily, sensing the shift in tactics.

The next forty minutes are a carefully choreographed sequence of psychological pressure. We separate the prisoners, feed them contradicting information, and create the impression that their teammates are cooperating.

It's not pretty, but it's effective.

When we return to Drake for the third time, something has changed in his demeanor.

"Your boy Carver's singing quite a song," Ryan comments casually. "Seems he knows more about your operation than you gave him credit for."

"That punk knows shit," Drake snarls, but there's uncertainty now.

"He's talking about the warehouse in Billings," I say, watching Drake's reaction closely. "About the Kostic connection. About Reynolds's arrangement with the FBI field office in Helena."

Drake's eyes flicker for just a microsecond—that was validation enough. I'm on target with the intelligence Willow shared with me privately, but Drake doesn't need to know that.

"Your wounded man isn't going to make it without proper medical," Jackson adds. "Field dressing can only do so much for a chest wound."

Drake stares back at me, eyes hard as flint. His training is evident in the way he controls his breathing and his expressions.

He's not going to break.

Which makes him useless to me.

I nod to Ryan, and we step outside the shed, leaving Jackson with Drake. Martinez is already outside, having finished his session with Carver in the separate storage area we moved him to.

"Carver's starting to crack," Martinez reports. "He's young, scared. Claims he didn't know what he was getting into."

"What did he give you?" I ask.

"Not much yet. Says he was hired as muscle, doesn't know operational details. I'm not sure I believe him."

"Play them against each other," I decide. "Go back to Carver. Tell him Drake's already given us everything, including how Carver was more involved than he's admitting."

Martinez nods and heads back to the storage area where Carver is held. Ryan and I return to Drake.

"Your man Carver's quite talkative now that he's away from your influence," I tell Drake. "Smart kid, looking out for himself."

Drake's face reveals nothing, but the tension in his shoulders speaks volumes.

Twenty minutes pass. We alternate between prisoners, feeding each contradicting information, creating an atmosphere of mistrust and urgency. It's textbook psychological manipulation —and while Drake resists with the resilience of his training, Carver doesn't have the same reserves.

When Martinez finally emerges from Carver's makeshift cell, his expression tells me we've succeeded.

"Carver broke," he says quietly. "Gave up everything. Teams, timetables, operational parameters."

"And?" I prompt.

"One team from Billings, led by a former Ranger, a six-man squad. Another from Idaho Falls, four specialists. Their comm window is 0600 hours. When Drake misses it, they'll accelerate deployment."

When Martinez returns to us again, his expression is grim but satisfied.

"Carver's talking freely now," he reports quietly, well away from both detention areas. "Kid's scared. Says he only signed on for executive protection work, not whatever this is."

"What did he give you?" I check my watch—0430. Ninety minutes until their check-in window.

"Reynolds has a network that goes way beyond normal corrupt judge activities. Arms deals with Mexican cartels, evidence tampering, witness intimidation. But the real money's in connections to a Serbian weapons dealer named Drazen Kostic."

Ryan and Jackson exchange glances, recognition flickering in their eyes. Kostic is on multiple international watchlists—a ghost who supplies arms to terrorist groups across three continents.

"The thumb drive Willow has—Carver says it contains everything. Bank transactions, meeting recordings, names, dates." Martinez continues. "Reynolds isn't worried about a corruption charge. He's worried about treason. And the people he works with… They solve problems permanently."

"That explains the resources he's deploying to find her," Ryan observes. "How many people know she's alive?"

"According to Carver, everyone," Martinez answers. "Reynolds activated his entire network when she ran. FBI contacts, local sheriffs, and state police. There's a blanket cover story that she's mentally unstable, armed, and dangerous."

I process this information, constructing contingencies in my head. "Did he say anything about satellite coverage or air assets?"

Martinez nods. "Reynolds has a contact in the FBI field office in Helena. They've got a BOLO out for Willow, and they're monitoring air traffic. Carver said any chopper in this region will be tracked."

"What about Drake?" I ask. "Anything useful?"

Jackson shakes his head. "Stone cold. Won't give up a thing."

"Keep trying with the third one?" Ryan suggests.

"No time," I decide. "We've got what we need from Carver. Let's focus on extraction."

I process this information, constructing contingencies in my head. "The chopper—where will it land?"

"She won't make it to the chopper," Drake says, voice dripping with certainty. "Reynolds has satellite access through his FBI contact. The moment that bird is in the air, they'll track it."

"Mason." Ryan's voice cuts through the tension. "A word."

We step outside, leaving Jackson and Martinez to guard the prisoners. The cold hits like a physical blow after the claustrophobic heat of the shed. The pre-dawn sky is beginning to lighten, stars giving way to a slate-gray expanse.

"He's telling the truth," Ryan says without preamble. "About Kostic, at least. If Reynolds has that kind of connection…"

"Then this isn't just about a domestic abuse victim running from her husband," I finish. "It's national security."

Ryan nods grimly. "We need to get that drive to people who can act on it. And we need to get Willow somewhere Reynolds and his network can't reach her."

"Ideas?"

"Guardian HRS can help us. I've got contacts at their headquarters who operate outside official channels. They specialize in this kind of extraction, including hostage rescue and witness protection. They can provide secure transport, new identity, the works." He checks his watch. "But we've got a more immediate problem."

"The FBI BOLO."

"If it's legitimate, every law enforcement officer in the state will be looking for her. Your place is remote, but not invisible. Reynolds will have given them approximate coordinates by now."

"We move," I decide. "Immediately. Bring the chopper to the secondary LZ, northeast ridge. Three-mile hike. It's higher ground with better defensive positions."

Ryan nods, already reaching for his comm unit. "What about them?" He jerks his head toward the shed.

The question hangs between us.

What about them indeed?

"We patch up the wounded one as best we can, then leave them," I decide. "It's up to Reynolds to find them when he realizes they've failed. Not our problem if they survive until then." My voice is clinical, detached.

"And Drake?"

I think of what Willow told me in the privacy of the cabin. How Drake watched, participated, and violated her on her husband's orders. How he hunted her through the storm, determined to bring her back to more torture.

"He doesn't leave this mountain," I say finally.

"Why?" Ryan's eyes narrow, understanding immediately.

"Because he touched her. Hurt her." I nod once, jaw tight. "Because he enjoyed it. Because some men don't deserve oxygen."

"And the others?" Ryan's expression remains impassive. He doesn't judge. Doesn't question. Just nods once.

"Carver seems salvageable—he didn't know what he was getting into. Give him a fighting chance. Jackson can patch him up, leave him with some supplies."

"And the last one?"

"Your call."

Ryan considers this, then nods. "I'll handle it."

"Prep for immediate departure. I'll brief Willow after I handle one last thing." My voice is even, controlled.

Ryan studies me for a moment, understanding crossing his features. "We'll be ready in twenty."

I return to the shed where Drake is secured. There's a cold clarity settling over me—a familiar feeling from combat zones.

The tactical mind takes over, emotions filed away, replaced by pure intent.

Drake watches me enter, his eyes tracking every movement. He's still calculating, still looking for a way out. That's what made him good at his job. That's what kept him alive this long. It's why I'm going to kill him.

"Your boy Carver sold you out," I tell him, voice conversational as I crouch in front of him. "Told us everything about Reynolds's operation. About Kostic. About what you did to Willow."

Drake's face reveals nothing, but his pulse jumps visibly at his throat.

"My team is leaving," I continue. "Taking Willow somewhere Reynolds and his network will never find her."

"You're dead, you know that, right?" Drake finally speaks, voice hoarse. "Reynolds won't stop. He has resources you can't imagine."

"I'm counting on it." I lean closer. "Because when he comes, I'll be waiting. And after I'm done with him, I'll start working through his network. One by one."

"Big talk from a washout hiding in the woods."

I smile, and Drake's confidence falters for the first time. There's something in my expression that triggers his survival instinct—too late.

"I want you to know something before you die." My voice drops lower. "She told me what you did to her. How you watched. How you took pleasure in hurting her. How you violated her on Reynolds's orders."

For the first time, uncertainty flashes in Drake's eyes.

"I served with men like you," I continue. "Men who enjoyed inflicting pain. Who got off on power and fear."

"Just following orders," Drake manages, but there's no conviction in it.

"No." I shake my head. "You enjoyed it. And that's why you don't leave this mountain."

My hands find his throat. Not a combat choke designed for quick unconsciousness, but something slower. More deliberate.

Drake struggles, but the restraints hold him firmly. His eyes widen as he realizes what's happening—that there's no escape, no rescue coming.

I maintain eye contact as I apply steady pressure. I want him to know why he's dying. Want him to feel the same helplessness Willow felt.

"This is for Willow," I say quietly.

Drake's eyes bulge as his oxygen depletes. The fear in them is primal, all calculation and bravado stripped away. His face reddens, then begins to turn blue. Purple. His struggles weaken.

The light in his eyes dims, and I see the moment he accepts his fate—the moment he knows that he's already dead.

I don't look away until it's done.

TWELVE

Mason

When I emerge from the shed five minutes later, Ryan is waiting. He takes one look at my face and nods. No questions. No judgment. Just the silent understanding of men who've shared battlefields.

"We're ready," he says. "Jackson's got the wounded one stable. Martinez gave Carver enough supplies to make it to the next town if he's smart about it."

"And the third one?"

"He'll have a headache when he wakes up. Fifty-fifty chance he survives until Reynolds's people find him."

"Let's brief Willow." I wipe my hands on my pants.

I pause at the edge of the tree line, taking a moment to truly see my cabin for what might be the last time. Early morning light catches on the snow-laden roof, giving the structure an almost ethereal glow against the backdrop of endless pines.

From the outside, it looks rustic, unassuming—just another mountain retreat for someone seeking solitude.

The perfect cover for what it really is.

Two years ago, I built this place with meticulous attention to every detail. Triple-reinforced walls capable of withstanding small arms fire. Cutting-edge security systems disguised as rustic fixtures. Solar arrays concealed beneath snow guards. A defensive perimeter that would make military installations envious.

Not just a cabin. A fortress. A bunker. A place to disappear.

And that was the point, wasn't it?

After Syria, after Rachel, after everything went to hell, I needed somewhere to contain the damage I might cause. Somewhere, I couldn't hurt anyone else.

Cerberus Securities continued to run without me at the helm. The company I built from scratch after leaving the military, utilizing my combat skills to create a multi-million-dollar private security operation. Ryan and the others kept it profitable, kept our clients protected, while I retreated to lick wounds that wouldn't heal.

The irony doesn't escape me. I created a security company to protect others, then built this place to protect others from me.

Cooper emerges on the porch, spotting me immediately despite my position in the shadows. He raises a hand in acknowledgment, then disappears back inside.

I approach slowly, allowing myself this moment of recognition. Of farewell. This cabin has been a sanctuary and a prison. A place where I could let the nightmares come without risk to anyone else. Where Bear and Chaos could roam free. Where I could pretend the world beyond these mountains didn't exist.

Where I could heal.

Then Willow stumbled through the snow, bringing that world crashing back in all its messy, violent, beautiful complexity.

Inside, the warmth hits me immediately—physical heat from the fire, but also the warmth of purpose and action after two years of stagnation. My team moves, packs equipment, checks weapons, and establishes communications. The familiar buzz of an operation in progress heats my blood and brings purpose back to my life.

Willow sits at the kitchen table, hands wrapped around a steaming mug of coffee. Her borrowed clothes hang loose on her petite frame, but there's a steadiness in her posture that wasn't there before—a warrior's stillness beneath the surface vulnerability.

My gaze sweeps the space I once designed to be a fortress.

Bookshelves line the walls—volumes I devoured during sleepless nights, seeking escape in someone else's story because I couldn't survive in my own. Half of them are unfinished. Just like me.

The weapons rack stands bare now, stripped for the mission. Custom-built, each piece once a promise of control, a way to keep the world at bay. Now, it's a hollow frame.

Like ribs without a heart.

The kitchen gleams with steel and solitude. I taught myself to cook in that space. Quiet routines. Precision. Control. A ritual to keep the darkness at the door. No one else ever sat at the island. No one else ever tasted what I made until she stood barefoot, licking sauce off her finger and smiling like I wasn't broken.

The bed still holds the shape of her. Sheets tangled, warmth lingering. Last night, I wrapped myself around her like a man anchoring his soul. Held her like I could hold back the nightmares. For one night, I wasn't a soldier or a monster.

I was human. And alive.

My chest tightens as my gaze lands on the bathroom door. That wall knows every inch of her. Every ragged breath, every whispered plea. I lost myself in her there. Found something I never thought I'd feel again—a need that wasn't about pain.

I turn slowly, taking inventory of everything I built to survive.

The underground tunnels that took months to dig with my own hands. My escape plan carved into the earth. The armory, hidden beneath layers of reinforced steel, stocked well enough to supply a black-ops team. The comms center—my lifeline to every operative in the field, encrypted to ghosts.

All of it, meticulously designed. All of it mine.

And yet, none of it matters now.

Not when they're hunting her.

Not when my world has narrowed to the single, blistering purpose of rescuing her.

"Ten minutes to departure," Ryan announces, breaking my reverie.

I take one last look around. This place served its purpose. It gave me what I needed: isolation, safety, and time to process. But it was always a retreat, not a life. A pause, not an ending.

With Willow, I have purpose again. A mission beyond mere survival. A reason to step back into the world I left behind.

The cabin will remain, of course. A fallback position. A resource for future operations. Perhaps even a place to return to someday, under different circumstances.

But it's time for my self-imposed exile to end.

Willow looks up as I approach, her eyes finding mine with that uncanny ability to see past my barriers.

"Everything okay?" she asks softly.

"Yes," I tell her, surprised to find it's not a lie. "It's time to go."

She scans me for injuries, for signs of what happened in the shed.

"How did it go?" she asks.

I hesitate, unsure how much detail to share.

"We got what we needed."

"Drake?" Her gaze is too perceptive, seeing past the professional mask to the violence beneath.

"You don't need to worry about him anymore."

Understanding dawns in her eyes. She doesn't ask for confirmation, doesn't seek reassurance that her abuser still lives. She nods once, accepting what needed to be done.

"We're moving," I tell her, crossing to where she sits. "Reynolds has more resources than we anticipated. We need to get you and that evidence to safety."

"Where?" Fear flickers across her face, quickly mastered. "How?"

"Northeast ridge. Defensible position for extraction by helicopter." I drop to one knee beside her chair, bringing us to eye level. "It's a three-mile hike, uphill in deep snow. Not easy."

"I can handle it." Determination hardens her features. "Tell me what to do."

I reach out, tucking a strand of hair behind her ear, the gesture far more intimate than our current circumstances warrant. "We've got one shot at this. If anything happens to me—"

"Don't." Her fingers press against my lips, silencing me. "Don't say it."

"Willow." I take her hand, my thumb circling her wrist where her pulse flutters. "Listen to me. If we get separated, if things go wrong, you stay with Ryan. He will get you somewhere safe, and get that evidence to people who can use it."

She shakes her head, stubborn. "I'm not leaving you."

"This isn't about us. It's about making sure Reynolds pays for what he's done."

"I know that." Her voice firms. "But I've spent three years planning this. I survived him. I survived Drake. I'm not running scared anymore."

Pride swells in my chest, unexpected and fierce. With her survival instincts and razor-sharp mind, this woman's capacity to endure is extraordinary.

"Just promise me you'll follow orders," I say. "When things get chaotic, when decisions need to be made in split seconds, you need to trust me. Trust my team."

"Yes, sir." The formality in her tone carries an intimacy that hits low in my gut, stoking a fire I can't afford to feed right now.

Cooper clears his throat, a subtle reminder that we're not alone. "Perimeter's clear for now. We've got maybe twenty minutes before we need to move."

"Gear up. Martinez, you're on point. Ryan takes the rear with me. Cooper, you're with Willow. No one gets within fifty yards of her."

Cooper nods, already moving to prep his rifle. I turn back to Willow, extending my hand to pull her to her feet.

"One more thing," I say, voice pitched low for her ears only. "The flash drive. We need to duplicate it, spread the risk."

She reaches into her pocket, producing the small device that's cost her so much pain. Her fingers tremble slightly as she places it in my palm, the weight of years of evidence, of her suffering and courage.

"I'll get it back to you," I promise.

"It doesn't matter." Her eyes hold mine. "As long as he pays. As long as it was worth something."

The lump in my throat makes it difficult for me to speak. I wrap my fingers around the drive, a silent vow to ensure her suffering wasn't in vain.

We move quickly after that—packing essential gear, distributing supplies, checking weapons. Bear and Chaos sense the tension, staying close, their bodies vibrating with alertness. They'll accompany us—Bear to break trail through the snow, Chaos to run security ahead and behind.

Ten minutes later, we stand at the cabin's threshold. Six humans and two dogs preparing to traverse three miles of snowbound wilderness with unknown threats converging. Outside, the light paints everything in shades of silver, the snow gleaming like diamond dust.

"Ready?" I ask Willow, who now stands dressed in my spare winter gear, too large for her, but better protection against the elements than anything she arrived with.

She nods, eyes focused on the path ahead. "Ready."

THIRTEEN

Mason

As we step out into the snow, leaving behind the safety of my cabin, I can't help but feel that Willow and I are crossing a threshold in more ways than one. Behind us lies the sanctuary we found in each other's arms—a fragile, beautiful moment carved from fear and fire. Ahead lies uncertainty, danger, and a reckoning three years in the making.

Martinez takes point, gliding through the trees with an eerily-silent gait. Cooper falls in beside Willow, rifle up, body shield angled subtly between her and every possible threat. Jackson moves behind them, scanning our six. Ryan and I bring up the rear, eyes always moving, weapons ready.

Bear leads the way, forging a path through the deep drifts like a living snowplow. The massive Newfoundland throws his full two hundred pounds into each step, muscles bunching beneath thick fur, breaking the crusted snow so we can follow without sinking knee-deep. His breath puffs in great white clouds, tongue lolling out the side of his mouth in sloppy, uncontainable happiness.

Despite the tension threading through our group, Bear radiates unfiltered joy—tail wagging in wide, snow-flinging arcs, ears flopping with each bounding step like he's charging into battle and Christmas morning all at once. He snorts and snuffles as he barrels through the powder, occasionally glancing back as if to say, *See? I got you. Just try to keep up.*

It's impossible not to feel lighter just watching him—like the big brute doesn't know or care that we're marching into danger, only that he's leading his pack and doing exactly what he was built to do. With every joyful leap, he reminds me that sometimes, even in war, there's room for something pure.

In contrast, Chaos is all business. The sleek Malinois ghosts through the trees, working the perimeter with laser focus. His gait is silent and economical; his eyes scan constantly, his body taut with readiness. Every few steps, he circles back to check on us, then melts into the shadows again—an ever-present phantom keeping danger at bay.

I watch them both—Bear's open exuberance, Chaos's silent vigilance—and feel something shift in my chest. Gratitude, maybe. Or awe. Or just the sheer comfort of being part of a pack for the first time in my life.

Protected. Seen. Needed.

Even now, with danger close and dread coiled in my stomach, Bear's joy makes me smile. Chaos's steadiness helps me breathe. Between them, I feel less alone.

And for me, that's everything.

As for Bear, his snowplow exuberance breaks the snow and hastens our pace, but it leaves one hell of a trail. Not breadcrumbs. The fucking whole loaf of bread.

Our path is clear.

Too clear.

It's a calculated risk. Within the tree line, the thick canopy conceals most of our tracks. Overhead drones can't see us, but each time we reach a clearing, a pale wound in the forest where the trees fall away into open meadows, we slow to a crawl.

Ryan lifts a fist, signaling a halt at the edge of the first one. The team sinks instinctively to one knee, melting into the shadows. We wait. Listen. Scan.

Nothing but wind.

I give a low whistle, and Bear veers left. We double back, tracing a wide arc around the open space to avoid leaving a path visible from above. The detour adds fifteen minutes, but it's worth it.

Lives are worth it.

Chaos ranges like a phantom between front and rear, paws silent on the snow. He vanishes into the trees, reappears beside Willow, then disappears again. Constant motion. Constant protection. His ears twitch at every sound, eyes sweeping left to right in tandem with the sweep of Cooper's barrel.

We keep moving.

Two miles in, lungs burning in the cold, legs leaden from the uneven terrain, Ryan's hand clamps down on my arm. He freezes, tilting his head slightly, breath misting in the air.

I hear it a second later—the faint, rhythmic thump of rotor blades. Helicopter. Still distant, muffled by the dense canopy, but closing.

"Incoming," Ryan murmurs. "Northeast."

I check my watch. "Too early for our extraction."

"Exactly."

Understanding passes between us. Not friendlies.

"Get Willow to the LZ," I order quietly. "I'll delay them."

Ryan's expression hardens. "Not alone, you won't."

"That's an order, not a request."

"With respect, sir," Ryan says, using the formal address to make his point, "that's just dumb."

His flat stare leaves me shaking my head. Classic Ryan. I'd dismiss his comment, or dress him down for the insult, except Ryan's tactical mind is formidable. It's why the team respects him, and why he's the one I trust to hold the line when everything goes to hell.

Before I can argue further, the chopper sound grows louder. Soon, everyone hears it. Willow turns, fear and question in her eyes.

"Move!" I shout, abandoning stealth for speed. "Cooper, get her to the LZ. Now!"

Martinez leads the way, one step behind Bear's thundering bulk. Cooper doesn't hesitate, grabbing Willow's arm and breaking into a run, following Bear's path through the snow. Jackson falls in behind them, providing additional cover.

Ryan and I drop back, seeking defensible positions among the trees. Chaos stays with us, hackles raised, sensing the imminent threat.

"They can't land in these trees," Ryan says, scanning the sky. "They'll either drop troops at the cabin or try to cut us off at the LZ."

"Split the difference. Two teams." I unshoulder my rifle, checking the chamber. "How many birds?"

"Just one."

The helicopter appears over the ridge line, a sleek black shape against the pale morning sky. Not military—private security, which confirms our suspicions. Reynolds isn't using official channels for this extraction.

"Dropping at the cabin." Ryan tracks the chopper through his scope.

I nod, already moving toward a better vantage point. "They'll secure the location, check the shed."

"Where they'll find nothing but blood." Ryan's grim satisfaction is evident. "That should keep them busy for a few minutes. Then, they'll follow."

We're two miles ahead of them, but we've broken the snow. Made it easy for them to follow us.

The helicopter reappears overhead, heading straight toward the ridge line—exactly where our extraction LZ is located.

"Fuck. They're cutting us off," I mutter. "How the hell did they know?"

"Reynolds has better intel than we thought," Ryan suggests. He peers through his scope. "Shit, dropping four lines." He waits a beat. "Dropped four men near the LZ."

"Fuck. We circle back." There's no time to dwell on it. The helicopter is deploying a second team, fast-roping them into a clearing just ahead of where Willow, Martinez, Cooper, and Jackson are headed.

"Chaos, track," I command, sending the dog ahead on a silent mission to locate and trail our team. To Willow.

Ryan and I move quickly through the trees, staying low, using the terrain for cover. We need to reach our people before Reynolds's men cut them off.

A burst of gunfire erupts ahead—short, controlled, professional. My blood runs cold.

"Contact," Ryan confirms unnecessarily.

We redouble our pace. I am no longer concerned with the noise of our approach; all that matters is reaching Willow before Reynolds's men get to her. The thought of her back in their hands, of what would happen to her…

No. That's not an option.

More gunfire—this time a different weapon. Cooper's rifle, the distinctive crack unmistakable.

"They've engaged," Ryan says, breathing hard as we push through a snow drift.

"Cooper's good," I remind him, though I'm unsure whether I'm reassuring him or myself. "Jackson's with them. Martinez. And Bear."

We crest a slight rise, and the scene unfolds below. Cooper positions Willow behind a fallen tree, covering her with his body while returning fire. Jackson flanks their position, creating cross-fire with interlocking fields of fire. Bear stands guard over Willow, his massive body tense and ready to attack anyone who approaches. Martinez is nowhere. Probably circling to get behind the threat.

Four men in tactical gear have my men pinned down, advancing in textbook fire-and-movement patterns. Professionals. Well-trained.

Dangerous.

"High-low," I tell Ryan, who nods, instantly understanding the plan. He'll take the high ground, providing overwatch, while I circle low to flank their position.

As Ryan moves off, Cooper takes a hit to the leg, his body jerking from the impact. He stays up, still firing, but the wound slows him down, limiting his effectiveness.

My world narrows to the mission: protect Willow.

Eliminate the threat.

I circle behind the attacking team, using the trees for cover, moving silently despite the deep snow. Chaos appears beside me, materializing like a ghost. He's already assessed the situation, already chosen his target. Movement to my right, and I spot Martinez, doing precisely as I imagined.

We trade hand signals.

"On me," I murmur, and Chaos falls in, his body vibrating with anticipation.

Ryan's first shot cracks through the air, dropping one of the attackers instantly. The remaining three immediately seek cover, scanning for the new threat.

Perfect.

I signal Chaos, pointing to the nearest attacker. "Kill."

The Malinois launches like a missile, silent until the moment of impact when his snarl fills the forest. The man goes down screaming, Chaos's powerful jaws locked around his throat, applying enough pressure to kill instantly.

Martinez and I engage the other two simultaneously. Martinez shoots first. A clean hit through the shoulder, disabling the man's weapon arm. I close in with the second. His eyes widen in surprise as I emerge from the trees, but he recovers quickly, bringing his weapon to bear.

Too late.

My first shot hits him in the thigh, staggering him. The second catches him in the chest, the impact throwing him backward into the snow.

Just like that, the fight is over. Four attackers neutralized in less than thirty seconds.

"Clear!" Ryan calls from his position.

"Clear," I confirm, already moving toward where Willow huddles behind the fallen tree.

Cooper is slumped against the log, hand pressed to his leg where blood seeps between his fingers. "Ate some lead," he manages through gritted teeth. "Think it missed anything vital."

"Let me see." Jackson appears at his side, medical kit already open.

I crouch beside Willow, who stares at me with wide, shocked eyes.

"Are you hurt?" I ask.

She shakes her head, seemingly unable to speak. Her gaze shifts from me to the men on the ground, then back to me.

"I need to check their communications and find out what we're up against." I cup her cheek, forcing her to focus on me rather than the carnage. "Stay with Jackson. Don't move until I come back."

"Yes, sir." Her voice is barely a whisper, but there's trust in it. Trust I haven't earned, and may not deserve, but will fight to be worthy of.

I move to the downed attackers, checking for survivors. Three dead—Ryan's target, the one I shot in the chest, and the one Chaos took care of. The fourth—the one Martinez shot in the shoulder—watches me approach with terror in his eyes.

"Please," he gasps. "I'm just doing my job. I have a family."

"So does she." I nod toward Willow. "The woman your boss has been torturing for three years."

His eyes widen. "I don't know anything about that. We were just told to retrieve a fugitive. Armed and dangerous. That's all."

I crouch beside him, close enough to keep my voice low. "Here's what happens next. You tell me everything you know— how many more teams, their positions, their orders. In return, you get to live. Do we understand each other?"

He nods frantically, already talking.

FOURTEEN

Willow

The world narrows to heartbeats and gunshots.

I huddle behind the fallen tree, snow seeping through my borrowed pants, while Cooper's blood stains the pristine white beside me. His breathing is labored, and his face is pale as Jackson works on his wound. The coppery scent of blood mingles with gunpowder and pine, a surreal cocktail that makes my stomach lurch.

Four men lie in the snow. Three dead. One is alive, but neutralized.

Four men who came to take me back to Steffan. One of Mason's men is wounded and bleeding because of me.

Bear presses against my side, his massive warmth anchoring me to reality as my mind threatens to float away on waves of shock. The Newfoundland's presence is solid, real. His deep, rumbling growl has subsided, but his body remains tense, alert to any further threat.

Mason moves among the fallen men, questioning the survivor, his voice too low for me to hear. The ease with which he and his team neutralized the threat should terrify me. Instead, it fills me with a strange, terrible relief.

For the first time in three years, the violence isn't directed at me. Men with weapons are using their skills to protect me rather than harm me.

"Stay with me, Cooper," Jackson mutters, working efficiently to stem the bleeding. "Just a through-and-through. You've had worse."

"Beirut, '18. That was worse." Cooper manages a tight smile despite the pain.

"Much worse," Jackson agrees, taping a pressure bandage in place. "You'll live to complain about this one, too."

Their camaraderie wraps around me like a protective blanket —these men who've clearly faced death together and speak a shorthand born of shared battlefields and mutual trust.

Ryan appears from the trees, rifle slung across his back as he approaches. "Chopper's gone. They likely had fuel constraints after dropping the first team at the cabin."

"There's another team?" The words hit hard. "The cabin?"

Ryan nods, his expression grim. "They dropped a team there before coming here."

Mason returns, face tight with focused intensity as he crouches beside me.

"You okay?" His voice is low and intimate, despite our audience.

I nod, not trusting my voice.

His eyes search mine, looking for truth beyond my automatic response.

"We've got a problem. The team that dropped off at the cabin will be following our tracks. Bear's been making a clear path. They're maybe ten, fifteen minutes behind us."

"What about Cooper?" I glance at the wounded man.

"I'm good," Cooper interjects, already struggling to his feet with Jackson's help. "Just a flesh wound."

Even I can see that's a lie. His face is ashen, jaw clenched against pain as blood continues to seep through the pressure bandage.

"We're splitting up." Mason's hand finds mine, squeezing gently before he turns to Ryan. "Martinez, Jackson, take Cooper and Willow to the LZ. Bear goes with you—they'll need his strength to break trail."

"And you?" Ryan asks, though his tone suggests he already knows the answer.

"You, me, and Chaos double back. Intercept the pursuit team before they can reach the others."

"Mason—"

The tactical logic is sound, but fear spikes through me at the thought of separation.

"This isn't a debate," he cuts me off, his voice gentle but firm. "Cooper needs extraction. You need extraction. The evidence needs to get out. Ryan and I can handle a single team."

I want to argue, to demand we stay together, but the steel in his eyes stops me. This is the soldier, the protector, making decisions that will keep me alive. My desire to stay with him is selfish when measured against the reality of our situation.

"How far to the LZ?" Martinez asks, already moving to Cooper's side.

"Half mile, northeast," Ryan supplies. "Clear path most of the way, then a steep climb at the end. Martinez on point, Bear following, Willow behind Bear, Cooper and Jackson bring up the rear."

The precision of their planning and the lack of wasted words or movement steadies me. These men know what they're doing. This isn't the first time they've had to adapt under fire.

"Go. Stay close to Martinez and Bear." Mason turns to me,

his hand cupping my cheek briefly. "We'll be right behind you once we deal with the pursuit team."

"Promise me." I search his face, memorizing every detail—the scar that bisects his eyebrow, the steel-gray of his eyes, the tight line of his mouth.

"I promise. Now go." Something flickers in his gaze—a shadow of doubt, quickly mastered.

The simplicity of the words belies their weight. In three years of marriage to Steffan, I never heard a promise that wasn't eventually broken. Yet from Mason, a man I just met, the words feel like gospel truth.

We move quickly through the forest, our group splitting up. Mason, Ryan, and Chaos head back the way we came, weapons ready, moving like shadows through the trees. The rest of us turn northeast, toward the extraction point where our ride awaits.

Bear takes the lead, moving with surprising stealth despite his size. His massive body creates a path through the deeper snow that the rest of us follow. Martinez comes next. I stay close behind him. Cooper and Jackson bring up the rear. Cooper's labored breathing is the only indication of how badly he's hurting.

The forest grows thicker as we climb, old-growth pines towering overhead, branches heavy with snow. Every step is a battle against gravity and exhaustion. My borrowed clothes are soaked with sweat beneath, and snow-covered outside; my muscles are screaming from the steep ascent.

But I don't complain. Can't complain. Not when Cooper is pushing forward despite a bullet wound, not when Mason is risking his life to buy us time.

Gunfire erupts in the distance—behind us, where Mason and Ryan have gone to intercept the pursuit team. The sound echoes through the trees, making it impossible to count individual shots.

My steps falter. Martinez notices immediately, turning back to grab my arm.

"Keep moving," he says, not unkindly. "Ghost and Brass know what they're doing."

Ghost. It fits him—the way he moves through the forest, the way he appeared out of the storm to save me, the way his eyes go distant sometimes, lost in memories I can't share.

The gunfire continues, sporadic now. Individual shots rather than clusters—aimed, deliberate. I try not to think about what each report means, about the men behind those triggers, about Mason in the crossfire.

We crest a slight rise, and Martinez signals for a halt. "LZ is just through those trees. We wait for my signal before crossing the open ground."

Cooper sinks to one knee, his breathing shallow, face gray with pain and exertion. Jackson crouches beside him, checking the bandage, which is now soaked through with fresh blood.

"Need a new dressing," Jackson mutters, already pulling supplies from his med kit.

"No time," Cooper manages through gritted teeth. "I'll make it."

"We've got time for me to slap a bandage on that leg." Jackson ignores Cooper and sets to work.

Bear circles back to me, pressing his warm bulk against my legs. I rest my hand on his massive head, drawing comfort from his solid presence. His ears suddenly prick forward, head turning toward the forest behind us.

"What is it?" I whisper.

"Listen." Martinez is already moving, rifle raised.

At first, I hear nothing beyond the rasp of Cooper's breathing and the whisper of wind through pine boughs. Then—a mechanical growl, growing louder. Not the distinctive thump of helicopter rotors, but something else.

Something moving fast through the forest.

"UTVs," Jackson says, voice tight. "Multiple. Reynolds must have a team stationed nearby."

"How did they—" I begin, but Martinez cuts me off.

"Doesn't matter. They're coming, and they're coming fast." He turns to Jackson. "How mobile is Cooper?"

Jackson's expression is grim. "He'll make it to the LZ, but he's not fighting anyone off."

"Then I'll hold them here while you three make the extraction." Martinez's voice leaves no room for argument.

"Like hell," Cooper grunts, struggling to his feet. "I can still shoot."

Martinez opens his mouth to argue, but a new sound cuts through the air—the unmistakable thump of helicopter rotors approaching from the east.

Our extraction.

"LZ, now," Martinez orders, already turning to cover our retreat. "I'll buy you time."

We move as one, breaking from the cover of the trees into the small clearing that serves as the landing zone. The helicopter appears over the ridge line, a sleek black silhouette against the pale morning sky. Not military—private security, with the distinctive profile of a modified civilian craft.

The mechanical growl of the UTVs grows louder. Closer. Through a gap in the trees, I catch a glimpse of movement. Three all-terrain vehicles race through the forest, each carrying two men in tactical gear. Six more of Reynolds's contractors are closing fast.

The helicopter descends toward the center of the clearing, snow billowing beneath the downdraft of its rotors.

Martinez takes a defensive position at the forest edge, rifle braced against his shoulder. "Go!" he shouts over the roar of the approaching helicopter. "I'll hold them until you're aboard!"

Jackson half-carries Cooper towards it, Bear loping alongside them, his dark fur stark against the pristine white.

I hesitate, torn between the safety of the aircraft and the wrongness of leaving anyone behind. "What about Mason and Ryan?"

"They'll find another way out!" Martinez fires three shots into the tree line, forcing the approaching UTVs to take cover. "That's what Ghost does. Now move."

The helicopter touches down, its side door sliding open to reveal a man in tactical gear, gesturing frantically for us to hurry. Jackson pushes Cooper towards it, the wounded man summoning a final burst of strength to cross the clearing.

I follow. Bear stays close to my side. Behind us, Martinez fires controlled bursts that keep the enemy pinned down.

The gunfire from the other direction—where Mason and Ryan went—has stopped entirely. The silence is somehow worse than the sounds of battle. Does it mean they've won? Or that they've fallen?

"Hurry!" the man at the helicopter door shouts. Jackson boosts Cooper inside, then turns back to help me.

Martinez retreats towards us, still firing as he moves. One of the UTVs breaks cover, racing toward the clearing. Martinez drops to one knee, takes careful aim, and fires. The driver slumps forward, the vehicle veering wildly before crashing into a tree.

I reach the helicopter, Jackson's strong hands pulling me aboard. Bear leaps in after me, his massive weight rocking the aircraft slightly. Martinez is twenty yards out, running full-tilt toward us as the remaining UTVs emerge from the tree line. Jackson lifts his weapon, firing over Martinez at the UTVs closing in.

"Come on!" I scream, though my voice is lost beneath the rotor noise.

Martinez makes it to the helicopter just as bullets begin to ping off its armored exterior. He dives through the open door, rolling to create space as the crew chief slams it shut behind him.

"Go! Go! Go!" he shouts to the pilot.

The helicopter lurches upward, the sudden acceleration pressing me back against the seat. Through the window, Steffan's men spill from the UTVs, weapons raised but no longer firing as we climb beyond effective range.

But it's not them I'm searching for.

I scan desperately across the forest, seeking any sign of Mason, Ryan, and Chaos. Nothing. Just endless pines and pristine snow, broken only by our tracks and the gouges where the UTVs passed.

"Mason," I whisper, pressing my palm against the cold glass. "Where are you?"

The helicopter banks sharply, turning east toward safety, toward the Idaho border and whatever sanctuary awaits beyond it. With each second, the distance grows between me and Mason.

Cooper groans as the medic aboard works on his wound. Bear settles beside me, his massive head resting on my lap, dark eyes watching me with what seems like understanding. Martinez and Jackson exchange low words—tactical assessments, contingency plans, things I should care about but can't focus on.

All I can think about is Mason's promise: *"I'll be right behind you."*

A promise I desperately want to believe, even as the Montana wilderness recedes beneath us, taking with it the only man who's ever made me feel safe. The only man who saw me beneath the bruises and the fear.

"They'll be okay," Martinez says, his voice calm despite the urgency vibrating through the helicopter's frame. He doesn't look at me—his gaze is fixed on the tablet in his lap, monitoring aerial feeds, heat signatures, and satellite data with surgical focus—but he must notice the way I'm glued to the window, straining for one last glimpse of Mason. "Ghost has gotten out of worse situations. Much worse."

The nickname pulls my attention away from the blur of snow and treetops. I turn toward him, blinking against the stinging wind leaking through the doorframe.

"Why do you call him Ghost?"

He taps the screen, zooming in on a flicker of movement in the trees, then relaxes slightly. "Because the man's a stealthy bastard. Recon mission in Aleppo went sideways. He infiltrated a fortified compound, extracted two hostages, and ghosted out before the enemy even knew he was there. No comms. No backup. No trail. Surveillance showed nothing but shadows—until he signaled for evac." He glances over, one brow raised. "We started calling him Ghost because he could vanish in plain sight and reappear only when he decided it was time."

I let that settle, trying to picture the man I'd shared a bed with, trembling in the snow, doing something that superhuman.

"Wow." My voice feels small over the thrum of the rotors. "Do you all have them?"

"Call signs?"

"Yeah."

Martinez smirks, fingers still flying across his screen. "Ryan is Brass. Cooper's Whisper. Jackson's Fuse."

I nod slowly, each name painting a clearer picture now that I know the men behind them.

"And you?" I glance at him sidelong. "What's yours?"

He finally looks up, that signature crooked grin curving his mouth. "Halo."

I arch a brow. "Like the video game?"

"Nah." He leans back, checking the distant horizon through the glass. "Like a guardian angel's always watching over me."

A soft laugh slips out before I can stop it. Somehow, despite the gunfire still echoing in my bones and the fear anchoring deep in my gut, I smile.

The moment stretches for a beat, held there in the thrum of the blades, the steady hum of electronics, and the growl of our escape across the Montana wilderness.

My fingers find the flash drive in my pocket—three years of evidence, of suffering, of careful documentation. The key to destroying Steffan and everything he's built.

It should feel like triumph. Like victory. Instead, it feels like another loss—another price paid in blood that isn't mine.

"Where are we going?" I finally ask, pulling my gaze from the window.

"Safe house in Idaho," the medic answers without looking up from Cooper's wound. "Guardian HRS facility. You'll be secure there until we can arrange more permanent arrangements."

"Guardian HRS?"

"Friends of Cerberus. Guardian Hostage Rescue Specialists. They're going to help us make you disappear."

"What about Mason and Ryan?"

Martinez meets my gaze steadily. "They have extraction protocols. Secondary and tertiary rendezvous points. They'll make contact when they're clear."

If they're clear, the words hang unspoken between us.

I lean back, exhaustion suddenly crashing over me like a physical weight. Bear shifts, pressing his warm bulk more firmly against my legs, offering silent comfort. My hand rests on his massive head, fingers buried in thick fur.

"He meant what he said," Cooper manages, his voice thin with pain. When I look over, his eyes are clearer than they have any right to be, given his injury. "Ghost always keeps his promises. Always."

I want to believe him. Need to believe him. But as the helicopter carries me away from Montana, away from Mason, I find myself adrift between terror and hope. For the first time in three years, I'm not someone's property. Not a victim. Not a target.

I'm just me.

Willow.

The thought carries me into uneasy sleep, my dreams filled with gunfire and snow, with Mason's steel-gray eyes and his final promise: *I'll be right behind you.*

But as the miles between us grow, I wonder if that's a promise even he can keep.

FIFTEEN

Mason

———

THE HELICOPTER CLIMBS RAPIDLY, BANKING EAST TOWARD IDAHO and safety. I watch until it's nothing but a dark speck against the pale sky. Willow is safely aboard and beyond Reynolds's immediate reach.

I allow myself exactly three seconds of relief before turning back to the threat at hand.

"They made it," Ryan confirms, lowering his binoculars. "Package secure."

My chest loosens marginally. After the firefight with the cabin team—four against two plus Chaos, no contest—I wasn't sure we'd make it to the LZ in time. Those four operators had training, but they lacked the tactical cohesion Ryan and I developed through years of combat.

We left them zip-tied and unconscious in the snow, rushing toward the extraction point when we heard the UTVs and gunfire.

"UTVs still active," I note, tracking the mechanical growls echoing through the trees. "Martinez must have taken one out, but the others are still operational." It could've been Jackson or

Cooper, but I know my men. Jackson was supporting Cooper, and Martinez held the lead. I'm pretty damn sure Martinez took one out.

Ryan nods grimly. "Five hostiles remaining by my count. One driver down, one wounded."

"Chaos, hunt." The command sends the Malinois racing toward the tree line where the mechanical growls are loudest. I follow, using the terrain for cover, moving like the ghost that earned me my callsign.

We approach from the east, using the rising sun to our advantage. The light at our backs makes us more challenging to spot, while we can see them clearly. Five men in tactical gear, gathered around their vehicles, gesturing as they debate their next move.

"I'll take the two on the right," Ryan murmurs. "You and Chaos handle the other three."

I give a curt nod, signaling Chaos. The dog understands immediately, his body lowering into attack position.

"On three," I whisper. "One… Two… Now."

We move simultaneously, emerging from the tree line with the precision that speaks to years of operating together. Ryan's rifle cracks twice in rapid succession, dropping his targets before they can react. I take out one with a clean headshot while Chaos launches at another, taking him down with savage efficiency.

The fifth man manages to fire a single wild shot before my second bullet finds his chest. He drops, weapon clattering uselessly into the snow.

Silence falls over the clearing, broken only by the idling engines of the UTVs and Chaos's low growl as he stands guard over his downed target.

"Clear," Ryan calls, moving to check his targets.

"Clear," I confirm, approaching the UTVs. One of the vehicles has a body slumped over the steering wheel—Martinez's handiwork from earlier. Another has blood spattered across the passenger seat where the wounded man must have been sitting.

"All neutralized," Ryan reports after checking the men. "What's the plan?"

I survey the three UTVs, already calculating the fastest route to our fallback position. "We take one. Head north."

We approach the lead UTV—a tactical model with a reinforced frame, expanded cargo area, and what appears to be light armor plating. Military-grade, not your typical recreational vehicle. Reynolds spared no expense.

I check the fuel gauge—three-quarters full. More than enough. Ryan collects the men's weapons and secures them with ours. I start the engine, the powerful motor rumbling to life in the stillness.

"Let's move," I say, swinging into the driver's seat.

Before Ryan can claim the passenger side, Chaos leaps up, planting himself firmly in the seat. His expression can only be described as smug as he looks at Ryan, then back at me.

"Seriously?" Ryan stares at the dog in disbelief. "Did he just call shotgun?"

I can't help the smile that tugs at my lips—the first genuine one since watching Willow's helicopter disappear. "Looks that way."

"Un-fucking-believable." Ryan shakes his head but climbs into the back cargo area without further complaint. "Your dog's an asshole, you know that?"

"He's earned it." I reach over to ruffle Chaos's ears, the dog leaning into my touch. "Good boy."

Chaos settles into his seat with the satisfaction of a king on his throne, ears perked forward as we begin to move. The UTV handles well on the snow-packed terrain, its oversized tires gripping where regular vehicles would struggle to find traction.

I navigate through the forest with the instinctive knowledge of a man who's made these mountains his home. Every ridge, every valley, every game trail is mapped in my memory. Reynolds's men would have been lost trying to track us through this wilderness, even with their high-tech equipment.

"How far?" Ryan asks, bracing himself as we navigate a particularly steep incline.

"Fifteen miles northwest," I answer, guiding the vehicle around a fallen tree. "Old mining complex. Abandoned in the sixties. One of my emergency caches."

"And from there?"

"Secondary extraction. We've got a bush plane on standby at Jenkins Lake. Small enough to avoid radar detection, fast enough to get us to Idaho."

Ryan nods, understanding the plan without needing further explanation. It's why we work so well together—years of shared missions have given us a shorthand that transcends words.

Chaos suddenly stiffens, ears pricked forward. I immediately slow the UTV, scanning our surroundings. The dog's senses are far more acute than ours, and he's never given a false alarm.

"What is it?" Ryan asks, already reaching for his rifle.

I don't answer immediately, trusting Chaos's instincts. The Malinois is focused intently on something to our left, a low growl building in his chest.

Then I hear it—the distant thump of helicopter rotors. Not from the east, where Willow's extraction headed, but from the south. Another aircraft is approaching fast.

"Reynolds's reinforcements," I mutter, immediately veering the UTV into denser tree cover. "Birds aren't part of the UTV team's equipment."

"Must be the Billings crew Carson leads," Ryan says, referencing Carver's intel. "Ex-Rangers with air support."

I cut the engine, killing our noise signature as the helicopter sound grows louder. Chaos remains alert but not agitated, which tells me they haven't spotted us yet.

Through gaps in the canopy, I catch a glimpse of the aircraft—a sleek black helicopter with no visible markings. Definitely private military contractors, not law enforcement. It circles the area where the UTV firefight took place, then hovers for several minutes.

"They're assessing the scene," Ryan observes. "Wondering where their men went."

"And where we are," I add.

The helicopter continues its slow circle, expanding outward. It's executing a standard search pattern, methodically covering the terrain. Eventually, it will spot our UTV tracks unless we move deeper into cover.

Ryan pulls out a small handheld device, scanning the UTV. His expression darkens. "Found it. Tracker embedded in the chassis. Military-grade. That's how they're following."

"Shit." I glance at the helicopter's search pattern. "We need to move. Now."

"Options?" Ryan asks.

I consider our position, the terrain, and our resources. "We ditch the UTV. Proceed on foot to the mining complex. It's about 15 clicks northwest."

Ryan nods, already gathering essential gear. "Old school. I like it."

"Chaos, security," I command. The dog immediately takes up a watch position while Ryan and I quickly strip the UTV of anything useful—weapons, ammo, survival gear, and comms equipment.

"We leave the tracker active," I decide. "Let them chase ghosts."

Ryan plants a small surprise under the UTV's seat—nothing

lethal, but enough to discourage pursuit. "Present for whoever comes looking."

"Ready?" I ask, shouldering my pack.

"Born ready," Ryan responds, securing the last of his gear.

"Chaos, on me." The dog falls in beside me as we disappear into the dense forest, leaving the UTV behind as bait.

We wait in tense silence as the helicopter completes its search pattern, gradually moving toward our position, honing in on the tracker's signal. We don't stick around, moving again, heading northeast toward the ravine.

"Still 15 clicks to the mining complex," Ryan notes, checking his GPS. "Terrain's rough. ETA four hours if we push it."

"Then we push."

The pace I set is punishing—fast enough to put distance between us and our pursuers, but sustainable for trained operators like us. Chaos moves effortlessly through the snow, occasionally ranging ahead to check for threats before circling back.

The eastern ravine appears ahead—a deep cut in the landscape with steep walls and dense vegetation—perfect for evasion. We slip into it silently, the ravine's walls closing around us, providing natural cover from aerial surveillance.

"Chopper's almost on the UTV," Ryan confirms, checking a small tracking device of our own. "Your surprise should be waiting for them."

As if on cue, a muffled thump echoes in the distance. I allow myself a grim smile. "That should keep them busy for a while."

We push deeper into the ravine, moving through knee-deep snow.

"You know," Ryan says after a while, "I've never seen you like this."

"Like what?"

"Invested. Personal." He pauses. "Even with Rachel, you kept a certain distance."

The mention of Rachel sends a familiar pang through my chest—not the searing guilt it once was, but a duller ache of regret. "This is different."

"I see that." Ryan's tone holds no judgment, just observation. "Just be careful, brother. You've got a lot at stake."

I don't respond immediately, as I focus on navigating a particularly treacherous section of the ravine. Chaos moves ahead, testing the snow depth, finding the safest path.

"She's worth it," I finally say, the words emerging with a conviction that surprises even me.

Ryan accepts this with a simple nod. He knows better than to push further.

The ravine gradually widens, eventually opening onto an old logging road overgrown with vegetation but still passable. I increase our pace, knowing we're on a direct path to the mining complex.

"How much of a head start does Willow have?" Ryan asks as we push forward.

"About thirty minutes by air. They'll be at Guardian HRS's safehouse before we reach the mine. I trust the Guardians to evade any pursuit by Reynolds."

"And the evidence?"

"She has the primary drive. I have a backup we made at the cabin." I check my watch. "Once we reach the mine, I'll contact Guardian HQ, confirm her arrival and status. We'll get the location."

Three hours of hard marching later, the mining complex finally comes into view—a collection of weathered buildings nestled against the mountainside, partially reclaimed by nature. My fallback point.

I signal for caution as we approach, scanning for any signs of disturbance or danger. Everything appears undisturbed, exactly as it should be.

"Home sweet home," Ryan mutters as we reach the largest structure—an old processing facility with reinforced walls and minimal windows. Perfect for defense.

Chaos immediately circles the building to check for threats. His training is impeccable—he never assumes safety until confirmed.

"Let's get inside and establish comms," I say, pulling out my keys. "I want to confirm Willow's status before we do anything else."

Ryan nods, helping me secure the perimeter. "And then?"

"We finish this." My voice hardens with resolve. "Reynolds, his network, his entire operation—all of it goes down."

"Like old times, then," Ryan says with a grim smile.

"Better," I correct him. "This time, we're not bound by ROE or political considerations. This time, we're free to do what needs to be done."

Rules of Engagement were always the bane of our existence in official combat zones—the restrictions that often prevented us from effectively eliminating threats. Now, operating as private contractors against a criminal network, those constraints no longer apply.

Chaos returns from his perimeter check, giving a soft woof to indicate all clear. He falls in beside me as we approach the building, his warm body pressing against my leg in silent solidarity.

"I'm coming, Willow," I whisper to the wind. "Just like I promised."

The mining complex door creaks open, revealing the emergency cache I established years ago—communications equipment, weapons, supplies, everything needed to continue the fight. We step inside, closing the door on the Montana wilderness.

SIXTEEN

Willow

The helicopter blades slice through the Montana air, carrying me away from Mason, away from danger, and into a future I never dared to imagine. I stare out the window as mountains and forests blur beneath us, my mind replaying those final moments.

Mason's promise, the gunfire, and the way he looked at me before turning back to face Steffan's men.

I'll be right behind you.

Four simple words that feel like both a lifeline and a lie. I've heard too many promises from too many men. Even with the best intentions, words are just that—air shaped by teeth and tongue, carrying no more weight than the clouds we're flying through.

But I believe those words.

My gaze shifts to Cooper, his ashen face tight with pain as the medic tends to his wounded leg. The stark red of his blood stands in violent contrast to the sterile interior of the helicopter. He took that bullet for me. They all risked their lives for me, a woman they'd never met before today.

Bear's massive head nudges my hand, pulling me from my

thoughts. His dark eyes hold a kindness that seems impossibly deep for an animal. When I hesitantly scratch behind his ears, his eyes close in contentment, massive body leaning against my legs like he's been mine forever instead of mere days.

"He likes you," Martinez comments from his seat across from me, barely looking up from his tablet. "Bear doesn't warm up to many people that fast."

"He's a good boy." My voice sounds strange in my own ears, hollow and distant. The massive Newfoundland responds to my praise by shifting closer, nearly pushing me off my seat.

"Status report," the pilot's voice crackles through the comms. "We've got company on our six. Range eight miles, closing."

Jackson tenses immediately. "Reynolds's people?"

"Likely," the pilot confirms. "They're tracking our heat signature. We need to shake them."

Martinez exchanges a glance with the medic. "We have to get off this bird. It's too easily tracked."

My stomach drops. "But Cooper—"

"Needs medical, I know." Martinez's fingers fly across his tablet. "Rerouting now. There's a fallback position twenty miles east. Emergency landing zone with ground transport waiting."

The helicopter banks sharply, descending toward a valley carved between two mountains. My hands grip the seat as vertigo washes over me, the abrupt change in altitude making my ears pop.

"What's the plan?" I ask, struggling to keep my voice steady.

"We're getting you off this bird and onto the ground," Martinez explains. "Helicopters are too easy to track. We've got multiple vehicle exchanges planned. By the time Reynolds's people figure out where we went, you'll be three states away."

Bear shifts with the helicopter's movement but remains steady against my legs, his warm weight an anchor in the chaos. The massive dog seems to understand the gravity of the situation; his usual playfulness has been replaced by an alertness that speaks to his training.

"Two minutes to LZ," the pilot announces over the roar of the rotors.

My heart jackhammers in my chest. I glance toward Cooper, still pale and blood-soaked on the stretcher. "Cooper?"

"Stays with the 'copter," Martinez answers without looking back. He's already unzipping a thick canvas duffel secured beside the door. "They'll fly him to the hospital. With any luck, the tail we picked up will follow them there."

I glance out the side window, the Montana wilderness flashing by below. "Won't they know we landed?"

The two Guardian operators exchange a look that says more than words ever could.

"Hopefully not." Jackson's mouth tugs into a grin as he pulls out a second harness.

Martinez hands him a bundle of webbing and turns to face me. "On your feet, luv. Time to earn your wings."

"Wings? Wait—what are you doing?"

He crouches in front of me like he's gearing up a rookie. "Can't land. That bird following us? If they see us touch down, they'll know this was the drop point. So we stay airborne. Fast, clean exit."

My stomach sinks as I realize what he's saying. "You're not landing?"

"Nope." Jackson loops thick webbing around Bear's massive chest. The Newfoundland huffs, more curious than concerned. "We drop."

"Drop? As in—out of the air? While it's still flying?"

"Controlled descent," Martinez says, cinching a strap around my waist. "We're rappelling, sweetheart. And you're with me."

I freeze as he lifts a padded harness, guiding my arms through the loops. "I've never—"

"Didn't ask if you had," he says, buckling the straps tight. "I'm your brake. You just hold on, and let me do the work."

"How is that supposed to make me feel better?!"

Jackson laughs from across the cabin, double-checking Bear's rig. "He says the same thing to every recruit."

"I'm not a recruit."

"You are today."

Martinez clips me to his harness. The click of the carabiner sends a jolt down my spine.

"You'll come down with me," he says, voice calm and steady. "Jackson's taking Bear. Dog's done this before."

"He has?"

"We train for weird," Jackson says, giving Bear's harness a tug. The dog gives a happy bark like he's just been promised bacon.

Martinez kneels to check our tether lines, his hands confident, methodical. He meets my eyes. "You trust me?"

I nod, because words have fled. My pulse thunders in my ears. My legs are shaking.

"Good. Just hang on."

The pilot shouts, "Thirty seconds!"

Doors slide open, and the world fills with wind and white and the shrieking chop of rotors. Cold slaps my face like a warning.

Jackson swings out first with Bear strapped to his chest, descending into a snowy clearing like it's just another Tuesday.

"Your turn, Willow." Martinez steps up to the edge, our harnesses clipped together. He glances down, then at me. "Deep breath. One step. That's all it takes."

I squeeze my eyes shut and nod.

"Count of three. One... Two... Three."

We step into the void.

The world falls away.

Wind whips past, bitter and biting. Martinez brakes the

descent, guiding us down. The earth rushes up to meet us, and just when I think we'll crash, his feet hit snow with a controlled crunch.

We're down.

I collapse into his side, legs barely holding me up.

"See? Easy," he murmurs.

"Remind me to define that word for you later."

He laughs, unhooking our harnesses.

Jackson's already unclipping Bear, the dog bounding forward through the snow, tail wagging like this is all a big game.

The helicopter banks hard, veering east, carrying Cooper and our would-be tail with it.

Hopefully.

A black SUV waits at the edge of the trees, engine running, two figures in tactical gear standing beside it. They approach quickly.

"The other bird is three minutes out," Martinez says. "We need to move."

"Roger that." The man turns to me. "Ma'am, I'm Axel with Guardian HRS. We're going to get you somewhere safe."

"In the vehicle, please." Axel guides me toward the SUV. "Time is critical."

Bear jumps into the back without command, making himself comfortable across the rear seat. I slide in beside him, his warm bulk immediately pressing against my side. Martinez and Jackson take the middle row, while Axel slides behind the wheel.

"Seat belts," he reminds us, then immediately accelerates down what appears to be a logging road, the SUV's suspension absorbing the worst of the bumps but still jostling us roughly.

"Where are we going?" I ask, one hand gripping the door handle, the other buried in Bear's thick fur.

"First vehicle exchange is three miles ahead," Axel explains.

"Then we'll take back roads to a secondary location for another swap."

"They're good at this." Jackson notices my confusion. "Guardian HRS specializes in extracting high-value targets from hostile situations. They've got protocols for everything."

"Reynolds has FBI connections," I remind them. "They'll be looking for us."

"Exactly why we're switching vehicles multiple times," Martinez says without looking up from his tablet. "First rule of evasion—never stay in one vehicle too long. Second rule—change your signature as often as possible."

The SUV barrels down the rough road for exactly eight minutes before Axel abruptly turns onto what appears to be a game trail barely wide enough for our vehicle. The branches scrape against the windows as we push through, emerging into another small clearing where a nondescript white van waits.

"Transfer point," Axel announces. "Everyone out."

The switch happens quickly. Bear leaps from vehicle to vehicle like he does this every day.

"What about the SUV?" I ask, looking back at the SUV.

"Axel will drive to a different location, creating a false trail."

Minutes later, we're moving again, this time in a commercial plumbing van with faded lettering on the sides. The driver identifies himself as Griff. The van's interior has been stripped and retrofitted, but from the outside, it looks like any service vehicle that might be traveling through rural Idaho.

"Thirty minutes to the next switch," Griff announces.

The next swap occurs at an abandoned gas station miles from any main road.

"These should fit better than what you were wearing." Griff tosses me a bag of fresh clothes—jeans, a sweater, and a heavy jacket, all in subdued colors that won't stand out.

Mason's borrowed clothes were practical but enormous on

my frame. These new garments fit properly, allowing for easier movement. I run my fingers through my hair, catching sight of my reflection in the cracked bathroom mirror. Beneath the fatigue and fear, something new glimmers in my eyes—determination, maybe. Or hope.

Bear is waiting when I emerge, pressing immediately against my legs like he can't bear to be separated from me. His steadfast presence grounds me in a way I can't articulate.

"You're good with him," Martinez observes as we prepare for the next vehicle transfer. "He's usually Mason's shadow."

"He's a sweetheart," I say, scratching behind Bear's ears. The massive dog leans into my touch, nearly knocking me over with his enthusiasm.

Martinez snorts. "Don't let him fool you. That 'sweetheart' is a trained protection animal who could take down a man at a single command."

I look down at Bear's gentle eyes and struggle to reconcile that image with the war machine Martinez describes. "Right now, he just seems like a big love muffin."

"Love muffin?" Jackson laughs. "I'm definitely telling Ghost you called his tactical assault dog a 'love muffin' when he catches up to us."

When, not if. The subtle confidence in Jackson's phrasing eases something tight in my chest.

Our next vehicle is a modest RV—the kind retirees might use to tour national parks.

"Perfect cover," Martinez explains as we get underway. "Tourist vehicle, common in these parts. We'll take back roads to a private airfield."

"Airfield?" I glance out the window. "We're flying again?"

Jackson nods. "Small plane, off the radar. It'll take us deeper into Idaho."

I sink into a seat, exhaustion suddenly crashing over me. Bear immediately jumps up beside me, his massive head resting on my lap as if sensing my need for comfort. His warmth and steady presence lull me into a light doze as the RV winds through mountain roads, putting more distance between us and the Montana border.

I dream of Mason—his steel-gray eyes, the scar bisecting his eyebrow, the way his hands cupped my face with both strength and tenderness. In my dream, he's running through endless snow, always just out of reach, always calling my name…

"Willow." A hand gently shakes my shoulder. "We're here."

I blink awake to find Jackson standing over me. Through the RV's windows, we've stopped at what appears to be a small private airfield. A single-engine plane waits on the runway, propeller already turning.

"Time to move." Jackson's voice is gentle but urgent.

Bear jumps down, stretching his massive body before nudging my hand. I follow Jackson outside, the cold air instantly clearing the fog of sleep from my mind.

The plane is smaller than I expected—a six-seater.

"Is this safe?" I ask, eyeing the small plane dubiously.

"Yes," Martinez assures me.

Bear boards without hesitation, somehow squeezing his massive frame into the limited space as if he's done this a hundred times before. I follow with more trepidation, strapping myself into the seat beside him.

The takeoff is smoother than I expected, the small plane lifting effortlessly into the afternoon sky. Through the window, the landscape changes beneath us—forests giving way to mountains, valleys, and eventually a massive lake gleaming like polished silver in the distance.

"That's our destination," Jackson explains, noticing my interest. "Guardian HRS has a facility on that lake. We'll land on the water and transfer to boats."

"Land on the water?" I look at him in alarm.

He grins. "Floatplane. Another change in transportation signature to throw off any pursuit."

The pilot expertly maneuvers the aircraft lower as we approach the lake, the pontoons beneath us now visible as we prepare for landing. I grip the armrests, heart pounding as we descend toward the water's surface.

The landing is surprisingly gentle—a slight bump, then the sensation of gliding across the lake as the plane slows. A boat approaches.

"We're almost there," Martinez announces.

SEVENTEEN

Willow

Bear perks up at the sight of the water, his tail thumping excitedly against the seat. Despite everything, I find myself smiling at his enthusiasm.

The transfer from plane to boat is tricky. Bear leaps into the boat without prompting, turning to watch expectantly as I carefully step from the plane's pontoon.

The boat—a sleek, powerful craft clearly built for speed—carries us across the lake.

"How are you holding up?" Jackson asks, settling beside me.

"I'm..." I pause, considering the question. "I'm still processing everything. It doesn't feel quite real."

He nods understanding. "First extractions are always surreal. Like you're watching a movie of your own life."

"Does it get easier?" I glance at him, curious.

"In some ways." His expression turns thoughtful. "You get used to the protocols, the constant movement. But the reasons behind it—those never get easier."

I think about Mason, about Ryan, about Chaos.

Cooper and his injuries.

I think about the gunfire that echoed through the Montana forest as we lifted off.

"Any word from Mason and Ryan?"

Jackson shakes his head. "Not yet. They'll make contact when they're secure."

Bear shifts closer, as if sensing my concern, his warm weight pressing against my side. I run my fingers through his thick coat, finding comfort in the simple, tangible connection of a four-footed friend.

The boat ride lasts exactly twenty-three minutes before we reach the opposite shore. True to Martinez's word, another SUV waits.

"Final leg of the journey." Jackson guides me toward a forest-green pickup truck.

Bear jumps into the vehicle bed, making himself comfortable with a contented huff.

"Stubborn beast," Jackson mutters, but there's affection in his tone.

The drive takes us up winding mountain roads, climbing higher into dense forest that seems to swallow us whole. After nearly an hour of relentless ascent, we round a final curve and the "safehouse" comes into view.

"Whoa," I breathe, taking in the sprawling structure.

"Guardian HRS doesn't mess around," Jackson says with evident pride. "This is one of their premier facilities. Completely off-grid, self-sufficient, and virtually impenetrable."

The "safehouse" is more like a fortress disguised as a luxury mountain retreat—a massive log structure nestled into the mountainside with commanding views of the valley below. Solar arrays gleam on the expansive roof, and I spot what looks like a helipad partially concealed by trees on one side.

"Home sweet home, at least for now." Martinez offers me a hand as I exit the vehicle.

Bear is out before the engine fully stops, bounding up to the porch where he's greeted warmly by a petite woman with a long brown hair pulled back in a tight ponytail.

"Bear! You handsome devil," she exclaims, kneeling to receive his enthusiastic greeting. "Where's your daddy, huh?"

"Ghost's on his way," Jackson answers, helping me from the truck. "Willow, meet Skye Summers, co-founder of Guardian HRS and head of their medical division."

Skye straightens, her green eyes sharp as she assesses me with professional interest. "Mrs. Reynolds. Welcome."

"Just Willow, please." The sound of Steffan's name makes my skin crawl. "I'm not his wife anymore. Not in any way that matters."

Understanding flashes across her face. "Willow, then. Let's get you inside." She turns to Martinez and Jackson. "Just got an update on Cooper. He's in surgery and he's going to be fine."

"That's great to hear." Jackson and Martinez exchange a relieved look.

"Well, come inside." Skye looks up. "We aren't tracking anyone in the air or the woods, but best not to hang out here for too long." She turns to me. "You'll get a full safety briefing later, but rule number one is no going outside where anything flying, or spying, can confirm your identity."

"Makes sense." I follow her inside.

The interior of the mountain retreat is even more impressive than its exterior, featuring soaring ceilings, massive windows that overlook the valley, and state-of-the-art security systems that blend seamlessly with rustic luxury. Despite its size, the space feels warm and welcoming in a way I hadn't expected from a high-security facility.

"This way." Skye leads us through what appears to be a great room toward a hallway lined with doors. "We've prepared a suite for you. You can rest, shower, eat—whatever you need. Bear can stay with you if you'd like."

At the mention of his name, the massive dog trots to my side, looking up at me with those soulful eyes that seem to understand everything.

"Yes," I say without hesitation. "I'd like that very much."

Skye smiles. "I thought so. Mason mentioned he's taken quite a shine to you."

"Mason?" I stop mid-step. "You've heard from him?"

"Brief transmission about twenty minutes ago," she confirms. "He and Ryan are en route. ETA tomorrow morning at the earliest."

Relief crashes through me with such force that my knees nearly buckle. "He's okay? They're both okay?"

"Apparently," Skye's expression softens. "Mason Blackwood is notoriously hard to kill. Now, let's get you settled."

The suite is larger than any hotel room I've ever stayed in—a sitting area with plush sofas, a bedroom with a king-sized bed, and a bathroom featuring both a massive shower and a deep soaking tub. Fresh clothes wait on the bed, and a tray of food sits on the coffee table.

"Everything you need should be here," Skye says. "If not, just use the intercom. Someone will come."

"Thank you." The words feel inadequate for what these people have done for me—risking their lives, creating this elaborate escape network, and treating my wounds, both visible and hidden.

Skye pauses at the door. "Oh, Mitzy will be by in about an hour. She's our tech specialist. She'll want to discuss the flash drive."

With that reminder, my hand immediately goes to my pocket, confirming the small device is still there—three years of evidence, of suffering, of careful documentation.

"Get some rest," Skye advises, then closes the door softly behind her.

Alone for the first time in what feels like days, I sink onto the edge of the bed, emotions finally catching up with me. Bear immediately jumps up beside me, his massive weight making the mattress dip dramatically. He settles with his head in my lap, eyes watching me with what seems like genuine concern.

"It's okay," I tell him, though the tears now falling freely suggest otherwise. "We're safe."

Bear whines softly, shifting to press more of his warm bulk against me. His steady presence anchors me as I finally allow myself to fully feel everything—the terror of the past days, the grief for years lost to Steffan's abuse, the strange, fierce hope that bloomed in Mason's arms. The fact that I think I might be in love with a man I've known for barely a handful of days.

I don't know how long I sit there, crying, while Bear offers his silent comfort. Eventually, the tears slow, then stop altogether, leaving me hollow but somehow lighter.

"Thank you," I whisper to the dog, who responds by licking my hand once, then jumping down and padding to the bathroom door, looking back at me expectantly.

"Good idea." I manage a watery smile. "A shower would help."

The hot water is glorious, sluicing away the physical remnants of our journey—the sweat, the dirt, the lingering scent of fear. I stand under the spray until my skin pinks, letting the heat soak into muscles I didn't even realize were tense.

By the time I emerge, wrapped in the plush robe provided, I feel almost human again. Bear has made himself comfortable on the bed, massive body sprawled across the crisp white duvet, but he immediately sits up when I appear.

"Make yourself at home, why don't you?" I tease, the

normality of the moment striking me as both absurd and precious.

I dress in the clothes provided—soft leggings, a cashmere sweater, thick socks—all in my exact size. The attention to detail is both impressive and slightly unnerving. How much does Guardian HRS know about me?

A knock at the door interrupts my thoughts. Bear is immediately alert and moves to my side.

"Who is it?" I call, one hand automatically going to the dog's thick scruff.

"Mitzy," comes the response. "Here about the flash drive."

I open the door to find a woman with startling blue, purple, and black hair cropped in a pixie cut smiling at me. Her eyes carry the spark of intense intelligence, but her smile is as genuine as it gets.

"Willow, right? I'm Mitzy." She extends a hand. "Head of tech operations here at Guardian HRS. May I come in?"

I step aside, and she enters, immediately dropping to one knee to greet Bear. "Hey, big guy. Long time no see." Bear accepts her affectionate ear scratches with dignified patience before returning to the bed.

"You know Bear?" I ask, surprised.

"Oh yeah. Ghost brings him whenever he visits. That dog's had more security clearance than most agents." She straightens, her expression turning serious. "So, the flash drive. Mason mentioned it contains critical evidence."

I nod, retrieving it from my pocket. "Three years' worth. Financial records, witness tampering, weapons deals with terrorist organizations, and offshore accounts. Everything needed to bring Steffan down."

Mitzy whistles low. "No wonder he wants you dead." She produces a sleek laptop from her messenger bag. "Mind if we take a look? I'd like to make multiple secure backups immediately."

"Please." I hand her the drive, the weight of responsibility lifting slightly as it passes from my possession. "The more copies that exist, the less power Steffan has."

We spend the next two hours going through the drive's contents, Mitzy occasionally mutters technical jargon I don't understand as she creates encrypted backups and routes them to secure servers.

"This is…" she pauses, staring at the screen. "This is explosive stuff. Your husband wasn't just corrupt—he was running a full-scale operation."

"Former husband," I correct automatically. "And yes, I know. That's why I spent three years gathering evidence. I needed to make sure when I finally escaped, he couldn't just make it all disappear."

Mitzy looks at me with new respect. "Smart. Dangerous, but smart."

Mitzy's eyes narrow as she scrolls, her fingers tapping a steady rhythm against the keys. "The files on this USB are a chaos of data—no unifying titles, no structured folders, just fragments of financial statements, security protocols, court transcripts, energy contracts. Like a hoarder's hard drive."

"I took what I could when I could. That's no surprise, but is it enough? Enough to take him down?"

"Definitely. The problem is this is messy," Mitzy mutters.

"That's what I said."

"But not messy enough."

"I don't know what that means."

"These files shouldn't connect."

"What do you mean?" I ask, watching her brow furrow deeper.

"They do," she says slowly. "Barely. But, then they don't. It's like a shadow running through the metadata. Version histories, revision comments, internal notes."

I have *no* idea what she's talking about.

Mitzy leans in, typing faster. "Most of these files were scrubbed or anonymized—some of them encrypted in layers. But not perfectly. There's a tag that keeps showing up, buried in old edits and hidden fields."

"A tag?" I shake my head. "Sorry, but you've lost me."

"Obsidian."

"What's Obsidian?"

"No idea," Mitzy replies. "But it's an odd reference, occurring across many of these files—legal, military-adjacent, even biotech. Some are scanned memos, while others resemble early-stage research proposals or covert budget approvals. All of it smells black-ops adjacent. It's as if someone was quietly pulling strings behind federal walls. It's just weird. You may have snagged a thread tied to an unsanctioned ghost project."

"I'm not surprised. Steffan and integrity are like oil and water."

Mitzy turns back to the screen. "I'm still digging, but this could be more than we realize. It could explain why Steffan wasn't willing to let you go."

"It was worth the risk." I think of the bruises, the humiliation, the years of careful planning while enduring systematic abuse. "It has to be."

A soft knock interrupts us. Bear's head lifts, but he doesn't seem alarmed, which I take as a good sign.

"Come in," I call.

The door opens to reveal a man who can only be described as a giant carved from mountain stone. He has the kind of height that makes doorframes nervous—to my best guess just shy of seven feet—and a body built like a battering ram. Tree-trunk legs, shoulders broad enough to block sunlight, and hands the size of dinner plates.

His hair is a shock of white blond, thick and unruly, falling over ice-blue eyes that crinkle with warmth when they land on Bear. A small scar slices through his left brow, barely noticeable, but enough to hint at stories not easily told.

"There's my favorite fur missile." His voice rolls through the room like distant thunder, like boulders crashing against each other in some forgotten canyon. Low. Deep. Resonant. A sound you feel in your chest more than your ears.

Bear launches off the bed, barreling into the newcomer with such enthusiasm that a lesser man would have been knocked flat. The giant merely laughs, absorbing the impact and rubbing Bear's ears.

"Willow, meet Forest Summers," Mitzy says, her tone suggesting this introduction is significant. "Creator and head of Guardian HRS."

EIGHTEEN

Willow

Forest straightens, offering me a smile that softens the sharp angles of his face. "Mrs. Reynolds. Welcome."

"Just Willow, please." I rise, feeling oddly formal in my borrowed clothes. "Thank you for everything your team has done."

"Mason Blackwood asked for help." He shrugs those massive shoulders like the weight of the world barely registers. "That's all I needed to know."

"You know Mason well?"

"Yeah." Forest's smile tilts, half-respect, half-history. "Guardian HRS subcontracts with his company when we need elite-level personal protection support, or when we need to help people disappear."

I blink. "His company?"

Forest nods. "Cerberus Personal Security Systems. Blackwood built it from the ground up. Field work, tactical logistics, high-risk extractions—he's one of the few we trust to run solo ops if things get ugly."

He glances at the laptop where my evidence is displayed. "Mitzy getting you set up with backups?"

"Yes, she's been incredibly helpful."

"Good. Once everything's secured, I'd like you to join us for dinner. There are some people you should meet—the core team who'll be helping with your situation."

"I'd like that." The prospect of a normal meal, of conversation not dominated by immediate survival concerns, appeals more than I expected.

After Forest leaves, Mitzy finishes creating the backups, confirming that the evidence is now stored on multiple secure servers, encrypted with protocols even the NSA would struggle to crack.

"There," she says with satisfaction. "Now, even if Reynolds somehow manages to find and destroy every physical copy, the data still exists. He can't bury this."

The realization hits me with unexpected force—Steffan can no longer make the evidence disappear. For the first time in years, I hold genuine power over my own fate.

"Thank you," I say, the words inadequate for what this means.

Mitzy nods understanding. "Dinner's in thirty minutes. Great room. You remember the way?"

"I do. Thanks."

After she leaves, I spend a few minutes gathering myself. Bear watches from the bed, his dark eyes following my movements as I pace the room, trying to process everything that's happened in the past forty-eight hours.

Two days ago—three?—I was fleeing through a Montana blizzard, certain I would die. Now I'm in a secure mountain fortress with a team of professionals dedicated to my safety and bringing Steffan to justice.

And somewhere between Montana and Idaho, Mason is making his way to me, keeping the promise he made as we parted.

I'll be right behind you.

Bear jumps down from the bed, padding to my side and pressing against my leg as if sensing my thoughts. I scratch behind his ears, finding comfort in this simple connection.

"Let's go to dinner," I tell him.

Dinner is held in a massing room adjacent to the Great Room. A large dining table is set for seven, although it could easily seat twice that number. A fire crackles in the stone fireplace, and the delicious aroma of real home-cooked food fills the air. Forest stands near the fireplace, deep in conversation with someone I haven't met yet.

He turns as Bear and I enter, beckoning us over. "Willow, come meet the rest of the team."

The man beside Forest is tall, although Forest stands head and shoulders over him. His frame is leaner, but still packed with muscles. There's a solidness to him, evident in the watchful intensity of his gaze as it sweeps over me, assessing.

"CJ," he introduces himself simply, offering a calloused hand. "Head of Field Operations and the Guardian teams."

Skye joins us, followed by Mitzy. Martinez and Jackson are barely a step behind. Dinner conversation flows surprisingly easy, touching on everything from Cooper's successful surgery to the security measures in place around the mountain.

"Any updates from Mason and Ryan?" I ask during a lull in conversation.

Forest's expression turns serious. "Last communication puts them about twelve hours out. They had to take an alternate route after encountering resistance."

My heart stutters. "Resistance? They're okay?"

"Ghost and Brass?" Jackson scoffs. "Takes more than a few mercenaries to slow them down."

The meal continues, but my thoughts remain fixed on Mason and Ryan, somewhere in the wilderness, making their way to us. I push food around my plate, no longer hungry despite the excellent cooking.

"You should rest," Skye suggests gently, noticing my distraction. "Tomorrow will be here before you know it."

I nod, grateful for the escape. "Thank you for dinner. It was lovely."

Bear follows me back to the suite, his steady presence a comfort as I prepare for bed. Despite my exhaustion, sleep proves elusive. I lie awake in the unfamiliar room, listening to Bear's soft snores from his position at the foot of the bed.

My mind replays everything—the storm, finding Mason, the night in his arms, the firefight, the extraction, the journey here. So much has happened in so little time that it feels impossible to process everything.

Somewhere beyond these walls, Mason is keeping his promise, fighting his way back to me. I cling to that thought as exhaustion finally claims me, dragging me into dreamless sleep.

Morning comes with soft light filtering through the windows and Bear's cold nose pressing against my cheek. I blink awake to find him staring at me, tail thumping against the mattress.

"Morning to you too," I murmur, reaching up to scratch his ears.

A knock at the door sends Bear bounding across the room, his entire posture alert but not alarmed. When I open it, Skye stands there with a tray of food.

"Breakfast," she explains. "And news. Mason and Ryan made contact thirty minutes ago. They'll be here within the hour."

"They're okay?" Relief floods through me, so intense it makes my knees weak.

"Tired, dirty, and according to Mason, 'severely caffeine-deprived,' but otherwise unharmed." She sets the tray on the coffee table. "Thought you might want to eat and get ready before they arrive."

"Thanks."

"And I'll take Bear out, if that's okay with you. Big guy needs to run and stretch those legs."

"Sure." I shower and dress with renewed energy, anticipation building with each passing minute.

After my shower, I head to the great room to wait.

I pace the length of the great room, nerves buzzing under my skin like static. The fire crackles in the hearth, its warmth doing little to calm the restless energy twisting inside me.

Bear lies near the window, massive body stretched out, chin resting on his paws. Suddenly, he lifts his head.

Every muscle in his frame goes taut. His ears snap forward. He sniffs the air once—twice—and then he's on his feet, tail swishing in tight, eager arcs.

"Bear?" I take a step toward him, but he's already trotting to the door, nails clicking on the wood floor. Not tense. Not on guard.

Excited.

He lets out a short, happy bark, his tail now wagging hard enough to thump against the entryway wall.

And then I know. I feel it before it happens.

I'm already halfway to the front door by the time the handle turns.

It swings open to reveal Ryan first, dusty, scraped up, but upright. He's already unlatching his gear as he steps inside, his rifle slung loose over one shoulder.

"Hey, sweetheart," he says with a tired grin. "Someone's been waiting for you."

Bear barrels past him with a joyful woof, launching himself toward the doorway.

Then Mason steps into view.

Filthy. Bruised. Alive.

His broad shoulders fill the doorway like he was built for it. His jacket is torn. There's dried blood at his collar, soot on his face, snow melting in his hair. He looks like hell.

But he's never looked more handsome to me.

Bear reaches him first, nearly knocking him back on his heels in his exuberance. Mason drops to one knee, arms open to catch the full brunt of two hundred pounds of ecstatic Newfoundland.

"Hey, buddy," Mason murmurs, ruffling Bear's thick fur, laughter rough in his throat. "Missed you too."

The moment Mason opens the door wide enough, Chaos slips past his side. Bear meets him mid-run. The two dogs collide with grunts and excited yips, paws batting, tails whipping like propellers. Chaos leaps up, licking Bear's jowls, and Bear answers with a playful snarl before nudging Chaos with a massive paw. It's pure joy—chaotic and animal and full of the kind of reunion that needs no words.

Then Chaos turns to me.

He charges forward with a full-body wiggle, tongue lolling, and skids to a stop just short of knocking me over. He nuzzles my side, tail wagging furiously as he presses his head against my thigh, whining in that high, happy way that says he's missed me.

I drop to my knees, threading my fingers into his warm fur. "Hi, boy," I whisper, my voice cracking. "I missed you too."

He licks my cheek once, snuffling like he's cataloguing every inch of me.

I glance up, and Mason is there. The room disappears. Ryan, the fire, the cold wind curling in from the open door—none of it exists.

Only Mason. Only us.

I throw myself into his arms, and he catches me with a grunt, hauling me against his chest like he might never let go.

His arms wrap around me like armor, like tethering, like he needs to feel that I'm real just as much as I need to feel him.

I bury my face in his chest, breathing in the wild, masculine scent of him—smoke, snow, pine, and something purely Mason. My fingers fist into the back of his jacket, refusing to let go.

"You smell terrible," I mumble into his ear.

He huffs a laugh into my hair.

I pull back just enough to look at him, to take in the days of stubble, the exhaustion etched into his face, the bruising along his temple.

His gaze sharpens at that—something primal lighting behind his eyes.

"You're okay," I whisper, breath catching, face buried in the curve of his neck. "You're really okay."

"Yeah." His voice is rougher than I remember, lower. "Told you I'd be right behind you."

He pulls back just enough to frame my face between his hands. His touch is reverent, thumbs brushing along my cheekbones. Emotion flickers across his face—relief, heat, hunger—and then he kisses me.

Not soft. Not sweet.

It's ferocious. Hot. Possessive.

It's a kiss that says *I survived for you.*

I melt into it, into him. I taste smoke and adrenaline and Mason, and I give in to the press of his body, the heat of his hand sliding into my hair.

His other arm locks around my waist, holding me so tight I can't tell where he ends and I begin.

Tension simmers just beneath his skin. Restraint barely holding him together. His tongue slides against mine, and I moan, my legs going weak beneath the onslaught of need and memory and overwhelming relief. My fingers curling in his jacket. There's nothing careful in the way he takes me in that moment—only claiming, only certainty.

Somewhere across the great room, someone whistles, followed by a familiar voice shouting, "Get a room, Ghost!"

When Mason finally pulls back, his forehead rests against mine, both of us breathing hard.

"Miss me?" he murmurs, the corner of his mouth lifting just slightly.

I try to laugh, but it comes out as a gasp when his hand skims under the hem of my shirt to rest on bare skin.

"I wasn't sure I'd ever see you again," I whisper, my voice raw.

"You'll always see me again," he says, pressing his forehead to mine, breath ragged. "I'll always come for you, Willow. Always."

Behind us, Bear lets out an impatient huff, nudging Mason's thigh as if to say, *Alright, alright, now pet me again.*

Mason chuckles and glances down, scratching the big dog's ears. "Jealous bastard." His mouth brushes mine again—softer this time, full of promise. "I'll never let you out of my sight again."

"Good." I kiss him this time, short and hard.

From behind us, Bear gives a louder grunt, clearly annoyed to have been displaced. I laugh, pressing my face to Mason's chest as he leans down to give the giant dog a consoling scratch.

Mason straightens, scanning the room with a slow, predatory smile. "I think someone mentioned a room?" His steel-gray eyes drop to mine, heat flaring behind them. "I like that idea."

Before I can react, he wraps an arm around my waist and lifts me clean off the ground. I yelp, laughing as he hauls me up and over his shoulder like I weigh nothing at all.

"Mason!"

He smacks my ass lightly. "No talking." Then he turns,

striding toward the hallway while Bear trots happily behind us, tail wagging like we're all playing the best game ever.

"Anyone disturbs us," Mason calls over his shoulder, "they die."

Laughter breaks out behind us, but I barely hear it—because Mason's hand slides higher up the back of my thigh as he carries me away, and my heart is already racing for what comes next.

NINETEEN

Willow

MASON BARRELS DOWN THE HALL LIKE A MAN POSSESSED, HIS stride long and loaded with intent. I'm slung over his shoulder, laughing breathlessly, the steady bounce of his gait sending blood straight to places that are already pulsing with need.

Bear trots ahead, tail wagging like this is his victory lap. Chaos flanks us with the focused contentment of a soldier on leave, his tongue lolling out in doggy delight.

Best. Day. Ever.

Mason doesn't stop until we reach the suite at the far end of the hall—the one I've been calling mine since they brought me to Guardian HRS's mountain retreat. Bear noses the door like he means to open it himself, but Mason plants his feet and sets me down, one palm on the doorframe.

"Not today," he says, not unkindly, but with enough steel in his voice that both dogs immediately obey. "You don't get to watch."

Bear whines in protest. Chaos lets out a resigned huff. But they retreat without argument.

"Sorry, boys," Mason mutters as he opens the door and nudges me through.

The second the door clicks shut, I'm pinned.

His hands are on me before I can breathe. One tangled in my hair, the other gripping my waist as he slams his mouth down on mine with no warning, no hesitation, no gentleness.

Heat erupts under my skin like a brushfire. I gasp into him, fingers clawing at his jacket, trying to get closer, always closer. He backs me into the wall with a growl, his body pressing hard against mine, all rough lines and pure male heat.

Clothes are the enemy now.

I yank his shirt over his head. He tears at the buttons of mine with zero finesse, fabric ripping under his hands as his mouth never leaves mine. His tongue claims me, wild and hungry, like he's been starving for this—for me—and I kiss him back with equal desperation.

His hands slide under the waistband of my leggings, dragging them down along with my panties. I toe off my socks, one at a time, kicking free as he curses and struggles with his boots.

"Fucking hell," he mutters, trying to shove them off with one foot and failing. "Should've left the damn things at the door."

A gasp swallows my laugh as he gives up and yanks his pants down anyway, boots still attached. It's chaos and clumsiness and so goddamn sexy I could scream.

Then he's there. Right there.

His hands find my thighs, lifting me like I weigh nothing, and I wrap around him instinctively. My back slams into the wall again, and in the next breath, he's inside me.

I cry out—sharp, broken, utterly overwhelmed.

He doesn't give me time to adjust. Doesn't give me space to think.

He thrusts into me with a savage rhythm, his mouth on my

throat, his body slamming into mine, over and over, until I'm not even sure where I end and he begins.

"You feel like fucking heaven," he growls against my skin.

I can't speak. Can't breathe. I just cling to him, fingers digging into his shoulders, every inch of me unraveling.

And God, I want it. I want him—this raw, consuming need. This overwhelming, violent passion. The way he fucks like he's trying to claim my soul through my body.

Every thrust drives me closer. I'm already close, already shaking, already there.

"Come for me," he growls. "Let me feel you fall apart."

His words are gasoline to the fire.

I shatter around him, gasping his name, clenching so tightly it rips a groan straight from his chest. He slams into me one last time, deep and hard, and endless, as he finds his release with a curse and a shudder.

For a moment, there's nothing.

Just panting. Sweaty skin. My cheek against his shoulder, his arms locked around me like he can't bear to let go.

He lowers me slowly, gently, until I'm on my feet but still pressed to the wall. His forehead rests against mine, breath hot and uneven.

"You okay?" he asks, voice hoarse, eyes dark and unguarded.

"Not even close," I whisper, smiling like I've survived a storm and want more. "Do it again."

Mason chuckles—low, smug, that gravelly rasp soaked in male satisfaction—and leans in to nip my bottom lip.

"Round one was just a preview," he murmurs. "But first…" He pulls back slightly, glancing down. "The fucking boots come off."

Still panting, still pressed to the wall, I watch as he sinks to the floor in front of me. He tugs off one boot, then the other, muttering something about "damn stubborn soles" and "next time, barefoot from the start."

When he finally looks up at me, his grin is wicked. Ferocious. Arousal ripples through me again—swift and hot.

"Shower or bed for round two?" he asks, breath hitching like he already knows the answer. "Because I need to fuck you again. Right now."

I laugh, unable to help it, the tension between us sharp edged but laced with joy. "Definitely shower," I say, wrinkling my nose as I tug his shirt from where it's bunched behind my back. "You smell like blood, sweat, and wilderness."

"Good." He stands in a single, powerful motion, scoops me into his arms like it costs him nothing. "Now I get to make you beg while I wash it all off."

The shower is oversized, stone tiled, has multiple nozzles, and is steamy the second he turns the water on. He sets me down, grabs the soap like he's been waiting his whole life to do this. Then he starts to clean me, slow and teasing, but I stop him with a firm shake of my head.

"My turn."

He lifts a brow, amused. "Gonna pamper me now?"

"Shut up and hold still."

I take the bar of soap and drag it across his chest, watching suds bubble over those hard planes and deep-cut ridges. He watches me, silent; the air between us shifting—less cocky now. More reverent. Hungrier. The intimacy of it slices through whatever wall he might've tried to rebuild.

My hands move lower. Over his abdomen. Down his thighs. I wash him with aching care, like touching him might fix something broken in both of us.

When I glance up again, he's not grinning. He's watching me too closely, his mouth set, eyes dark with something more than lust.

His hands frame my face, thumbs stroking just beneath my cheekbones. The water cascades over his broad shoulders, flattening his hair to his skull and sluicing down the hard ridges of his chest, but his expression is dead serious. Quiet.

A little uncertain.

"I need to ask you something," he says softly. "Back at the cabin… We kinda played with some things. The *Sir* thing. The control."

My breath catches.

"I don't want to assume, and I don't want what happened with your husband to—to taint what this is."

I blink hard. My heart presses against my ribs.

He lowers his hands but stays close, watching me, waiting. That's what undoes me—the waiting. The space he gives me. The restraint in a man built to destroy.

"Does it bother you when I call you that? When I let you take control?"

His groan is low and immediate—visceral.

"Shit," he mutters, voice thick with hunger. "That punches all my fucking buttons, Willow. Every. Single. One." His jaw flexes. "I love it. All of it. And more. I just…" He swallows hard. "I don't ever want to cross a line you're not ready for. Especially because of what that bastard did."

My breath leaves me in a rush, not from fear, but from understanding. Relief.

I hear the message beneath his words. That I'm safe. That what we shared wasn't a mistake. That he's not afraid of what I want—only of hurting me.

I rise on tiptoe and press my lips to the edge of his jaw, my breath warm against his ear. "I'm yours to command, *Sir*," I whisper. "I love what you did before. Don't stop because of him."

The air changes between us. Instant. Sharp.

He pulls back, just enough to look at me. His eyes blaze—hot, greedy, possessive—and something low and dark sparks inside them.

He takes my wrist and guides it downward, slow and sure, until my fingers brush the length of his cock—already thick, already hard.

Already waiting.

His hand closes around mine, folding it over his arousal with unmistakable intent.

"Finish washing me." His voice is as rough as gravel, "Especially down here."

"Yes, Sir!" My thighs clench. Heat pulses low and deep.

I obey, lathering soap between my hands as water pounds around us. I touch him slowly, deliberately—my palm sliding along him, working the slickness over every inch. His breath stutters. His fingers curl into fists at his sides.

Everything between us crackles—want, need, permission—wrapped in the kind of trust I never thought I'd feel again.

Steam coils around us as I kneel, naked and soaked, my breath shaky with anticipation. The tile presses against my knees, but I barely feel it. Every nerve in my body is tuned to him.

Mason stands above me, broad and beautiful and dangerous, water running down the muscle-sculpted lines of his abdomen. His cock juts thick and hard between us, slick from my touch, flushed and pulsing at the tip.

He watches me. Silent. Waiting. Letting me choose.

I wrap my fingers around the base of him. He hisses through his teeth, low and sharp.

"Fuck, Willow…" His voice is shredded silk. My name in his mouth tastes like reverence and ruin. "You feel—so fucking good."

I press a kiss to the crown, just a whisper of contact—and his hips shift, the control in him unraveling thread by thread. I slide my tongue along the underside, tracing the thick vein, and he groans, one hand flying out to brace against the wall.

When I take him deeper—inch by inch—his knees almost buckle.

"Jesus Christ." His fingers tangle in my wet hair. Not pulling. Not forcing. Just anchoring. "That mouth…"

I hollow my cheeks and suck him deep, loving the way he twitches, the rough rasp of his praise above me.

"Look at you." His voice is hoarse, awed. "On your knees for me. So fucking beautiful."

The water keeps falling, heat curling through the shower like fog, but it's his approval that scorches me.

His other hand joins the first, cradling my skull. I let him guide me, surrendering to the slow rhythm he sets. He doesn't thrust. He claims. Deep strokes, deeper moans, his cock thick against my tongue.

"Tell me if it's too much," he says, barely holding on. "I'll stop. I'll always stop for you."

I dig my nails into his thighs in answer—*don't you dare stop.*

And he doesn't.

He fucks my mouth slow and possessive, hips flexing just enough to feed me more, groaning like the sound's ripped from his core.

When I reach up and roll his balls in my palm, he chokes on a curse and pulls out fast, gripping the base of his cock to keep from coming.

His chest heaves. His whole body shakes.

"You keep that up," he growls, "and this ends with me painting your throat and whispering apologies."

I grin up at him, lips swollen and slick. "So don't keep me waiting."

He stares at me like I've gutted him. "Holy fuck."

Then he grabs my arm and yanks me upright, his mouth crashing down on mine in a bruising, punishing kiss.

I taste him. He tastes me. And everything else—fear, history, doubt—burns to ash.

He spins me, crowding me back against the tile wall. One knee shoves between mine, spreading my legs. His hand slides down, fingers finding how wet I am, how ready.

He growls, the sound primal. Then he's inside me—one hard, perfect thrust that stretches me to the edge of pain and rips a cry from my throat.

He doesn't give me time to adjust. He fucks me hard.

Against the wall. In the steam. With his name on my lips and his cock driving into me like he owns my soul.

I claw at his shoulders. He bites my throat. We don't make love. We burn. His hand snakes between us, fingers rubbing my clit just right, just rough enough to shove me over the edge.

I come screaming his name, clenched tight around him, writhing between him and the wall as the orgasm rips through me.

He groans, thrusts once more, twice—and explodes inside me, biting my shoulder, emptying himself with a violence that makes the world tilt.

For a long moment, we don't move. Just breathe.

Steam curls around us. My legs tremble. He holds me like I might disappear.

"I've got you," he whispers, forehead pressed to mine. "I'll always have you."

I believe him.

Even as my body pulses from the aftershocks, even as he carries me from the shower and lays me gently on the bed, this isn't just *sex*. It's surrender. Devotion. Fire and trust and healing wrapped in skin and sweat.

And I want more.

So much more.

"Mason," I whisper, chest rising and falling with rapid breath. "You mentioned you want *more*."

He goes still.

"Show me what that means to you."

His eyes darken—not just with arousal, but with something deeper. Worship. Possession. Love, raw and unnamed, but undeniable.

"You sure about that?"

"Yes, please."

He shows me with his hands—slow and reverent as he binds my wrists with his belt, not to restrain, but to center me. To remind me I'm safe. That he'll never take more than I give.

He shows me with his mouth—kissing every scar, every bruise that still lingers beneath the surface, until I'm trembling not from pain, but from being seen.

He shows me with his voice—low, commanding, patient. Teaching me the rhythm of his world. How to bloom beneath his control.

He shows me what it means to be cherished and claimed, to be taken again and again until I forget what it feels like to be afraid.

We don't leave the room all day.

When we finally emerge—hours later, freshly showered and walking a little slower—I wear one of his shirts and a smile I can't contain.

The moment we step into the dining room, every conversation halts.

Ryan smirks over his coffee. Jackson gives Mason a mock salute. Mitzy just raises a single eyebrow, fighting a grin. Chaos trots in behind us, tail wagging like we haven't all just walked through fire.

No one says a word.

They don't have to.

My cheeks heat, but Mason rests his hand on my lower back with quiet pride. He doesn't hide. Doesn't flinch from what we've become.

We take our seats at the long table, Bear flopping at my feet with a satisfied sigh. The warmth of camaraderie hums in the room, easy and familiar—until Mitzy sets her coffee down with a decisive click and levels her gaze on me.

"Now that you've had your *reunion*," she says, voice calm but cutting straight to the bone, "we need to talk about Steffan Reynolds."

Silence falls like a hammer.

I straighten in my seat, pulse kicking up again—not from desire this time, but from the familiar edge of dread.

"We have the USB," Mitzy continues. "Names. Accounts. Transactions. Enough to put half a dozen high-ranking officials behind bars. Maybe more."

Forest leans forward, arms crossed over his mountain of a chest. "And enough to make us all targets if we move too fast."

CJ taps a tablet beside him, data scrolling rapidly. "We've verified the files. Arms deals. Foreign deposits. Payments to officials, agents, even judges in neighboring districts."

Mason's hand finds mine beneath the table. Grounding me. Reminding me I'm not alone.

"The question," Mitzy says, "is what we do next."

"Do we go public?" CJ asks. "Drop the files to a secure leak site, force the DOJ's hand?"

"Or keep it in-house?" Forest counters. "Build our case, get Reynolds stripped of his power before he knows we've struck."

Mitzy's eyes don't leave mine. "And then there's you, Willow."

My breath catches.

The room goes quiet.

Not the uneasy silence of fear—but the kind that comes

before impact. Like the pause between thunderclaps. Everyone is watching me. Waiting.

Mitzy meets my gaze, steady and unflinching. "You're the key witness. We need to know what you want. Do you testify? Go public? Help us bring him down from the inside?"

"Or disappear," CJ adds, his tone low. "New name. New life. You'd be safe—but always looking over your shoulder."

The breath catches in my lungs.

Disappear. Safe, quiet, forgettable. No courtrooms. No microphones. Just shadows. I could be a ghost, and survive.

Or…

Testify. Speak the truth aloud. Name names. Face Steffan in a courtroom and drag him into the light.

Mitzy lays it out in two clear paths. Forest folds his massive arms across his chest. His voice is deep, calm, and final. "If we do this, it's scorched earth. We go after everyone."

Skye, poised and calm beside him, adds softly, "And we paint a target on your back. Testifying means exposure. Hearings. Media. And Steffan will come after you with everything he has left."

Ryan speaks next, voice quiet but fierce. "But it's the only way to make it stick."

Jackson leans forward, scarred knuckles braced against the table. "You want him buried, not just wounded?" His stare pins me. "You need to look him in the eye when you slam the cage shut."

I stare down at my hands, laced in Mason's. His thumb strokes slow circles across my knuckles. The heat of his skin grounds me.

They're all right.

One path means safety, but silence. The other—is fire.

And I'm so tired of being afraid.

I lift my head. My voice is quiet, but steady.

"I want to testify."

The tension shifts. Not gone—but different now. Controlled. Directed.

Ryan lets out a short breath and slaps his palm against the table. "Let's burn this motherfucker down."

A low rumble of agreement moves around the room. Forest nods once. Jackson smiles—grim and satisfied. Skye is already opening her laptop. CJ starts tapping on his tablet. All I can feel is Mason's hand tightening around mine. His eyes on me, full of pride and something deeper I can't name.

Because I didn't choose to survive.

I chose to fight.

TWENTY

Mason

Sunlight slices through the window blinds, casting gold bars across Willow's sleeping form. I've been awake for almost an hour, just watching her breathe. The rise and fall of her chest. The soft flutter of her eyelashes against her cheeks. The way her body curls instinctively toward mine, even in sleep.

Ten days. Ten days since we arrived at Guardian HRS's mountain fortress. Ten nights with her in my arms. Ten mornings waking up beside her, still half-disbelieving that she's real.

That we're real.

Bear snores softly at the foot of the bed, his massive body taking up more space than should be physically possible. Chaos is curled in the corner, one eye open, always on guard.

My boys. My team. And now, my woman.

Willow stirs, her body stretching languidly against mine. Even half-asleep, she moves with a new confidence that wasn't there when I first found her in the Montana snow. She's softer now in my arms—but stronger in every other way.

"Morning," she murmurs, voice husky with sleep as her eyes flutter open. Green-gold and clear, meeting mine without fear.

"Morning, beautiful." I brush a strand of hair from her face, letting my fingers linger against her cheek. "Sleep well?"

She smiles, slow and satisfied. "Eventually."

The memory of last night flashes behind my eyes—her body arched beneath mine, her wrists pinned above her head, her voice breaking as she begged for release. The way she surrendered to me so completely, her trust a gift I'm still not sure I deserve.

"You did at that," I agree, my voice dropping an octave as I roll her beneath me.

Her laughter is breathless as my mouth claims hers. Not gentle. Not patient. But hungry in a way that still surprises me after ten days of having her. Of learning her body. Of watching her bloom under my touch.

She isn't surviving anymore.

She's learning how to fight.

How to want.

How to live.

And fuck, if it isn't the most beautiful thing I've ever seen.

An hour later, freshly showered and thoroughly satisfied, we make our way to the kitchen where the rest of the team has already gathered. Skye stands at the counter, two mugs of coffee in hand. She passes one to Forest, who's hunched over a laptop, his massive frame somehow managing to make even the high-end wooden chairs look like doll furniture and the coffee mug like a child's toy cup.

"Look who finally decided to join the land of the living," Mitzy calls from her spot at the table, not looking up from her tablet. Her fingers fly across the screen with almost inhuman speed, lines of code reflecting in her glasses.

"Some of us actually sleep," I counter, reaching for the coffee pot.

Skye snorts. "Sleep. Is that what they're calling it these days?"

Willow's cheeks flush, but she doesn't shy away from the teasing. Instead, she moves to the refrigerator and begins pulling out eggs and vegetables. "Anyone hungry besides us?"

The casual domesticity of the moment hits me like a freight train. This woman, who escaped a monster, carries evidence that could topple a federal judge and his entire network, yet she makes breakfast as if she belongs here.

Like this is home.

And maybe it is.

Brass strides into the kitchen, data pad in hand. Chaos immediately perks up at his entrance. "Morning, lovebirds. Got the overnight drone footage." He tosses the device onto the table where Forest can reach it. "Site's been cleared."

"Cleared?" Willow asks, looking confused. "What does that mean?"

"Clean. Like it never happened." Ryan helps himself to coffee. "Cabin too. Professional job."

Forest's massive hands dwarf the tablet as he swipes through the images. "They're spooked," he rumbles, voice like distant thunder. "Covering tracks means they're afraid of what could be traced back to them."

"Good," Willow says, cracking eggs into a bowl with more force than necessary. "They should be afraid."

The steel in her voice makes me glance at her, pride swelling in my chest. Every day, she grows stronger. Every day, the woman who was buried beneath years of abuse emerges more fully.

"Any movement on the Reynolds front?" I ask, moving to help her with breakfast, my hand brushing the small of her back in silent support.

Skye taps her own tablet. "His public schedule continues uninterrupted. Court appearances. Charity fundraiser. Not a hint that his wife is missing or that he's under scrutiny."

"Classic narcissist move," Willow says, not looking up from the vegetables she's chopping. "He thinks he's untouchable."

"He's maintaining his routine," Forest adds, "but his security detail has doubled, and his communications have gone dark."

"Encrypted channels only," Mitzy confirms. "But I'm making progress cracking them."

Ryan gestures toward the tech wizard's tablet. "How's the case build going?"

Willow answers without looking up from her chopping. "Slow but steady. I want every 'i' dotted and 't' crossed. It's not just about Reynolds anymore—his network touches half a dozen agencies, two federal courts, and God knows how many politicians."

"And if we move too fast, we tip our hand," Mitzy adds, her focus never leaving her screen.

"We move carefully," Forest agrees. "Methodically."

"In the meantime?" Ryan asks.

"In the meantime," Skye says, moving to stand beside Willow, "we keep working. Legal prep, security protocols, extraction contingencies if things go sideways."

The front door opens with a gentle click that would be inaudible to most people, but sets both Bear and Chaos instantly on alert. Bear launches himself off his cushion by the fireplace, bounding toward the entryway with surprising speed for his massive bulk. Chaos moves to flank him, a low, happy growl rumbling in his chest.

"Right on time," Ryan mutters, a smile playing at the corners of his mouth.

I nod. Martinez left two days ago to retrieve Cooper from the hospital. Their arrival this morning is right on schedule.

Cooper appears in the doorway, favoring his left leg but otherwise upright and whole. The bandages that had wrapped his thigh are gone, replaced by a compression sleeve just visible beneath his cargo pants. He carries a duffel slung over one shoulder, and his face splits into a wide grin as Bear nearly knocks him over with an enthusiastic greeting.

"Easy, you beast," he laughs, scratching behind the Newfoundland's ears. "Don't rip out my stitches."

Willow is across the room in seconds, surprising everyone—maybe even herself—with how quickly she moves to hug him. "You're okay," she breathes, relief evident in her voice.

"Takes more than a little lead to keep me down, darlin'," Cooper drawls, returning her hug with his free arm.

I follow more slowly, letting her have her moment before clasping forearms with my sniper, my brother. "Good to have you back in one piece."

"Good to be back," Cooper replies, his eyes conveying what words can't—gratitude, brotherhood, the unbreakable bonds forged in battle. "Started climbing the walls after three days in that hospital bed."

"Climbing the nurses, more like," Martinez quips, appearing behind Cooper with a smirk. "Had to drag him out before someone married him."

Laughter ripples through the room, genuine and warm, breaking the tension that's been building for days. The team is whole again.

I watch them interact. Cooper settles at the table, wincing only slightly as he extends his injured leg; Martinez recounts the hospital escape with theatrical embellishment. Jackson enters from the training room to complete our circle. Ryan leans against the counter, steady as always. My brothers. My team.

And Willow, finding her footing among them, laughing at Cooper's outrageous flirtation, her shoulders relaxed in a way they haven't been since we arrived. The sight of her there, comfortable among these dangerous men, fills me with a fierce pride I can't quite name.

Skye steps into the kitchen, her expression shifting the mood instantly. "Briefing in fifteen," she announces. "We've got movement."

Forest follows, nodding toward Cooper. "Glad you're back. We'll need all hands for this."

The easy camaraderie fades, replaced by the focused energy that precedes action. We've been in a holding pattern for days—building the case, preparing Willow, waiting for the right moment to strike. That moment is approaching; I can feel it in the air like the static before a lightning strike.

Breakfast forgotten, we move as one unit toward the war room—the reinforced chamber at the center of the lodge where our most sensitive operations are planned. Forest takes his position at the head of the table. Skye and CJ flank him like sentinels. Mitzy immediately connects her tablet to the main display, fingers flying as she pulls up file after file.

"Let's review what we know," Forest begins, his deep voice commanding attention without effort. "Reynolds has maintained his public persona without interruption. No missing persons report for Willow. No sign he's concerned about his security breach."

"But his movements tell a different story," CJ adds, tapping a command that brings up a series of surveillance photos. "Increased security. Closed-door meetings with known associates. And this…" He taps again, enlarging an image of Steffan Reynolds entering what appears to be a nondescript office building.

"That's Drazen Kostic's front company," Willow says, leaning forward. "Serbian arms dealer. I documented at least three meetings between them last year."

Mitzy nods. "The USB confirms it. Reynolds has been facilitating weapons deals through his judicial position—sealed warrants, evidence 'lost' in transit, cases dismissed on technicalities."

"Not just weapons," Skye adds. "Human trafficking. Drug smuggling. Anything that pays."

I watch Willow's face as she absorbs this information. Ten days of suspicion confirmed. Three years of documenting his crimes while suffering his abuse. Her expression hardens, not with fear, but with righteous anger.

"We've discussed our options," Forest says, his massive hands flat on the table. "But let's be clear on how we're proceeding. Option one: we build the case quietly. Feed information to trusted DOJ contacts. Let them handle the takedown."

"Safer," Ryan notes. "Less exposure for Willow."

"But slower," Jackson counters. "And more room for Reynolds to wriggle out."

"Option two," Forest continues, "direct testimony. Willow presents the evidence herself, publicly. No room for coverups. No bureaucratic delays."

"But dangerous," I say, the words tasting like ash on my tongue. "Reynolds would know exactly where to strike."

Cooper leans forward, wincing slightly. "What about Kostic? If we move on Reynolds, Kostic won't sit idle."

"Precisely the concern," Forest rumbles. "We expose Reynolds, we potentially set off a reaction from everyone in his network—including an arms dealer with resources that rival small countries."

"We've been monitoring Kostic's movements," CJ confirms. "If he gets wind that we're moving on Reynolds, we need to be ready for him to activate his own assets."

All eyes turn to Willow, who sits perfectly still, processing. The room falls silent, waiting for her to speak.

"I still want to testify," she says finally, her voice firm. "Direct testimony. Public record. No shadowy dealings that can be dismissed as conspiracy theories."

I take her hand under the table, squeezing gently in silent support. The pride I feel threatens to burst through my chest. I've seen men crumble under less pressure, seen hardened operators balk at half the risk she's willingly taking on. Yet here she stands, bruised but unbroken, choosing to face her monster head-on.

"Then we prepare," Forest declares, the matter settled. "Mitzy, full analysis of the USB contents. CJ, security protocols for a public appearance. Skye, medical and psychological prep."

"And us?" Cooper asks, gesturing to our Cerberus team.

"Training," I say, my eyes still on Willow. "Starting today. We're officially on protective detail."

TWENTY-ONE

Mason

THE ENSUING DAYS FALL INTO A RHYTHM THAT FEELS BOTH foreign and familiar. Mornings begin with Willow in my arms, our bodies learning each other with increasing intimacy. Sometimes gentle, sometimes fierce, always with a hunger that shows no signs of abating.

Breakfast with the team becomes a touchstone—Willow joking with Martinez, learning intel lingo from Skye, gradually integrating into this strange family of warriors and spies as if she's always belonged.

Work sessions with Mitzy follow—legal analysis, reviewing evidence, and redacting sensitive names. Willow's law degree emerges from the shadows of her abandoned career, her sharp mind finding connections and precedents that even Mitzy's algorithms miss.

But as the days pass, her restlessness grows. The lodge, although spacious, remains a gilded cage. Security protocols mean she can't set foot outside where surveillance might spot her. Some days, I find her at the window, staring at the mountains with such longing that it makes my chest ache.

"I have an idea," I tell her one morning, seven days into our stay. "Meet me in the gym in fifteen."

The training room is Forest's pride and joy—a state-of-the-art facility with every piece of equipment an operator could want. Mats cover one half of the floor, weight machines and cardio equipment the other. A climbing wall dominates the far end, and reinforced glass separates a shooting range beyond.

Willow arrives precisely on time, dressed in the workout clothes Skye has acquired for her—leggings and a fitted tank top that reveal the subtle changes in her physique. Regular meals and reduced stress have filled out the hollows in her cheeks and added healthy curves to her frame.

"What's all this?" she asks, eyeing the hand wraps I'm laying out on the mats.

"Training," I say simply. "If you're going to face Reynolds in court, you need to know you can face him anywhere."

Fear flickers across her features, but she nods. "Okay. What do we start with?"

"Basics. Stance. Balance. How to fall." I move behind her and adjust her posture with gentle hands. "Your center of gravity is here," I place a palm against her abdomen. "Everything starts from this point."

We begin slowly. How to stand. How to breathe. How to move without telegraphing intentions. She absorbs every lesson, her frustration visible only when her body can't immediately perform what her mind understands.

"I'm never going to get this," she mutters after an hour, sweat dampening her shirt, hair clinging to her forehead.

"You will," I assure her, demonstrating the movement again. "Your body is learning a new language. It takes time."

Days turn into a week. Each morning, the patterns become more fluid. Each afternoon, her strikes grow stronger, her footwork more precise. I watch her transform—not into a soldier, but into something equally powerful.

A survivor who refuses to be a victim again.

One afternoon, after a particularly grueling session with defensive moves, she collapses onto the mat, frustration etched into every line of her body.

"This is pointless," she says, voice thick with unshed tears. "I'm never going to win a fight against men like Steffan. Against men like Drake."

I crouch beside her, about to offer reassurance, when a better idea strikes me. "Mitzy!" I call. "CJ! Got a minute?"

They appear in the doorway moments later—Mitzy with her ever-present tablet, CJ looking mildly amused.

"Need your help with a demonstration," I say, rising to my feet. "Willow needs to see something."

Understanding dawns in Mitzy's eyes. Without a word, she hands her tablet to CJ and steps onto the mat, kicking off her shoes as she goes.

"What's happening?" Willow asks, confusion replacing frustration as she watches Mitzy roll her shoulders, stretching her neck.

"A lesson," I reply, moving to stand beside CJ. "Mitzy, you ready?"

The tech wizard—all five-foot-three of her—nods. "Any boring rules to follow?"

"Ha-ha, Standard takedown. No permanent damage." I wink at her. "Try not to hurt me too badly."

"Wait, what?" Willow sits up straighter, looking between us in disbelief.

Before she can say anything else, I lunge at Mitzy with a controlled strike that would have connected with most opponents. Instead, my hand meets air as she sidesteps, redirecting my momentum with a twist of her forearm. In an eyeblink, I'm flat on my back, Mitzy's knee pressing lightly into my sternum.

"Again." I climb off the floor.

Mitzy backs away to reset.

This time, I approach more cautiously, feinting left before striking right. It makes no difference. Mitzy reads my movements like they're written in neon, using my force against me. Three attempts, three takedowns, each more emphatic than the last.

By the final one, Willow is on her feet, mouth slightly open in awe.

"Your turn, CJ," Mitzy says, gesturing him forward without breaking a sweat.

CJ hesitates only a moment before squaring off against her. Despite his greater size and obvious strength, the outcome is the same. In less than ten seconds, he's on the mat, arm twisted behind his back, Mitzy's expression never changing from mild boredom.

"How?" Willow breathes, looking at the diminutive woman with new eyes.

"Technique beats strength," Mitzy says, releasing CJ and straightening her shirt. "Always. I'm never going to overpower a man like Mason or CJ. But I don't need to. I just need to be smarter, faster, and better trained."

"We train all our female operatives to capitalize on momentum over strength," CJ explains, rubbing his shoulder where Mitzy manipulated a pressure point. "It evens the playing field. In a direct contest of strength, you'll more likely than not—lose. However, we train our female operatives to minimize this as much as possible. It's all about force, momentum, and physics. Gravity takes care of the rest."

"CJ's right," I add. "Men rely on power. We're taught to dominate through strength. We train against other men. Rarely against other women. Women like Mitzy are taught to redirect our power, use it against us."

Willow looks between us, then at her own hands, small like Mitzy's, but growing stronger every day. A slow smile spreads across her face, determination replacing defeat in her eyes.

"Okay," she says, retying her ponytail. "I'm back in. Show me again."

The next day's training session runs longer than usual. By the time we finish, the lodge has emptied—Forest and Skye gone to a secure meeting in Missoula. Mitzy is locked in her tech lab, working on a secret project. The rest of the team are on various assignments. The blessed quiet feels like a stolen luxury after days of constant company.

"You're improving," I tell Willow as she towels sweat from her face. "Your form is solid."

She flexes her fingers, examining the calluses beginning to form on her palms from striking the pads. "Still a long way from taking down Steffan."

"That's not the goal," I remind her, checking her hands for any serious bruising. "You're learning to defend yourself, to buy time. You've got an entire team of killers ready to handle the rest."

She laughs softly, the sound still new enough to make my chest tighten. "My own personal army."

"Damn right." I brush my thumb across her knuckles, the simple contact sending heat through my veins despite the exhaustion of training. "These look good. No serious bruising."

"I don't mind bruises if they're from you," she says quietly, her eyes lifting to meet mine.

I freeze, my thumb still tracing circles on her skin. The words, innocent on the surface, carry layers of meaning that make my pulse quicken. We've established a certain dynamic in our intimate moments—her calling me "Sir," me taking control—but we've never ventured into anything more intense than that.

"Willow," I say, my voice dropping lower. "What exactly are you saying?"

She steps closer, tilting her face up to mine. "I'm saying I like it when you overpower me. When you take control. And I don't mind a few bruises when the sex is steamy."

"After what Steffan did…" I choose my words carefully. "I never want to trigger those memories."

"This is different." Her fingers trace the line of my jaw. "With him, I had no choice. With you—I choose to submit. But…" She looks down, appearing deliciously shy. "What if I get to fight a little first? Let you overpower me."

My breath catches. "You want me to make you work for it?"

She rises on tiptoes, her lips brushing my ear as she whispers, "I'm yours to command. Yours to claim. But I want to make you earn it."

The dam breaks.

My hands find her waist, lifting her against me with a growl that comes from somewhere primal. Her legs wrap around my hips as I carry her to the wall, pinning her there with my body, my mouth claiming hers in a kiss that is pure possession.

"Tell me what you need," I demand against her lips, my control fraying with every soft sound she makes. "Tell me what you want."

"You," she gasps as my teeth find the sensitive spot where her neck meets her shoulder. "All of you. Don't hold back."

Those three words unleash something I've been keeping reined in tight.

I lower her slowly, letting her feel every inch of my restraint —then step back.

Not because I'm done, but because she asked for a fight.

"Prove it," I say roughly. "You want me to earn it? Then make me."

Willow's eyes flare with heat. She doesn't hesitate.

She rushes me.

The first move is sloppy—too much emotion in it—but her follow-up is clean. Low sweep to the knee, sharp twist of her hips. I let her take me down, rolling with the fall to gauge her momentum. She lands on top, trying to pin my arm.

"Good," I grunt. "But you're leaving your flank open."

I flip her.

She hits the mat with a thud but grins as she kicks out, catching me in the gut. I rip off her shirt, then stumble back a step, laughing.

She's not just playing now. She's fighting.

And she's damn good.

She dodges my grab and throws her shoulder into my ribs, using my weight against me. It almost works—almost. But then I plant, pivot, and catch her wrist mid-strike, yanking her off balance.

She goes down again.

This time, I follow.

I pin her beneath me, knees bracketing her hips, wrists caught in my hands and pressed to the mat above her head.

Her breath rushes out in a gasp, eyes wide, cheeks flushed, chest heaving beneath me.

She struggles.

Twists.

Fights.

It turns me on like nothing else.

"Fight all you want, Willow," I growl, voice thick with arousal. "You want to lose. You want to be overpowered. Admit it."

Her pulse flutters beneath my fingers. Her thighs tense around my hips, but she doesn't buck me off.

Her thighs squeeze me tighter.

"And you just lost, little warrior." I use one hand to pin her hands over her head. The other one strips her bare. I shove down my workout shorts, cock already thick and ready. She whimpers, eyes locked on mine, chest arching up into me.

I thrust into her in one long, claiming stroke, driving the breath from her lungs.

"Oh, fuck," she gasps, body bowing.

"Say it again," I rasp, hips rolling deep and slow. "Say you don't mind the bruises. Say you like when I take what's mine."

"I love it," she moans, arching beneath me. "God, Mason— please—don't hold back."

And I don't.

I fuck her hard, pinning her wrists, pressing her into the mat like the weapon she is—polished and fierce and mine. Her sounds grow ragged, desperate, echoing in the empty training room like music made of surrender.

Her climax slams into her with a strangled cry, her inner muscles clenching around me, dragging me with her. I thrust harder, deeper, until I break apart inside her, spilling with a growl that sounds more animal than human.

We stay like that for a long beat—panting, trembling, skin slick with sweat.

Then I slowly release her wrists, bringing one to my lips.

"You still with me?" I murmur, voice gentler now.

She nods, eyes shining. "That was—everything."

I kiss her forehead, then roll beside her on the mat, pulling her into my arms.

"You're dangerous," I murmur into her hair.

"So are you, Sir," she whispers, smiling against my throat.

And just like that, we've crossed another line.

Not into darkness. Into something real.

Something that belongs to us.

Once is never enough with Willow. I take her again, accepting the responsibility that comes with her surrender, only this time, she doesn't fight me. I claim her on the mat again.

Each touch is a celebration of what we've found in each other's arms.

Each kiss is a promise.

Each command given and obeyed a step further away from the shadows of her past.

And afterward, as we lie tangled together on the mat, her body curled against mine like she belongs there, I hold her as though she's sacred. Because to me, she is.

TWENTY-TWO

Mason

Evening finds us in the war room, the entire team assembled for what feels like a turning point. Forest stands at the head of the table, his massive frame casting shadows in the dimmed lighting. Skye and CJ flank him, their expressions grave. Mitzy runs point on tech, multiple screens displaying data that illuminate her face in blue-white light.

The Cerberus team completes the circle: Cooper, his injured leg now supporting his weight without visible discomfort, Martinez, unusually serious without his customary smirk, Jackson, cleaning his nails with a tactical knife, Ryan, stone-faced and ready.

And Willow, sitting beside me, her spine straight, her eyes clear. No longer the frightened woman who stumbled through a Montana blizzard seeking escape. A warrior in her own right now, preparing for the final battle.

"We've narrowed our options," Forest begins without preamble. "Based on the evidence and Willow's decision, we're taking this to court. Full disclosure. Full testimony."

"Timeline?" Cooper asks, leaning forward.

"Two weeks," Skye replies. "We've established back-channel communication with a federal prosecutor we trust. He's preparing the groundwork now."

"Security?" Ryan's question is directed at CJ, who taps his tablet in response.

"Three-layer protocol. Cerberus on the inner ring, Guardian operatives in the middle, and outer. Extraction plans for every scenario."

Mitzy picks up the thread, her fingers moving across her keyboard as she speaks. "The evidence has been authenticated, encrypted, and distributed to secure servers across four continents. Even if something happens to the physical drive, the data survives."

"And Reynolds?" I ask, my hand finding Willow's under the table.

In answer, Mitzy loads a satellite photo onto the main screen. Steffan Reynolds, immaculately dressed in a tailored suit, ascends the steps of what appears to be a government building. A senator walks beside him, their heads bent in conversation.

"Pentagon," Forest identifies the location. "Three days ago."

"He's not hiding," Skye observes. "He's reminding us who he knows."

"Who he thinks will protect him," CJ corrects.

The image changes to another—Reynolds at a charity gala, smiling for cameras, a blonde woman on his arm who is decidedly not Willow. The date stamp shows it was taken just yesterday.

"Already replaced you publicly," Mitzy says to Willow, her voice gentle despite the harsh reality. "Classic narcissist move."

Willow stiffens beside me, but when I glance at her, there's no hurt in her eyes. Only cold determination. "Good," she says. "Let him think he's won. It'll make his fall that much harder."

Forest nods approvingly. "We hit him, we better not miss. Once we go public, there's no going back."

"Then let's make damn sure we don't," Willow says, her voice steady and strong.

I look around the table at these people who have become her protectors, her allies, her family. At the woman beside me, who has faced her worst nightmare and chosen to fight back. Who is preparing to stand before the world and speak truth to power, regardless of the cost.

She isn't running anymore.

And I've never been more proud to stand beside her.

Forest is about to continue when Mitzy's tablet begins flashing red. She doesn't look alarmed—more intrigued, her head tilting slightly as her fingers fly across the screen.

"What?" Forest demands, instantly alert.

"Someone's probing our servers," Mitzy says, her voice calm but focused. "Exactly as anticipated." A slight smile plays at the corner of her mouth. She taps a few more commands, and a secondary screen illuminates with streams of code. "They're good. Not good enough, but definitely professional-grade hackers."

"Reynolds?" CJ asks, moving to look over her shoulder.

"Most certainly," Mitzy confirms. "The attack pattern matches what I've been monitoring from his encrypted channels. Sophisticated, but predictable."

I watch Mitzy work, understanding dawning. "You set a trap."

Her smile widens. "A very appealing one. Just enough genuine data mixed with carefully crafted false leads to make it irresistible. The moment they breached the outer firewall, my countermeasures activated."

"Can you trace it back to the source?" Skye asks.

"Already have. Three locations. Two are obvious decoys, but

the third…" She pauses, fingers flying across her keyboard. "The third is interesting. Private residence, Montana. Registered to a holding company that connects back to—"

"Drazen Kostic," Willow finishes, leaning forward to study the data.

"Exactly." Mitzy nods. "But more importantly, I can now see what they're after." She pulls up a list of filenames. "They're specifically targeting your financial records, Willow. The ones documenting Reynolds's offshore accounts."

Forest's expression darkens. "Money trail. The most damning evidence."

"Let them keep digging," Mitzy says with a predatory gleam in her eye. "Every attempt gives me more access to their systems. More intelligence about their operations. Meanwhile, they're getting exactly what I want them to see."

The main screen suddenly flickers, then resolves into a video feed. A man's face, familiar to all of us, but especially to Willow, who goes utterly still beside me.

Steffan Reynolds stares out from the screen, his expression calm, almost bemused. He adjusts his tie—a casual gesture that nonetheless radiates menace—then smiles directly into the camera.

"Hello, Willow," he says, voice smooth as poisoned honey. "Did you think I wouldn't find you?"

Willow's hand tightens in mine, but her face remains composed. Mitzy's fingers never stop moving across her keyboard, her expression one of cool calculation rather than alarm.

"That's impossible," Cooper mutters. "How did he—"

"He hasn't," Mitzy interrupts calmly. "This is a pre-recorded message they're broadcasting through their attack program. Standard intimidation tactic." She glances at Willow. "He's fishing. He has no idea where you are."

On screen, Reynolds continues, unaware that his psychological warfare has already been neutralized. "I've been patient, sweetheart. Given you time to come to your senses, but my patience is running out." His smile never wavers, never reaches his eyes. "You have something that belongs to me and I want it back."

"The evidence," Willow whispers.

"You've always been clever, Willow. Too clever for your own good, but this little game ends now." Reynolds leans closer to the camera. "I know where you're hiding. I know who's helping you. And I know exactly how to make them suffer if you don't return what's mine."

Forest signals to Mitzy, who cuts the feed with a keystroke. "He's bluffing," she says confidently. "If he knew our location, he wouldn't be hacking our decoy servers to deliver threats."

"Can you track the video source?" I ask, my arm instinctively wrapping around Willow's shoulders.

"Already done," Mitzy confirms. "Signal originated from the Montana location. I'm gathering everything I can about their systems, their security, their personnel." Her eyes gleam with a predatory light. "While Reynolds thinks he's frightening us, he's giving me full access to his operation."

I turn to Willow, expecting fear, trauma, regression. Instead, I find her sitting straighter, eyes focused, jaw set. "He always did underestimate me," she says quietly. Then, louder, "Mitzy, can you keep the connection open? Get as much as you can?"

"Working on it." Mitzy's fingers move like lightning across her keyboard. "I've already pulled their security protocols, personnel files, and…" She stops, a genuine smile breaking across her face. "And what appears to be Reynolds's complete financial records. The real ones, not the sanitized versions."

"The idiot just handed us everything we need," Ryan murmurs, shaking his head in disbelief.

"He never could resist showing off how clever he is," Willow says, and there's something in her voice I've never heard before. Not fear. Not anger. But satisfaction. The predator watching her prey walk into a trap of its own making.

"Keep him talking," Forest instructs Mitzy. "Let him think he's in control while we prepare to move."

Mitzy nods, reopening the video feed. Reynolds's face reappears, still speaking, still threatening, still completely unaware that his every word is strengthening the case against him.

Willow watches her husband, and for the first time since I've known her, she smiles at the sight of him. Not with warmth, but with the cold certainty of someone who knows the end is coming.

"Record everything," she says quietly. "Every threat. Every admission. I want it all for the court."

"Consider it done," Mitzy promises.

Reynolds continues his monologue, each word digging his grave deeper, each gesture providing more evidence for Willow to use against him. And all the while, Mitzy's trap closes around him, silent and invisible, gathering everything we need to annihilate him.

My focus remains on Willow, on the transformation happening before my eyes. She's no longer a victim. No longer hunted. She's a predator, hunting her prey.

Damn, I love this amazing woman.

TWENTY-THREE

Willow

STEFFAN CONTINUES HIS MONOLOGUE, UNAWARE HE'S PERFORMING for an audience that's already three steps ahead. "I've been patient, sweetheart. Given you time to come to your senses. But my patience is running out."

I can feel Mason beside me, his body radiating tension. His hand hovers near mine, not quite touching. Giving me space to process this moment.

"You've always been clever, Willow," Steffan says on screen. "Too clever for your own good, but this little game ends now."

Something clicks inside me. A final piece shifting into place.

"We need to use this," I say, my voice cutting through the room's tension.

Forest turns to me, one bushy eyebrow raised. "Use it how?"

"He thinks he's found us," I say, gesturing toward the screen where Steffan continues his threats. "Mitzy, does your trap show him a location? Something he believes is our hideout?"

Mitzy nods. "The decoy server farm is presenting as a remote property in northern Idaho. Basic security protocols, nothing that would suggest Guardian-level defenses."

"Then we set a trap." The words feel right as I say them. Powerful. "We let him come to us. Let him think he's found me. But we control the ground."

Mason shifts beside me. "Absolutely not. We move you to a more secure—"

"No." I meet his gaze steadily. "I'm done running."

The room goes silent. Mason's eyes darken with concern, but I see something else there too.

Pride.

"He expects me to be cowering," I continue. "Let's show him who I've become."

Forest strokes his beard, considering. "It has tactical advantages. Choose our ground, set the terms of engagement."

"It's too risky," Mason argues, but his tone lacks conviction.

I step closer to him, close enough that only he can hear my next words. "I need this. I need to face him on my terms. Not in a courtroom surrounded by his people, but somewhere I know I'm not alone."

His jaw works as he processes my words. Then, slowly, he nods.

"We'd need to secure a location," Forest says, already shifting to planning mode. "Not here, obviously. Somewhere we can control completely."

"The Blackwater safe house," CJ suggests. "It's been partially decommissioned. Perfect cover."

"We capture him alive," I say firmly. "He needs to face justice for everything he's done. His network needs to be exposed."

Forest exchanges a look with Mason that I can't quite interpret. Then he nods. "Capture, not kill. That's the mission."

As they begin hammering out details, CJ steps away briefly, phone to his ear. I catch fragments: "Charlie Team… Immediate deployment… Full tactical… Ethan, your team only…"

When he returns, he makes no mention of the call, but I

understand instinctively—he's creating layers of security even the rest of us don't know about.

Mason's hand finally finds mine under the table, fingers interlacing. "I don't like this," he murmurs.

"I know," I squeeze his hand. "But it's time."

On the screen, Steffan finishes his threats with that smile I once feared more than his rage. "I know where you're hiding. I know who's helping you. And I know exactly how to make them suffer if you don't return what's mine."

Mitzy cuts the feed. In the sudden silence, my resolve hardens like steel being tempered.

I am not his. Not anymore. Never again.

THE TRAINING ROOM SMELLS OF SWEAT AND DETERMINATION. My muscles burn pleasantly as Mitzy circles me on the mat, her petite frame deceptively relaxed.

"Remember," she says, "you're not fighting fair. You're fighting to win."

She lunges suddenly—a calculated attack designed to test my reflexes. I sidestep, redirect her momentum using her arm as leverage, just as she's taught me over these past few weeks.

Mitzy hits the mat with a grunt, then grins up at me.

"Perfect." She springs to her feet. "Now, men like Reynolds fight with their emotions. They get angry when they don't immediately dominate."

"Steffan always did have a temper underneath that controlled exterior," I confirm, readjusting my stance.

"Use it against him. Let him think he's winning. Let him over-commit." Mitzy demonstrates, telegraphing a wide swing that leaves her center exposed. "Then strike where it hurts."

We continue like this for another thirty minutes—Mitzy

attacking, me defending, then counterattacking. My body moves with a new fluidity, muscle memory taking over where conscious thought ends. By the time we finish, my tank top is soaked, and my lungs burn with exertion.

But I feel ready.

In the armory, Mason waits with a black case. His expression is solemn as he sets it on the bench between us.

"Non-negotiable," he says, opening the case to reveal a sleek, lightweight vest of ballistic material. "If you're doing this, you wear protection."

I nod, understanding this is his way of supporting my choice while still needing to keep me safe. He lifts the vest carefully, stepping behind me to help me into it. His hands are gentle as they position the plates, then firm as they tighten the straps.

"It's designed for women," he explains, his breath warm against my ear as he works. "Kevlar composite with ceramic strike plates. It'll stop anything short of a high-powered rifle round."

His fingers brush against my ribs, adjusting the side panels. Even through the tactical material, his touch sends electricity along my spine. He reaches around to secure the front plate, his palm resting briefly over my heart.

"It's lighter than I expected," I say, placing my hand over his.

"Latest Guardian tech. Doesn't mean you take unnecessary risks." His voice is gruff, but his eyes tell a different story when I turn to face him.

"I won't," I promise. "This isn't about revenge, Mason. It's about ending it. On my terms."

He nods, then helps me out of the vest. "We'll continue training with it on. You need to get used to moving in it."

As we exit the armory, I catch a glimpse of movement in a connecting hallway—six men in tactical gear. Their leader, tall with sharp features and watchful eyes, pauses briefly to acknowledge Mason with a curt nod.

"Ethan," Mason returns the nod. "Good hunting."

The man—Ethan—glances at me, his assessment quick but thorough. Then he's gone, his team disappearing like shadows into another section of the facility.

"Charlie Team," Mason explains, noting my curiosity. "Forest's elite tactical unit."

"Part of the operation?"

Mason's expression reveals nothing. "Insurance we don't talk about."

I understand then—they're the contingency no one mentions. The forces that only appear if everything goes wrong. Somehow, this knowledge doesn't frighten me. It reassures me.

We've planned for every possibility.

THE SAFE HOUSE SITS IN A SMALL CLEARING, SURROUNDED BY dense forest on three sides and a steep ridge on the fourth. To casual observation, it's just another remote cabin—weathered wood siding, metal roof, generator humming quietly behind the structure. But I know better.

The windows are bulletproof. The walls are reinforced with ballistic panels. The perimeter is rigged with motion sensors and infrared cameras. And somewhere out there, hidden even from us, Charlie Team waits in silence.

Inside, I adjust the lightweight body armor beneath my sweater. It feels strange, constricting yet reassuring. The weight of it grounds me in this moment.

"Thirty minutes," Mason says, checking his watch. "Mitzy confirms their convoy is on schedule."

I nod, trying to steady my breathing. We're in position in the main living area—the predetermined confrontation point. Floor-to-ceiling windows offer clear views of the approaching road, while strategically placed furniture creates cover if needed.

The plan is elegant in its simplicity. Steffan will send his team to secure the perimeter. They'll encounter moderate resistance—enough to seem realistic but not enough to deter them. Steffan will remain back until the initial breach is complete, then enter to retrieve me personally. Standard procedure for him—always letting others take the initial risks.

When he enters, he'll find me waiting. Mason and the others will be nearby but hidden, ready to move the moment Steffan is fully committed.

"You okay?" Mason asks, his voice low as he checks his sidearm one last time.

I take a deep breath, centering myself. "I'm ready."

He studies me, then nods. "Remember your training. Don't take unnecessary risks. And most importantly—"

"Trust the team," I finish. "I know."

"I'll be right over there," he indicates a hallway alcove with clear sightlines to our position. "You won't see me, but I'll see everything."

"I know," I repeat, this time with a small smile. "That's why I can do this."

"They're here. Get in position." He kisses me briefly, fiercely, then checks his earpiece. As Mason disappears into his hiding spot, I move to my designated position—standing before the main window, silhouetted against the late afternoon light.

Visible. A target.

Bait.

My heart doesn't pound with fear but with anticipation. The body armor presses against my ribs with each breath, a constant reminder that I'm protected.

Prepared.

Through the window, I catch the first glimpse of vehicles approaching—three black SUVs moving in tight formation up the access road.

Professional. Coordinated. Armed.

The first shots crack through the stillness, controlled bursts from the perimeter defense teams. The SUVs halt in a practiced formation, doors opening as tactical teams deploy in textbook cover patterns.

I watch dispassionately as the ballet of violence unfolds. Guardian operators falling back strategically, appearing to be overwhelmed while actually channeling Steffan's forces exactly where we want them. The gunfire is sporadic but intensifies as they approach the house.

Then I see him.

Steffan emerges from the middle SUV, hanging back as his security team secures the approach. Even at a distance, I recognize the set of his shoulders, the way he holds his head. The casual confidence of a man who expects the world to bend to his will.

My mouth goes dry; ancient instincts scream warnings that my mind no longer heeds. I force myself to remain still, visible in the window. Letting him see his target.

Radio chatter from Mason's position confirms what I'm seeing. Steffan's team has breached the outer perimeter. They're pushing toward the house, moving in coordinated pairs. Two men break off to flank the building while four approach the front entrance directly.

The sound of splintering wood echoes through the house as they breach the door. Boots on hardwood. Tactical commands shouted room to room.

"Clear!"

"Clear!"

I remain rooted in place, breathing controlled, eyes forward. Any moment now.

The living room door opens. Two men in tactical gear enter, weapons raised. They sweep the room, then one speaks into his radio.

"Primary target located. Room secure."

Then Steffan fills the doorway.

He's exactly as I remember and nothing like I remember. Impeccable charcoal suit. Silver temple wings accentuating his distinguished looks. That same commanding presence that once made me feel small.

But now I see what I couldn't before—the coldness in his eyes. The cruelty etched into the lines around his mouth. The emptiness behind the facade.

For a moment, he stares, clearly shocked to find me standing calmly before him rather than cowering or fleeing.

"Willow." My name in his mouth sounds wrong somehow. Possessive. Entitled. "This is—unexpected."

"Hello, Steffan." My voice remains steady, giving nothing away.

His surprise transforms into that familiar smile—the one that once preceded pain.

"There's my wayward wife. Though I must say, I'm disappointed to find you standing alone." His gaze sweeps the room. "Where are your protectors now?"

"I don't need protection from you anymore."

His laugh is genuine, which makes it all the more chilling. "Is that so?" He turns to his security team. "Secure the rest of the house. I'd like a private moment with my wife."

The men nod and exit, closing the door behind them. I know what they'll find—empty rooms and prepared ambush points where Ryan and the others wait.

Steffan loosens his tie slightly as he approaches. "You've led me on quite a chase. Weeks of considerable inconvenience." He circles me slowly, maintaining distance. Assessing. Looking for weakness. Finding none.

"The evidence you stole—" he begins.

"I didn't steal anything. I documented the crimes you committed. There's a difference."

His nostrils flare—the first sign of the temper simmering beneath his controlled exterior. "Semantics. You took confidential documents from my home office."

"Our home," I counter. "And those documents are evidence of arms trafficking, judicial corruption, and collusion with terrorist organizations."

"My God." He shakes his head with mock admiration. "Listen to you. So righteous. So certain." The smile returns, sharper now. "Tell me, did you practice this speech for your new boyfriend? The mountain man who's been hiding you?"

I say nothing, which irritates him more than any response.

"You think I don't know about him? About your—*protector*?" Steffan sneers the word. "Did he enjoy my leftovers? Did you spread your legs for him as easily as you did for me?"

The words are designed to humiliate. To reduce me to the powerless, frightened woman I once was, but they slide off me like water, leaving no mark.

"You always did talk too much." I take a single step forward. "It's time to end this."

His smirk falters at my advance. "Yes, it is." His hand moves to his jacket, and I tense, expecting a weapon. Instead, he pulls out his phone. "One call, and Drazen's men eliminate your little band of mercenaries. One call, and you come home with me. Where you belong."

"I'm not going anywhere with you."

"No?" He moves closer, confidence restored by my apparent defenselessness. "And how exactly do you plan to stop me? You're alone. You've always been alone. That's what you never understood."

He reaches for my arm, fingers extended to grasp, to control, to hurt—just as they have countless times before.

But this time, I move.

Sidestep. Redirect momentum. Just as Mitzy taught me.

His hand grasps empty air as I pivot away, sending him slightly off-balance. The surprise on his face is almost comical.

"What the—"

I don't let him finish. Strike palm-heel to sternum. Quick. Efficient.

Steffan stumbles back, more shocked than hurt. His expression morphs from surprise to rage in an instant.

"You little bitch." He lunges forward, abandoning pretense, reaching for my throat with both hands.

I duck under his grasp, using his forward momentum to push him further off balance. But Steffan recovers faster than I anticipated, years of racquetball and martial arts training evident in his reflexes. He pivots, catching my arm in a painful grip.

"Did you really think a few days of training could match years of experience?" he snarls, twisting my arm behind my back.

Pain lances through my shoulder. From Mason's hiding place comes the faintest sound—the whisper of movement, quickly stilled. He's fighting the instinct to intervene. Trusting me to handle this.

I slam my heel down on Steffan's instep, simultaneously throwing my head back toward his face. He dodges the headbutt but loosens his grip enough for me to twist free.

We circle each other, both breathing hard. A thin trickle of blood runs from his split lip where my earlier strike connected better than I realized.

"You've changed," he says, eyes narrowing. "Someone's been teaching you bad habits."

"You have no idea."

He attacks again, faster this time—a boxer's combination targeting my face and solar plexus. I block the first blow, absorb the second against the body armor beneath my sweater. His knuckles connect with the ballistic plate, and he hisses in pain.

"What the hell?"

I use his confusion to counter, driving my knee toward his groin. He blocks, catching my leg and shoving me backward. I stumble, my back hitting the wall hard enough to rattle picture frames.

Steffan advances, fury transforming his handsome face into something monstrous. "I'm going to enjoy breaking you all over again."

He grabs my throat, pinning me against the wall, his other hand drawn back to strike. From the corner of my eye, I see movement—Mason, unable to remain hidden, starting to emerge.

But I don't need rescue

As Steffan's hand tightens around my throat, I drive my palm up under his chin, snapping his head back. Simultaneously, I bring my knee up into his diaphragm.

Air whooshes from his lungs. His grip loosens. I twist away, creating distance.

"That's new," he wheezes, genuine surprise in his eyes.

"I've learned a lot since I left you."

He straightens, reassessing. This time, when he attacks, it's with cold calculation rather than rage. A precise strike to my kidney, followed by an attempt to sweep my legs.

I dodge the kidney punch, but the sweep connects, sending me sprawling onto the hardwood floor. Pain radiates through my hip where I land. Mason shifts forward again—I see his shadow move—but I shake my head minutely. No.

This is my fight.

Steffan stands over me, that familiar smirk returning. "Back where you belong. On the floor at my feet."

I roll as his foot lashes out, barely avoiding the kick aimed at my ribs. The body armor absorbs a glancing blow to my side, the impact dulled but still jarring.

"Enough games," Steffan reaches inside his jacket and pulls out a small pistol. "Get up."

The sight of the gun changes the equation.

"Drop it, Reynolds." Mason is visible now, his sidearm raised, stepping from concealment.

TWENTY-FOUR

Willow

Steffan whirls, keeping the gun trained on me while facing this new threat. His eyes widen with recognition, then narrow with calculation.

"The mountain man himself," he says. "How gallant."

"Drop the weapon. Last warning."

Steffan laughs, a hollow sound devoid of humor. "Or what? You'll shoot me? With my wife so close? I don't think so."

"He doesn't have to shoot you." I push up to my knees, then to my feet. "I've already beaten you."

Steffan sneers, glancing between us. "You call this beaten? I'm the one holding the gun, sweetheart."

"Are you?" I smile.

His expression falters as he registers what I've done—during my fall and recovery, I've positioned myself by the concealed panic button beneath the side table. My finger hovers just above it.

"One push, and this room fills with highly trained operatives," I tell him. "You're surrounded. Your security team has been neutralized. It's over."

Doubt flickers across his face. Then the familiar mask of control returns. "You're bluffing."

"Try me."

His finger tightens on the trigger. Mason tenses, ready to fire.

I push the button.

Silence.

Steffan's smirk returns. "As I thought. A bluff—"

The doors on either side of the room burst open. Ryan and Martinez enter from one, Cooper from the other, all with weapons trained on Steffan.

"Federal Judge Steffan Reynolds," Ryan announces formally, "you're being detained for questioning regarding charges of corruption, arms trafficking, and conspiracy."

The color drains from Steffan's face as he realizes how completely he's been outmaneuvered. The gun wavers in his hand.

"Don't," Mason warns. "That would be a very poor decision."

For one terrible moment, I think Steffan will choose violence over surrender. His finger twitches on the trigger. Mason steps in front of me, shielding me with his body.

Then, with a sound of disgust, Steffan lets the gun clatter to the floor.

"Hands behind your head," Ryan orders. "On your knees."

Steffan complies, his eyes never leaving mine. "This isn't over."

"Yes, it is." I step past Mason to face my husband—my abuser—one last time. "It is."

Ryan moves to secure him with zip ties, but freezes at a sudden burst of radio chatter. Mason's hand goes to his earpiece, his expression darkening.

"What?" I ask.

"Multiple vehicles approaching," Mason says grimly. "Fast. Professional."

"Reynolds's backup?" Cooper asks, weapon still trained on Steffan.

Mason shakes his head. "Something else."

From outside comes the staccato rattle of automatic weapons fire, different from the controlled bursts of earlier engagement. More intense. More deadly.

Steffan's expression shifts to one of confusion, then dawning hope. "Ah," he breathes. "Right on time."

"Who?" I demand.

Before he can answer, Mason's radio crackles with a new voice—one I haven't heard before. Tightly controlled but urgent.

"Ghost, this is Charlie One. We have multiple hostile teams approaching from the north and east. Professional operators. Heavy weapons. We're engaging but outnumbered."

Ethan. Charlie Team. The contingency I wasn't supposed to know about has now been activated.

Mason's response is immediate. "Acknowledged. Secure the prisoner. Prepare for immediate extraction."

Steffan laughs, the sound chilling in its confidence. "Oh, I don't think I'll be your prisoner for long."

My blood runs cold as understanding dawns. "Kostic," I breathe. "You called Drazen Kostic."

"Not exactly." Steffan's smile is triumphant. "But Drazen and I have—mutual interests. He doesn't like loose ends."

Mason grips my arm, eyes intense. "We need to move. Now."

The distant gunfire intensifies. Through the window, I catch glimpses of muzzle flashes in the gathering dusk. Charlie Team is engaging the new threat.

"Cooper, secure Reynolds," Mason orders. "Ryan, Martinez, prepare for extraction protocol *theta*."

Cooper moves to zip-tie Steffan, but the judge twists suddenly, driving his elbow into Cooper's recent wound. Cooper grunts in pain, momentarily stunned. Steffan lunges for his discarded pistol.

Everything happens in rapid sequence. Ryan shouts a warning. Mason pushes me behind him. Steffan brings the gun up.

Before he can fire, a cold voice cuts through the tension.

"Judge Reynolds. What an unfortunate situation."

Steffan freezes, his head snapping toward the doorway. His expression transforms instantly—rage giving way to unmistakable relief.

A tall, lean man in an immaculate suit stands in the threshold, flanked by four heavily armed men in tactical gear. His angular features could be carved from marble; his eyes, like chips of ice, survey the scene.

"Drazen," Steffan breathes, lowering his weapon slightly. "Thank God. Perfect timing."

The arms dealer steps into the room, his movements precise and economical. Not a wrinkle on his tailored suit despite the violence happening outside.

"It appears you've encountered—difficulties." Kostic's accent is barely perceptible, his English polished and deliberate.

Steffan laughs—a sound of genuine relief. "You could say that." He gestures toward us with his gun. "These people have stolen my property and sensitive information. They need to be eliminated."

Mason tenses beside me, shifting imperceptibly to better shield me. The air in the room thickens, charged with deadly potential.

Kostic steps closer, examining each of us in turn. His gaze lingers on me with unsettling intensity.

"Your wife," he observes. "The one who escaped."

"Yes," Steffan's voice hardens. "She's taken documents that could compromise our operations."

"I see." Kostic circles the room slowly, like a predator

assessing prey. "And the information she took—it contains details of our arrangement?"

"Potentially." Steffan straightens, clearly emboldened by Kostic's arrival. "Which is why this needs to be handled permanently." His eyes find mine, cold with triumph. "No loose ends."

"No loose ends," Kostic repeats thoughtfully. "We agree on that principle."

Mason's hand finds mine, squeezing once—a signal to be ready to move. Ryan and Martinez have repositioned slightly, prepared for whatever comes next.

Steffan steps forward, gesturing with the gun. "I'll handle my wife. Your men can deal with the others."

"That won't be necessary, Judge Reynolds." Kostic's voice remains perfectly calm.

"What?" Steffan frowns, confusion flickering across his features.

"I said that won't be necessary." Kostic moves to stand between us, facing Steffan. "The situation has changed."

Steffan's smile falters. "What are you talking about? Get me out of here. We'll eliminate them together."

"I'm afraid our arrangement has become a liability." Kostic straightens the cuff of his immaculate shirt. "Your obsession with retrieving your wife has become—problematic for my organization."

The blood drains from Steffan's face as understanding dawns. "Drazen, wait—"

"I dislike complications, Judge Reynolds," Kostic says, as if he's discussing the weather. "Your personal vendetta has created unnecessary exposure."

Steffan raises his gun, panic replacing confidence. "You need me. My position, my contacts—"

"Are replaceable." Kostic's hand moves in one fluid motion.

The deafening crack of a shot fills the room.

Steffan staggers backward, stunned disbelief etched on his face as he looks down at the hole in his chest. His expression cycles through shock, betrayal, and finally, terrible understanding. His eyes find mine one last time before he crumples to the floor.

"Drazen," I whisper, frozen in place as the arms dealer lowers his weapon, smoke still wisping from the barrel.

In death, Steffan looks smaller somehow. Less threatening. Just a man on a hardwood floor, blood pooling beneath him, all his power gone in an instant.

Kostic studies me dispassionately, then nods once to Mason. "Mr. Blackwood. Your reputation precedes you."

Mason shifts slightly, keeping his body between me and this new threat. "I'd say this is a surprise, but that would be a lie."

"Indeed." The arms dealer steps further into the room, his men flanking him with weapons at the ready. "Our mutual problem has been resolved."

My husband's body lies on the hardwood floor between us, blood pooling beneath his head. I should feel something—horror, grief, satisfaction. Instead, I feel only a strange numbness.

"Why?" I ask. "He was your business partner."

Kostic's lips curve in the barest approximation of a smile. "Judge Reynolds became a liability. His obsession with retrieving you and the evidence you carry compromises our operations."

"So you eliminated the threat," Mason says flatly.

"Business," Kostic shrugs elegantly. "Nothing personal."

Outside, the gunfire diminishes, replaced by an eerie silence broken only by an occasional, distant shot.

"Your men—" I say.

"Unfortunate misunderstanding. Professional operators responding to perceived threats." Kostic gestures, and his men lower their weapons. "I'll order my forces to disengage immediately."

Mason's radio crackles. "Ghost, this is Charlie One. Hostiles are pulling back. Repeat, hostiles are withdrawing. We have two wounded, none critical."

Relief floods through me. Ethan and his team are alive.

Kostic continues smoothly. "I have no quarrel with Guardian HRS or Cerberus. My business is with Reynolds alone." His cold gaze fixes on me. "And now, with you."

My spine stiffens. "With me?"

"Yes." Kostic turns his full attention to me. "The rather extensive documentation of operations involving me and your late husband."

My mouth goes dry. "I don't know what you're talking about."

"Please." Kostic looks genuinely disappointed. "Let's not insult each other's intelligence. The flash drive. The offshore accounts. The meetings in Belgrade and Zurich."

I say nothing, mind racing. If Kostic knows about the evidence, knows he's implicated...

"The files you gathered," he continues, "are they comprehensive?"

An unexpected question. I hesitate, uncertain where this is leading.

"Yes," I finally admit. "Three years of documentation. Every meeting. Every transaction."

Kostic nods thoughtfully. "And my organization? We feature prominently?"

"Yes. Extensively." I meet his gaze steadily.

His expression doesn't change, but something shifts in his eyes —a cold calculation moving behind them like shadow beneath ice. He takes a moment, considering.

"I hear Guardian HRS technology is especially savvy," he says. "Particularly when it comes to digital manipulation."

Mason tenses beside me. "What are you suggesting?"

"I wish to make a deal." Kostic straightens his already immaculate tie.

"No deal," Mason says immediately, voice hard.

I place a hand on his arm. "What do you have in mind?"

Kostic smiles—not the practiced social expression, but something genuine and therefore more frightening.

"Simple," he says, spreading his hands. "Remove my organization from your files. Eliminate all references to our operations. Do that, and we have no quarrel." He gestures to Steffan's body. "With Judge Reynolds dead, there will be no trial. No testimony. The corruption in his network can still be exposed without—certain complications."

"You want us to tamper with evidence," Mason states flatly.

"I want a business arrangement," Kostic corrects. "You get what you need—the dissolution of Reynolds's network. I get what I need—continued operational security."

"And if we refuse?" I ask.

Kostic doesn't answer directly. Instead, he looks out the window where the sporadic gunfire has completely ceased. "Your Charlie Team fought admirably. Professional. Disciplined. But significantly outnumbered." His eyes return to mine. "I would prefer that our organizations maintain a respectful distance rather than an—antagonistic relationship."

The threat is clear without being explicit.

"Mason," I say quietly. "Reynolds is gone. The immediate threat is neutralized."

"He's a weapons dealer, Willow," Mason replies, voice low. "Responsible for arming terrorists, cartels—"

"And I will continue those operations with or without your interference," Kostic interjects smoothly. "The only question is whether we part ways peacefully today or become permanent adversaries."

I weigh the options quickly. The evidence we have could implicate dozens of corrupt officials, judges, and law enforcement. We could still dismantle Reynolds's network without Kostic's organization being mentioned.

"If we do this," I say slowly, "you guarantee you'll never come after us. Never interfere with the cases against Reynolds's other associates."

"You have my word." Kostic places a hand over his heart, the gesture somehow not appearing theatrical despite its formality. "Remove my organization from your files, and we have no reason to ever speak again."

Mason and I exchange glances. The tactical reality is clear—we're outnumbered, and the priority has always been dismantling Reynolds's corruption.

"This ends here," Kostic states, not a question but a command. "Reynolds disappears. His corruption is exposed. My name remains unmentioned. Agreed?"

Mason and I exchange glances. What choice do we have?

"We have a deal," I say finally. "Mitzy can alter the files. No trace of your organization."

"Agreed," Mason echoes.

"Excellent." Kostic buttons his suit jacket with an air of finality. "My men will retrieve the body. No traces will remain." He turns to leave, then pauses. "Mrs. Reynolds—"

"I'm not Mrs. Reynolds," I interrupt. "I haven't been for some time."

A flash of genuine amusement crosses his features. "Indeed. My apologies." He studies me with newfound interest. "You're a formidable woman. Far more than your husband deserved." He inclines his head slightly. "Until our paths cross again."

"Let's hope they don't," I reply.

His smile deepens. "Let's hope." Then he's gone, his men following silently, leaving us with the cooling body of the man who once controlled my every breath.

Mason immediately calls out on his radio to coordinate the

extraction. Ryan and Martinez secure the room while Cooper checks the perimeter. Organized chaos as the operation pivots from capture to evacuation.

I stand motionless, staring at Steffan's body. The man who terrorized me for years is reduced to an empty shell on a hardwood floor. Blood stains the expensive Italian leather of his shoes. Eyes vacant, staring at nothing.

Mason approaches cautiously. "Willow? We need to move."

I nod, unable to look away from the body. "Is it wrong that I feel nothing?"

"No. It's not wrong." His hand finds mine, warm and solid.

"I wanted him to face justice. Real justice."

"I know." Mason gently turns me away from the sight. "But maybe this is justice. Just not the kind we planned for."

Outside, the low *thump-thump-thump* of an incoming helicopter breaks the quiet. Kostic's forces withdraw, melting into the forest as suddenly as they appeared.

As Mason leads me to the helicopter, I glance back at the house where my nightmare ended. At the husband who was my abuser. The past I'm finally, and truly, leaving behind.

"I stood up to him," I say quietly as we board the helicopter. "I wasn't afraid."

Mason's arm tightens around my shoulders as we lift off. "You never have to be afraid again."

"I know." The certainty in my voice surprises even me. I rest my head against his shoulder, watching the safe house shrink beneath us. Kostic's men will retrieve Steffan's body, erasing all evidence of what happened here.

It's not the justice I wanted. Not the ending I planned. But it's an ending nonetheless.

"What do we do now?" I ask as we head toward the Guardian HRS safe house in Idaho.

Mason's fingers lace with mine, strong and steady. "Whatever you want."

Below us, the forest stretches, endless and dark. Above, the first stars pierce the dusk. And ahead—for the first time in years—lies a future that belongs only to me.

#Mason takes my hand, his thumb tracing circles on my palm. "You did it, Willow. You brought him down."

"We did it," I correct, leaning into his solid warmth. "I couldn't have done this without you."

His lips brush my temple. "You would have found a way. You're the strongest person I've ever known."

The compliment warms me from within, but I shake my head. "Strong doesn't mean doing it alone. I tried that route for three years. Nearly got myself killed."

He's quiet for a moment, eyes tracing my face with that intensity that still makes my heart race. "How are you feeling? Really?"

I consider the question, searching for the truth he deserves. "Relieved. Vindicated. Exhausted." I swallow hard. "And sad, strangely enough. Not for Steffan—never for him—but for the years I lost. The person I might have been if I hadn't met him."

"You didn't lose those years," Mason says softly. "You survived them. Used them to gather evidence that's now dismantling criminal networks across three states." His hand squeezes mine gently. "And the person you might have been wouldn't have been as strong, as resilient, as extraordinary as the woman sitting beside me now."

Tears prick at my eyes, but they're different from the ones I've shed over the past six months—not tears of pain or fear, but of release. Of understanding that even our darkest chapters shape us in ways that matter.

"Take me home," I whisper, suddenly eager to shed the formal suit, the careful makeup, the public persona I've maintained throughout the trial. "I'm ready for this day to be over."

TWENTY-FIVE

Willow

Six Months Later

Home is a renovated waterfront property north of Seattle —close enough to the city for our work, remote enough to provide the security and privacy we both crave. Floor-to-ceiling windows overlook Puget Sound, the water reflecting the late afternoon sun in rippling gold.

I kick off my heels at the door, a small act of freedom that still brings me joy. In Steffan's house, shoes were always worn, appearances always maintained, even in private. Here, with Mason, I exist without performance.

"Wine?" he asks, shrugging off his suit jacket and loosening his tie. Today's deposition was the last one—the final thread in the unraveling of Steffan's criminal network. Even with Steffan gone, the evidence I gathered over those three years continues to topple corrupt officials, one after another.

"Please." I pad toward the bedroom, already unbuttoning my blouse. "I'm going to change."

He murmurs low in acknowledgment as I step into our bedroom—the space we've shaped over the past six months. Not his Spartan precision, not my carefully curated luxury. Something new lives here.

Comfortable yet elegant. Secure. Welcoming. Ours.

I pull on soft leggings and one of Mason's worn t-shirts. The fabric carries his scent, a comfort I never tire of. In the adjoining bathroom, I wash away my makeup, revealing the woman beneath.

The mirror doesn't lie. Six months have carved change into every line of my face. The haunted shadow behind my eyes has lifted, replaced by something steadier—calm, anchored, resolute. I don't flinch when doors slam anymore. My spine holds straighter. My gaze meets the world without apology. And I move like someone who no longer expects pain for being seen.

I touch the fading scar at my temple—a souvenir from the crash in the Montana snow. It's barely visible now, a thin white line hidden by my hairline. Mason says it's my battle scar, proof of survival. I'm learning to see it that way too.

When I return to the living room, Mason has changed as well, trading court formality for jeans and a Henley that does nothing to hide the powerful build beneath. Two glasses of wine wait on the coffee table, along with a small wrapped package I didn't notice before.

Bear and Chaos lounge by the fireplace, the picture of contentment. They've adapted to Pacific Northwest living faster than any of us expected. Bear still chases waves at the private beach below our property, while Chaos patrols the perimeter with the same vigilance he showed in Montana.

"What's this?" I gesture toward the package as I curl into my favorite corner of the sofa.

Mason hands me a glass of wine, then settles beside me. "Open it and see."

The box is small, wrapped in simple blue paper. Inside, nestled in tissue, lies a delicate silver bracelet. A single charm hangs from the fine chain—a mountain peak crafted in polished silver.

"Mason," I breathe, lifting it carefully.

"A year," he says quietly. "Since Montana. Since you found me in that storm, or I found you—I'm still not sure which way it went." His fingers trace the mountain charm gently. "Thought you might want a reminder that not all defining moments are painful ones."

I extend my wrist, offering it to him silently. He understands immediately, securing the bracelet with careful fingers. The metal is cool against my skin, the weight barely noticeable yet somehow grounding.

"It's perfect," I whisper, blinking back sudden tears. "Thank you."

His thumb traces my pulse point, that unconscious gesture of possession that still sends warmth flooding through me. "Have you decided what you want to do next?"

The question we've been circling for weeks. We've both focused so intently on dismantling Steffan's network that we've neglected looking beyond. I sip my wine, gathering my thoughts.

"I want to finish setting up the new legal clinic," I say finally. "The foundation approved the funding last week. I can start offering services to domestic violence survivors as early as next month."

Pride flashes in his eyes. "You're going to change so many lives."

"That's the plan." I twist the bracelet absently. "And I think… I want to start writing. Not a memoir—the media circus around that would be unbearable. But maybe something that could help other women recognize the warning signs I missed." I meet his gaze. "What about you?"

He sets down his wine glass, expression thoughtful. "It's time for me to return to Cerberus. Ryan's done a great job during my self-imposed exile, but I'm ready for the work again."

"Based here?" I try to keep my tone neutral, though the thought of him leaving sends a spike of anxiety through me.

"Based wherever I want," he says, eyes never leaving mine. "And as it turns out, we're headquartered in Seattle."

Relief floods through me. "So you're staying."

"If that's what you want." There's a hesitancy in his voice I rarely hear—a vulnerability that reminds me he carries his own doubts and fears. His biggest fear is that he might hurt me, but since that first time in the cabin, he hasn't had a single PTSD flare. He says it's me. I say it's all the exceptional sex he's having.

I set my wine aside and move closer, eliminating the space between us. "You're what I want." My hand cups his face, feeling the stubble beneath my palm. "These past six months, building a life together—it hasn't always been easy, but it's been right."

His arms encircle me, drawing me against the solid warmth of his chest. "Even the hard parts?"

"Especially those," I say softly, thinking of our early struggles —the nightmares that used to wake me, the moments when trauma intruded on healing, and the careful negotiation of boundaries and needs.

His hand slides to the nape of my neck, exerting just enough pressure to make my breath catch—that perfect balance of dominance and care that speaks directly to my deepest needs.

"And this part? Still figuring this out too?"

The subtle shift in his tone sends a shiver down my spine. In Montana, our connection had been immediate, intense, almost desperate—two broken people finding unexpected salvation in each other's arms. Here, in the aftermath, we've moved more carefully, rebuilding trust and relearning intimacy without crisis as its catalyst.

"I think we're getting pretty good at that part." I tilt my head to give him better access as his lips find the sensitive spot beneath my ear.

"Good enough that I can try something new tonight?" His chuckle vibrates against my skin.

"What did you have in mind?" Curiosity and heat stir low in my belly.

His fingers thread through my hair, tightening just enough to guide my gaze to his. "Something we've talked about but haven't tried yet. But tonight should be about celebration, about reclaiming something for ourselves. If you want that."

I search his face, finding only open desire and careful restraint—the hallmarks of the dominant I've come to trust implicitly. With Steffan, dominance was a weapon, a tool of control and punishment. With Mason, it's an exchange, a gift freely given and received.

"Yes," I whisper, the word carrying all the trust I've rebuilt over these months. "Show me."

His eyes darken, pupils dilating as he reads the desire in my response. "Go to the bedroom." His voice drops to that commanding tone that makes my knees weak. "Take off your clothes and kneel by the bed. I'll be there in five minutes."

The instructions thrill me, and anticipation builds as I stand. This is nothing like the fear-based submission Steffan demanded. This is a conscious choice, freely given—the surrender of control to someone who has earned my absolute trust.

In our bedroom, I comply with his instructions, removing my clothes before kneeling beside the bed, back straight, hands resting on my thighs. The position feels natural, right—a physical manifestation of the dynamic we've been carefully exploring.

When Mason enters, I feel his presence before I see him— that shift in the air that accompanies his focused attention. He moves around me, not touching, just observing with appreciation that feels tangible on my skin.

"Beautiful," he murmurs, finally coming to stand before me. "Look at me, Willow."

I raise my eyes, finding him changed—still in his jeans but shirtless now, his powerful upper body bearing the scars of his military service. The contrast between his clothed state and my nakedness emphasizes the power dynamic in a way that sends heat flooding through me. The bulge straining beneath his zipper shows his arousal and need.

"Tonight is about reclamation." He reaches out and tilts my chin. "Taking back what was stolen from you—the joy of submission freely given, the pleasure of surrender on your terms." His thumb traces my lower lip. "Do you trust me to guide you through that?"

"Yes, Sir." The honorific comes naturally now, no longer shadowed by past abuse.

Approval warms his expression. "Good girl. Remember your safe word?"

"Snowbound," I confirm, the word we chose together—a reminder of where we began, a symbol of moving from danger to safety.

"Use it if you need to, without hesitation," he reminds me, as he always does. "Ready?"

At my nod, he guides me to my feet and toward the bed, arranging me as he likes—on my back, arms stretched above my head. From a drawer in the nightstand, he retrieves soft leather cuffs I haven't seen before.

"May I?" he asks, the simple request for permission underscoring that this exchange remains mine to control, even in surrender.

"Yes," I breathe, offering my wrists willingly.

The leather is butter-soft against my skin as he secures the cuffs, then attaches them to hidden anchors on our headboard. The restraint is secure but not tight, a symbolic restriction rather than a genuine confinement.

"Test them," he instructs, watching me pull gently against the bonds. "Comfortable?"

I nod, a strange sense of peace settling over me as I accept the restraint. With Steffan, restraint meant terror, pain, degradation. With Mason, it becomes the opposite—a framework for trust, letting go, and receiving pleasure on terms we've established together.

"Close your eyes," he commands softly. "Focus only on sensation."

I obey, darkness enhancing my other senses—the sound of his movement around the bed, the scent of his skin as he leans closer, the anticipation building in my veins. When he finally touches me, tracing a path from my throat to my sternum, I arch into the contact like a flower seeking the sun.

What follows is nothing like the desperate, needy passion of our first encounter in his Montana cabin. This is a deliberate, methodical exploration. His hands and mouth map my body with exquisite tenderness. He alternates between feather-light touches that make me whimper and firm, possessive grips that remind me of his strength.

Words of praise flow continuously—"So beautiful," "So responsive," "Such a good girl"—each one a healing balm to wounds left by a man who used words as weapons. When pleasure builds to an almost unbearable peak, Mason's command comes against my ear—"Come for me, Willow"—and my body responds instantly, the release washing through me in waves that leave me trembling.

Before I can fully recover, he's positioning himself above me, his jeans discarded, his arousal evident. His eyes lock with mine, seeking final confirmation even now.

"Please," I whisper, arching toward him in silent invitation.

He enters me with exquisite control, his pace measured, giving me time to adjust to the fullness. When he begins to move, it's with the same deliberate patience—each thrust precise, angled to bring maximum pleasure. One hand holds my bound wrists, emphasizing the power dynamic without causing discomfort.

"Mine," he growls against my throat, the possessive claim sending a fresh surge of desire through me. "Say it."

"I'm yours," I gasp as he increases his pace, the coil of pleasure tightening again impossibly soon. "Only yours."

His control fractures slightly at my words, his movements becoming more urgent, more primal. Yet even as he chases his release, his focus remains on my pleasure—one hand slipping between us to ensure I join him in climax.

When it claims us both, the intensity leaves me breathless, tears streaming from the corners of my eyes. Mason releases my wrists immediately, gathering me against his chest as aftershocks ripple through us both.

"You're safe," he murmurs against my hair, seeming to understand that my tears aren't from pain but profound emotional release. "I've got you."

I curl into his warmth, letting the tears flow freely—not from grief or fear but from reclamation and healing. From the knowledge that what was broken in me is mending in ways I once thought impossible.

"Thank you," I whisper against his chest, but my words are inadequate for the gift he's given me. It's not just pleasure but the return of agency, the reclaiming of surrender as something beautiful rather than terrifying.

His arms tighten around me, a fortress against the memories, against the world. "Always," he promises, the single word carrying the weight of absolute certainty.

Later, wrapped in the soft sheets of our bed, I trace the lines of his face. The scar that bisects his eyebrow. The strong curve of his jaw. The tiny lines at the corners of his eyes that deepen when he smiles.

"I never thought I'd have this again," I admit softly. "Trust. Safety. The freedom to choose for myself."

His gaze holds mine steadily. "When I built that cabin in Montana, I thought I was done. With people. With connection. With feeling anything beyond guilt and regret."

"And now?" I ask, though I can see the answer in his gaze.

"I know better," he says. "That storm brought me more than a woman to protect. It brought me back to life."

Outside our window, waves crash against the shore, creating a gentle rhythm. Bear snores softly from his bed in the corner. Somewhere in the house, Chaos keeps his silent vigil, ever watchful.

"Tell me again," I whisper, needing to hear the words that have become our private ritual.

Mason's arms tighten around me, his voice a rumble against my ear. "You're safe. You're home. I've got you, and I love you dearly."

And in those simple words lies everything—the promise of protection, the gift of belonging, the certainty that whatever storms may come, we will weather them together.

I press my lips to the steady beat of his heart, silently offering my promise in return—that I will be his harbor as surely as he has been mine. That the strength he sees in me will continue to grow. The trust between us, hard-won and precious, will only deepen with time.

A year ago, I drove through a Montana blizzard with broken ribs and a desperate plan, sure I would die alone in the snow. Instead, I found a warrior with scars that matched my own. A protector whose strength became my shelter. A partner who shows me, every day, what love looks like when it's built on respect instead of fear.

"I love you," I whisper, the words no longer frightening but freeing.

His hand cups my face, thumb brushing away a tear I hadn't realized I'd shed. "I love you more." The simple truth reflected in his eyes. "Always."

As sleep claims us both, one final thought drifts through my mind—that sometimes, salvation arrives not as we imagine it, not in rescue from above or liberation from without, but in the simple, profound act of two broken souls recognizing each other across the darkness.

I found safety from the storm and a reason to weather it. I discovered even the deepest wounds can heal, given time, tenderness, and trust.

I discovered love, real love, doesn't diminish but magnifies. It turns victims into survivors. Survivors into warriors. And warriors into something greater still.

We saved each other. And that… That was enough for us to start again.

TWENTY-SIX

Willow

One year to the day:

Autumn paints the mountains in russet and gold as we drive the winding road to the cabin. One year to the day since I crashed in a Montana blizzard, fleeing a monster to find unexpected salvation.

Mason's hand rests on my thigh as he navigates the familiar route, occasionally squeezing gently in wordless communication. Bear and Chaos doze in the back of the SUV, older now but still alert, still protective of the humans they've adopted.

The cabin appears around a final curve, transformed from the tactical fortress of my memories into something warmer, more welcoming. The porch has been expanded, window boxes added, and a sense of permanence infused into what was once merely a survival outpost.

"Ready?" Mason asks as we pull to a stop, his eyes searching mine for any hesitation.

I look at the place where our story began—not with romance

but with survival, not with courtship but with necessity. The memories could be overwhelming, but instead, I find they've lost their sharp edges, softened by a year of healing, building, and reclaiming.

"Ready," I confirm, squeezing his hand before stepping out into the crisp mountain air.

The dogs bound ahead, reacquainting themselves with familiar territory as Mason retrieves our bags. Inside, the cabin has been transformed—still secure, still tactical in its bones, but warmer now. Bookshelves line the walls, filled with legal texts alongside military strategy. The kitchen gleams with new appliances, ready for the meals we'll prepare together over the coming week.

"What do you think?" Mason asks, setting down our bags and wrapping his arms around me from behind. "Too many memories?"

I lean against his solid warmth, surveying where everything changed. "Good memories now. Or at least, memories that led to something good."

His lips brush my temple. "I have something for you."

From his pocket, he produces a small velvet box—not the traditional shape for a ring, I note with curiosity. Inside, nestled on black velvet, lies a key.

"The deed transferred yesterday," he says, voice rumbling against my back. "The cabin is yours now. Or ours, if you want it to be."

I lift the key, turning to face him with questions in my eyes.

"This place saved me after Rachel," he explains, his hands settling at my waist. "Kept me sane when I thought I'd never rejoin the world. Then it brought you to me, gave us both shelter when we needed it most." His eyes hold mine, serious and intent. "Seemed right that it should be yours now. A safe place, whenever you need it. No matter what happens."

The gesture renders me speechless—not just the gift itself, but the profound understanding behind it. A safe place. A refuge. A choice that's truly mine.

"Ours," I say finally, pressing the key back into his hand and closing his fingers around it. "It should be ours."

Relief and something deeper flashes in his eyes. "You're sure? I wanted you to have something that was completely yours, without obligation—"

I silence him with a kiss, pouring everything I feel into the connection. When we part, I keep his face between my hands, ensuring he understands the importance of what I'm about to say.

"I spent three years trapped in a marriage where nothing was truly mine," I tell him, voice steady despite the emotion behind the words. "Where every gift came with invisible strings, every kindness with expected repayment. What you're offering—a safe place with no obligations—means everything." I press another kiss to his lips, gentle and affirming. "But I'm choosing us. Not out of fear or necessity or gratitude, but because it's what I want."

The tension in his shoulders eases beneath my touch. The warrior who faces every threat without flinching still struggles sometimes to believe in his worthiness, just as I struggle with trusting my judgment after Steffan.

"What we're building together—it isn't perfect," I continue, tracing the scar along his jawline with tender fingers. "We both carry too many scars for perfect. But it's real, and it's healing, and it's chosen freely, every day."

"Every day," he echoes, gathering me closer. "For as long as you'll have me."

His shirt shifts as he moves, revealing the edge of new ink over his heart—a small mountain range matching the charm on my bracelet. The tattoo is recent, acquired without fanfare just before our trip. His commitment is etched into skin that already bears so many marks of his past.

"I love you," I whisper against his lips—words we've exchanged before but that feel especially significant here, in the place where everything began. "Not despite your darkness but including it. Not because you saved me, but because you saw me as worth saving."

His answering kiss holds everything words cannot express—protection without possession, dominance without subjugation, love without conditions. When we finally separate, his forehead rests against mine, our breathing synchronized in the quiet cabin.

"Welcome home, Willow," he murmurs, the simple phrase carrying layers of meaning.

Home, I reflect as I look around the cabin that witnessed our beginning, is no longer a place I'm running from, but a feeling I've found—in my reclaimed sense of self, in the legal work helping others escape abuse, in the arms of a man who understands both my strength and my submission.

Outside, snow begins to fall—gentle this time, not the raging blizzard of a year ago. Through the window, I watch the flakes settle on the pines, transforming the landscape into the pristine beauty that first sheltered our unlikely beginning.

"Home," I agree, turning back to the man who has become my sanctuary. "At last."

READY FOR BOOK TWO IN THE CERBERUS SECURITY SERIES?
Read **BRASS** Today

Some secrets are worth killing for. Some passions are worth dying for.

HE'S ALL CONTROL. Ryan "Brass" Ellis never loses his cool. As second-in-command of Cerberus Security, he's the strategist, the levelheaded one, the man who makes the impossible possible. His legendary control has seen him through three combat tours and countless high-risk operations.

Until her.

SHE'S ALL DEFIANCE. Investigative journalist Sloane Hart has stared down warlords and exposed corruption across four continents. She's used to danger—it's practically her comfort zone. What she's *not* used to is being protected, especially by a bossy, infuriatingly competent ex-Delta Force operator who thinks he knows what's best for her.

What she's definitely not prepared for? The way he makes her want to surrender.

TOGETHER, THEY'RE EXPLOSIVE.

When Ryan witnesses an assassination attempt on Sloane in a DC subway, he intervenes without hesitation. What should be a simple extraction becomes a cross-country chase as professional kill teams hunt them at every turn. Forced into hiding together, their volatile chemistry ignites into something neither can deny.

But Sloane's investigation has uncovered a terrifying truth: an autonomous AI assassination program with full authority to identify and eliminate threats—*no human oversight required.* As they piece together the conspiracy, they discover connections that reach the highest levels of government.

Now they're not just running for their lives. They're fighting to expose a truth that could cost them everything.

ONE BED. ONE RULE. ONE BURNING DESIRE.

Trapped in hotel rooms with nowhere to run, Ryan and Sloane wage their own private battle—one of wills, trust, and a passion neither expected. He demands obedience to keep her safe. She challenges his every command. But when night falls and defenses crumble, they discover a connection deeper than either imagined possible.

Ryan will do anything to protect Sloane, even sacrifice

himself. But the stubborn journalist is determined to break through his carefully constructed walls, proving that surrendering control doesn't mean weakness—sometimes it's the greatest strength of all.

In a high-stakes game where trust is a luxury they can't afford and desire is a distraction they can't resist, they'll need to embrace what's building between them to survive the forces hunting them down.

Because the most dangerous weapon isn't the one pointed at them—it's the feelings neither can control.

BRASS IS A FULL-LENGTH, HIGH-HEAT ROMANTIC SUSPENSE novel featuring:

- A protective alpha hero who meets his match
- Forced proximity that ignites into scorching chemistry
- Edge-of-your-seat action with a steamy slow burn
- Passionate power exchange between equals
- Only one bed (and so much sexual tension)
- Life-or-death stakes with an emotionally satisfying HEA

No cliffhangers. Can be read as a standalone, but best enjoyed as part of the Cerberus Security Series.

"Control is his specialty until he meets the one woman who challenges everything—a fearless journalist who ignites a passion more dangerous than the killers pursuing them."

CRAVING MORE GUARDIANS?

If you've fallen for the fierce alphas of Cerberus, you're just getting started.

There's an entire world waiting for you—the Guardian

Hostage Rescue Specialists series—one built on danger, desire, and the kind of love that ruins a woman for anyone else.

Start with the *Alpha Team series*—because once you meet these men, you'll never forget them. Protective. Possessive. Unapologetically alpha. And the women who bring them to their knees? Equally unforgettable.

But if you want to feel **EVERYTHING**—if you want to understand where it all began, before Cerberus, before the Guardians, before the rescues—go back to the beginning.

Heart's Insanity, the first book in the *Angel Fire* rock star romance series, is where you'll meet Skye and Forest. It's raw. It's emotional. It's the origin story of the entire Guardian world. And trust me—once you see who Forest Summers was before Guardian HRS existed, you'll never look at him the same way again.

Start there.
Feel everything.
And then come back for more.
Start with Heart's Insanity
Or dive into the Alpha Team series.
The heat only gets hotter.
The danger only gets deadlier.
And the Guardians?
The mission isn't over. It's just getting started.

Keep current with Ellie Masters.
CLICK HERE
Receive news of her writing and new releases.

Shop Ellie Masters Romantic Suspense and Steamy
Contemporary Romance by series.

Angel Fire Rock Romance
Guardian HRS: Alpha Team
Guardian HRS: Bravo Team
Guardian HRS: Charlie Team
Guardian HRS: Delta Team
Cerberus Personal Security
The LaRouge Triplets
The One I Want Series
Angel's Peak Series
Billionaire Boy's Club
The Lovers
Changing Roles

ELLZ BELLZ

ELLIE'S FACEBOOK READER GROUP

If you are interested in joining the **ELLZ BELLZ**, Ellie's Facebook reader group, we'd love to have you.

Join Ellie's **ELLZ BELLZ**.
The **ELLZ BELLZ** Facebook Reader Group

Sign up for Ellie's Newsletter.
Elliemasters.com/newslettersignup

Also by Ellie Masters

The LIGHTER SIDE

Ellie Masters is the lighter side of the Jet & Ellie Masters writing duo! You will find Contemporary Romance, Military Romance, Romantic Suspense, Billionaire Romance, and Rock Star Romance in Ellie's Works.

YOU CAN FIND ELLIE'S BOOKS HERE:

ELLIEMASTERS.COM/BOOKS

Shop Ellie Masters Romantic Suspense and Steamy Contemporary Romance by series.

Angel Fire Rock Romance

Guardian HRS: Alpha Team

Guardian HRS: Bravo Team

Guardian HRS: Charlie Team

Guardian HRS: Delta Team

Cerberus Personal Security

The LaRouge Triplets

The One I Want Series

Angel's Peak Series

Billionaire Boy's Club

The Lovers

Changing Roles

SUGGESTED READING ORDER

START HERE
Rockstar Romance
The Angel Fire Rock Romance Series

EACH BOOK IN THIS SERIES CAN BE READ AS A STANDALONE AND IS ABOUT A DIFFERENT COUPLE WITH AN HEA.

IT IS RECOMMENDED THEY ARE READ IN ORDER.

Heart's Insanity

Ashes to New

Heart's Desire

Heart's Collide

Hearts Divided

Hearts Entwined

Forest's FALL

Hearts The Last Beat

CONTINUE HERE…
Military Romance
Guardian Hostage Rescue Specialists

Rescuing Melissa

*(*Get a FREE copy of Rescuing Melissa
when you join Ellie's Newsletter*)*

Alpha Team

Rescuing Zoe

Rescuing Moira

Rescuing Eve

Rescuing Lily

Rescuing Jinx

Rescuing Maria

Bravo Team

Rescuing Angie

Rescuing Isabelle

Rescuing Carmen

Rescuing Rosalie

Rescuing Kaye

Cara's Protector

Rescuing Barbi

Charlie Team

Rescuing Rebel

Rescuing Stitch

Rescuing Mia

Jenna's Protector

Rescuing Sophia

Rescuing Malia

Rescuing Ally (Part 1)

Rescuing Ally (Part 2)

Delta Team

Rescuing Ember

Rescuing Aria

STANDALONES IN THE GUARDIAN HOSTAGE RESCUE

Science Fiction

Ellie Masters writing as L.A. Warren

Vendel Rising: a Science Fiction Serialized Novel

If you enjoyed this book by Ellie Masters, the LIGHTER SIDE of the Jet & Ellie writing duo, and aren't afraid of edgier writing, you might enjoy reading BDSM themed books written by Jet, the DARKER SIDE of the Masters' Writing Team.

The DARKER SIDE

Jet Masters is the darker side of the Jet & Ellie writing duo!

Romantic Suspense

Changing Roles Series:

THIS SERIES MUST BE READ IN ORDER.

Command Me

Control Me

Collar Me

Embracing FATE

Seizing FATE

Accepting FATE

HOT READS

A STANDALONE NOVEL.

Down the Rabbit Hole

Light BDSM Romance

The Ties that Bind

Each book in this series can be read as a standalone and is about a different couple with an HEA.

Alexa

Penny

Michelle

Ivy

HOT READS

Becoming His Series

This series must be read in order.

The Ballet

Learning to Breathe

Becoming His

Dark Captive Romance

A standalone novel.

She's MINE

About the Author

Ellie Masters is a USA Today Bestselling author and Amazon Top 15 Author who writes Angsty, Steamy, Heart-Stopping, Pulse-Pounding, Can't-Stop-Reading Romantic Suspense. In addition, she's a wife, military mom, doctor, and retired Colonel. She writes romantic suspense filled with all your sexy, swoon-worthy alpha men. Her writing will tug at your heartstrings and leave your heart racing.

Born in the South, raised under the Hawaiian sun, Ellie has traveled the globe while in service to her country. The love of her life, her amazing husband, is her number one fan and biggest supporter. And yes! He's read every word she's written.

She has lived all over the United States—east, west, north, south and central—but grew up under the Hawaiian sun. She's also been privileged to have lived overseas, experiencing other cultures and making lifelong friends. Now, Ellie is proud to call herself a Southern transplant, learning to say y'all and "bless her heart" with the best of them.

Ellie's favorite way to spend an evening is curled up on a couch, laptop in place, watching a fire, drinking a good wine, and bringing forth all the characters from her mind to the page and hopefully into the hearts of her readers.

FOR MORE INFORMATION
elliemasters.com

Connect with Ellie Masters

Website:
elliemasters.com
Purchase Direct:
elliemasters.com/shopify
Amazon Author Page:
elliemasters.com/amazon
Facebook:
elliemasters.com/Facebook
Goodreads:
elliemasters.com/Goodreads
Bookbub:
elliemasters.com/Bookbub
Instagram:
elliemasters.com/Instagram

Final Thoughts

I hope you enjoyed this book as much as I enjoyed writing it. If you enjoyed reading this story, please consider leaving a review on Amazon and Goodreads, and please let other people know. A sentence is all it takes. Friend recommendations are the strongest catalyst for readers' purchase decisions! And I'd love to be able to continue bringing the characters and stories from My-Mind-to-the-Page.

Second, call or e-mail a friend and tell them about this book. If you really want them to read it, gift it to them. If you prefer digital friends, please use the "Recommend" feature of Goodreads to spread the word.

Or visit my blog https://elliemasters.com, where you can find out more about my writing process and personal life.

Come visit The EDGE: Dark Discussions where we'll have a chance to talk about my works, their creation, and maybe what the future has in store for my writing.

Facebook Reader Group: Ellz Bellz

Thank you so much for your support!

Love,
Ellie

Dedication

This book is dedicated to you, my reader. Thank you for spending a few hours of your time with me. I wouldn't be able to write without you to cheer me on. Your wonderful words, your support, and your willingness to join me on this journey is a gift beyond measure.

Whether this is the first book of mine you've read, or if you've been with me since the very beginning, thank you for believing in me as I bring these characters 'from my mind to the page and into your hearts.'

Love,
Ellie

THE END

www.ingramcontent.com/pod-product-compliance
Lightning Source LLC
Chambersburg PA
CBHW021041310726
48969CB00006B/1751